Strangers Are Like Children

Joan Baxter

Pottersfield Press

Lawrencetown Beach, Nova Scotia, Canada

Canadian Cataloguing in Publication Data

Baxter, Joan
    Strangers are like children
    ISBN: 0-919001-98-X

1. Africa — Fiction.	2. Aliens — Africa — Fiction.	I. Title
PS8553.A856S87 1996	C813'.54	C95-950342-0
PR9199.3.B3759S87 1996		

Pottersfield Press gratefully acknowledges the ongoing support of the Nova Scotia Department of Education, Cultural Affairs Division, the Canada Council and the Department of Canadian Heritage.

Cover art by Phyllis Koinange, photographed by Anthony Njenga.

Printed in Canada

Pottersfield Press
Lawrencetown Beach
R.R. 2 Porter's Lake
Nova Scotia, Canada, B0J 2S0

Contents

For my mother and father

Acknowledgements

Thanks to all those who helped with this book. For the happy endings, Dali Mwagore in Kenya and friends in West Africa. For their invaluable advice, patience and editing, Kathy Overholt, Helen van Houten, Katherine Snyder, Joanne Reilly (who visited the "witches" with me and wrote her own wonderful story about it), Debby Plestid, David Baxter. For the cover painting, Phyllis Koinange. For inspiration and "voices", the people in West Africa who tolerated, schooled and befriended me. For taking my breath away, that "special" group of expatriates who happened my way over the years, and spurred me to write rather than resort to violence. For getting it all into print, my publisher, Lesley Choyce. For their patience and understanding, Karlheinz, Anna-Sarah and Bobo. And for their assistance and unflagging interest, my parents.

Foreword

In 1992, I worked for some time in a "witches' village" in Ghana. The assemblywoman, who had become a good friend by the time I left her village, told me a lot about the plight of the women they called witches. She and the village chief took them in, cared for them, made sure they had enough to eat. There were about five hundred witches in the village — one-sixth of its population.

When I went back later to do a radio documentary on the village, the assemblywoman took me around from hut to hut to meet the witches. Although there was one male among them, most of the five hundred witches were old and feeble women, past childbearing age and no longer up to the heavy chores girls and women perform in Ghana's north, such as fetching firewood and water from distant rivers or dams.

"The women come with nothing," the assemblywoman told me, "not even a pot to cook in, and they come from villages throughout the north of the country, even from neighbouring countries. They have usually been beaten. Some die before they reach this place."

She said a very few came with a daughter or granddaughter, but mostly they came alone and lived in tiny huts the community helped build for them.

When I had been in the village before, it was in the company of young and "enlightened" men from the city. They had shared with me their fear of the old women we saw crouched in the doorways of the dark huts who stared out at us as we passed. They were men who had studied abroad, men who were there to assess the various options for a village water supply, men who told me they wouldn't spend a single night in that village. They said, but only after we were safely in the car and driving back home to the lights of the regional capital, that the assemblywoman was probably a witch too.

That I categorically denied, but some of their apprehension about the other women had rubbed off on me. So I was surprised and relieved when the assemblywoman led me into the compounds to meet one after another of the witches, and they emerged to welcome us, wearing huge smiles. The assemblywoman informed them of my "mission." I had come to hear their stories, she said.

One told me she had been accused of causing a man back home in her own village, about two hundred kilometres away, to be bitten by a snake and to die. "They said they went to a soothsayer and he said that I had caused the death," she said. She was seriously beaten but she escaped with her life. She said that since she had been proven innocent of her crime she had "peace of mind." But she maintained that she had never harmed anyone, certainly never killed a man. "I think it's a lie," she said, understating her case in that way so many Africans have of boiling down enormous hardship to the barest of facts. So that even obtuse foreigners can understand the gist if not the magnitude of what's being said.

Another woman said she was accused of killing her son, who died after he went into convulsions brought on by a high fever. "I don't believe it, though," she added. "It is not possible for a human being to give birth to a child and then cause the child's death. And I myself do not know this thing they call witchcraft; whether it's black or white, I don't know it."

The village is the home of one of the most powerful shrines in the country and the region. The shrine, called *malzugu*, is out of sight inside a small hut, distinguishable from the ones the witches inhabit by the white seashells that are embedded in the clay walls. The fetish priest said it was open only on Mondays and Fridays, the days he did the de-witching.

I sat with him and the assemblywoman in his dark hut, interviewing him about the procedure for de-witching.

"When a witch is brought here," he said, "I take her into the shrine yard. She brings a fowl and swears an oath. She says that the matter of whether she killed someone or not is now between her and that person. I kill the fowl and mix the blood with the shrine water and stir it with the knife I used to sacrifice the fowl. I give the blood and water to the old lady. If it is true that she caused the death, that very day the woman will die. This is my duty to the people."

"Have any of the women who have come here and been de-witched been proven to be witches and died in the shrine?" asked I, the brash intruder with a microphone.

"Such things *do* happen. The shrine will kill a woman who is a witch. I, the fetish priest, did not kill her."

"Such things *may* happen, but *has* this happened when you performed the rite?" I persisted.

"It has *ever* happened," he replied, meeting my eyes with a look that I interpreted as defiance.

"When?" I persevered. As usual, I needed hard, cold, rational evidence, on tape. I knew I was being overly aggressive, contravening all the cultural rules. But journalism itself did this by digging up information that is not meant to be brought out for airing. As I sat there, arguments for and against my work, which de-mystified the mystic, turned people's beliefs and cultural secrets into fodder for international broadcast, raged in my head.

"It has *ever* happened," he repeated.

We went through this a few more times before he edged the interview away from witches and onto the subject of the guinea worm that was emerging through a sore in his ankle. He wondered if I had medicine that could heal that.

I didn't. Instead, I took a photograph. He thought that was pretty good medicine. It was hard to focus in the hut and not just because it was dark inside the solid mud walls. My hands were shaking and I was anxious to get out from under his baleful stare. He had wrestled complete control of the interview and had managed to unnerve me in a way few politicians in that country — or elsewhere — ever did.

Still, it was all amiable enough. He somehow dodged my next question about whether the five hundred de-witched women living in the village were or ever had been witches. I found myself nattering on about how this was a far better system of dealing with witches than the one practised in Europe up until the end of the last century — where a witch would have to die to prove her own innocence, where there was no such thing as refuge in a village at a shrine that proved her innocent. He commented that the women he had de-witched were safe in the village and that they could live here in peace. They would not be accepted back home again, where people would say they had returned to kill.

Obviously the faith in the de-witching shrine didn't extend that far, but I decided not to go into that. It was clear I had asked enough. We wound up the session with a long round of farewells. When we emerged through the small doorway, the sun was, as the assemblywoman succinctly put it, "pounding pounding." After the relative cool inside the hut it made my head spin. She chatted as we moved back through the village, with the usual mob of curious and boisterous children following behind. She talked about the problems the women had getting water from a river two kilometres away. There was a steep climb at the far end that would challenge any able-bodied person, let alone aged and worn-out women with enormous water cans on their heads. She meant the witches, of course. She had no use for any traditions and beliefs that "no longer fit", which made life for women a living hell. She pooh-poohed the notion that any of the old women in the village were witches — the whole notion of witchcraft. She spoke of them as "my women".

We had almost reached the chief's palace and the shade of the huge baobab tree there when a boy caught us up. He had been sent by the fetish priest with a gift for me, he explained breathlessly in his meagre English. He held up a white dove, a beautiful white bird that looked dazed and as disoriented as I felt by the whole business. It was typical of people in villages to give visitors gifts no matter how wealthy the visitor or how poor the villagers. I was used to receiving bundles of yams or perhaps a few guinea-fowl eggs. But a white dove? What meaning, what symbolism here?

The boy extended his hand on which the dove was perched. I reached for it. As I did so, drops of blood began to pour out of the bird, dripping down the white feathers and onto the brown dust below. I recoiled, leapt backwards.

The assemblywoman quickly intervened, told the boy to take the bird to her compound, graciously releasing me from my dilemma of how to avoid accepting the gift dove.

Afterwards, on the way back to the town where I lived, I thought the whole thing through, rationally, with a level head — something we in eastern Canada pride ourselves on having. I decided that the answer was obvious. They had just plucked the dove's wing feathers so that it wouldn't fly off and the blood had come from the fresh cuts on the wings. I only *thought* it began to bleed as I reached for it, because I was still feeling I had revealed too much skepticism and was afraid that the fetish priest had noticed and decided to take his revenge, show me a little of his power. My guilt over what I had asked and what I was going to have broadcast had played havoc with my senses. That guilt made me susceptible to all sorts of hallucinations and easy prey for the slightest sign of witchcraft or juju at work. That's what I decided. With my *level head.*

But of course, I still don't know what really happened as opposed to what I thought I saw happen. As often as I have run that scene through my brain in the intervening years I still see the same picture. A pure white dove, cooing as it sat in the boy's hands. And blood suddenly appearing as I reached to take it.

Mysteries like these, enchanting, perplexing and tantalizing, are common in Africa and they are what lie beneath the stories on the pages of this book. I am fascinated — obsessed — by what occurs when cultures collide, as they did when my secular skepticism came up against the defiant glint in the eyes of the fetish priest. And he answered, or politely deflected, all those questions I put to him, as though we were discussing nothing more meaningful than recipes. While we both knew that what we were discussing was as mysterious as life itself.

This anecdote is real, taken right off that tape I made in the village, unlike the people, events and places in the stories in this book, all of which are taken right out of my imagination. They are all fictional reflections of what Africa has offered me, and others, who have ventured out here to live. People in Africa have patiently taught me to appreciate the dignity, insight and intelligence that are to me Africa's most outstanding features.

Africa is a magical continent brimming with life, wisdom and love. Yes, it is impoverished, rife with injustice and war, riddled with social and political ills that we hear about all too often — but perhaps not often enough? Africa is still the world's least understood and most misunderstood continent.

There are many complex reasons for the problems the people of Africa face today. Far too many of those reasons find their roots not in Africa, but in foreign capitals, where the arms dealers and power-brokers have their bases — power-brokers who allow, even encourage with their silence or their "quiet diplomacy", many African powers-that-be to pursue their maniacal dreams for immortality, which they seem to think will come true after they've stolen their country's future and stashed it away in foreign banks.

But that is another book, or a whole library of books, about a vast, intricate continent on a troubled and shrinking planet. This book is not about Big Men and Big Problems. This is a collection of tales about everyday people whose voices are never heard on international news dispatches from that "hopeless" continent called Africa.

Hopeless? Africa? The treasure of Africa is its people who despite hardship are full of hope. People embroiled in their own struggle for survival or a few of the most basic amenities and the justice, which elsewhere are so fundamental that life without them is almost inconceivable.

The Africans in this book attest to that. They are not real people, but I have met and known many individuals very much like them. The "strangers" are foreigners who land and then must find solid ground under their feet — anyone who has headed out for the first time to an unfamiliar place, to deal with unfamiliar people. Some fare better than others. Strangers are like children, they say.

I have given up trying to explain why I feel so deeply about this continent on which I am a guest, why I am compelled to write about it. But life *is* art, nowhere more so than in Africa — where, if you go back far enough, every one of us has roots.

Maybe these stories come from my own inability to put much of what I have seen and learned in Africa into any rational and logical framework, so there is nowhere for it but on the pages of a book of fiction. Or maybe it's as friends in Ghana have suggested — maybe someone has used powerful *juju* on me. Or maybe there's no difference — maybe fiction is juju.

Nairobi
October 1995

Flying to Africa

Annie can't believe she is actually on her way, flying to Africa. She has always loved flying, even before she had left the ground for the first time. And that is already twenty years ago — that awful year when she got braces and flew to Montreal on a cultural exchange program.

The braces are long gone and so is *that* Annie Minski, the homely teenager who lived in the pink bungalow at 17 Reed Street. This Annie Minski is going places. And this is no joy-riding holiday package. She is travelling business class on an all-expenses-paid trip, a monitoring mission for CDO.

She has a new cut that her hairdresser calls "sassy", a new seal-grey suit with a long, tailored blazer and low-heeled pumps to match. She is carrying her new powerbook PC and a slim briefcase as hand luggage.

This time she is on her own. Not trailing along in a pack of rowdy classmates on a cultural exchange program meant — through language — to promote understanding among young people. Annie remembers little of the girl who billeted her in Montreal, just that she was drab and quiet, too shy to even try speaking English. She lived in Montreal's inner city, in a drab tenement that smelled like cooked cabbage. That cultural exchange program had left Annie depressed and not the least impressed. How was such an experience supposed to make her appreciate another culture? All that she had liked about that experience was the flight.

In those days she wrote every detail of her life in a scrapbook. She had thought it worth noting, for example, that the airplane toilet flushed with blue liquid. On the same page she taped a bar of Air Canada soap taken from that airplane washroom. Underneath this she printed the word "Comments" and filled in the blank with the word "interesting".

At some point she had stopped writing things down — probably around the time she decided to put all her energy into succeeding at school and making her mark on the world. She thinks with chagrin about her naivety back then, scrawling pages full of trivia about the things she saw around her on that flight. Imagine saving that pathetic bit of soap.

Unsophisticated is the word. She prefers not to remember.

So far, though, things are not quite going according to plan on this trip. She intended to drink some wine over her dinner, watch a film on the individual video screen beside her seat and then listen to music on her Walkman, as the plane chased and overtook the dawn over Europe. Perhaps because of all the wine she drank with her colleagues at a popular new Italian *ristorante* before the flight she fell asleep during the stop-over in Halifax. She didn't wake up again until the air hostess gently shook her shoulder to offer her breakfast.

When she lands at Schipol she feels woozy, dazed and rumpled. She ducks into a washroom to make up her face and finger some life back into the curls flattened by a night of dry cabin air. She changes her panties, stuffing the worn ones into her make-up bag, brushes her teeth and moves close to the mirror to ensure that no blemishes have popped up on her face during the night. When she is happy with her appearance, she steps smartly out of the washroom, pulling her computer and briefcase on the portable metal pulley she purchased in the event of a lay-over. She is pleased that she knows the word "lay-over".

For good measure, she checks at the KLM counter to see that the boarding pass issued in Ottawa for the rest of the journey is in order. Outside, jumbo jets with insignia she has never seen before, from countries she has somehow missed hearing of, are nosing in and out of gates.

The transit hall has a half a mile of windows and is full of economizing passengers sprawled *sans dignité* on benches and institutional sofas. Annie heads towards the executive lounge, trying not to feel *too* smug as she enters.

It is dark and cool after the hot, bright transit hall. In one corner, a giant screen is playing music video hits. News headlines flash across a digital band over the bar in alarming red dot-matrix. She pauses, allows her glance to take in her fellow executive passengers. They are mostly middle-aged males. She spies the spot she wants and moves quickly to the empty armchair beside an attractive black man. He wears a flawless navy blue suit. She hopes he's a *real* African. She smiles at him and asks, "Is this chair empty?"

He lowers *The Economist*, glances up at her, glances at the empty chair, smiles and shakes his head. It is only as she is folding her skirt around her knees and leaning back into the chair with an exaggerated sigh that she realizes her question was ridiculous — in Canada someone might have retorted "Do bears shit in the woods?" She would have to remember to think before she spoke. She hasn't got to where she was by acting the frumpy, small-town girl from 17 Reed Street.

The interior of the lounge smells like expensive perfume. Just being in here makes her feel glamorous, part of an exclusive master plan. In her mind this looks like a globe sewn up tight as a baseball with its flight paths and telecommunication networks, of which she is now part. She reaches down and pulls a book from the zip-pocket of her computer case. She spent an afternoon in the bookstore choosing just the right reading material for the trip: Alice Walker's *The Colour Purple*, a Nobel prize-winning novel by a Nigerian with a name she can't pronounce, and because she thought she should be reading some serious non-fiction as well, an edition of Orwell's essays. It is this that she pulls out now, wondering if she should exchange it for the Nigerian novel. Surely the man next to her will notice her reading African literature and be impressed.

She casts her eyes around the lounge, checking again on her neighbour to see if he shows signs of wanting to strike up a conversation with her. He seems engrossed in the magazine. She begins to read, trying in vain to summon a healthy intellectual interest in what Orwell had to say in 1946. Why did she think she'd be able to fathom his essays when she hadn't even been able to get through *Nineteen Eighty-four*?

Her mind wanders automatically back to Canada and how it's all come together for her. The contract is a fitting reward for all her hard work. She and her colleagues had submitted a proposal twelve months earlier to the CDO West African desk, and she had almost given up on it altogether. Then, a week ago now, Mark called her office at five.

"Hi, Annie? Mark here. Listen, pack your bags. You're outa here. CDO wants you in Africa within five days, to do a preliminary study, sort of prepare the groundwork for the full-scale monitoring session. I'll fax the contracts over to you in the A.M. Have a look at them and give me a buzz. You and me'll have to get together to lay out the terms of reference. Get it all on paper."

"Mark, that's great. Wonderful, in fact."

"Ha," he snorted. "You haven't been to Talon yet, or you might not be quite so grateful. Talon's the end of the world as we know it. Worse shitholes might be out there but not on this planet. You all boostered up, got all your shots?"

"Yes, Mark. Just after we submitted the proposal."

"Ace. Normally we wouldn't send you out alone. George likes to supervise consultants in the field, but he's over in southeast Asia for a couple of months, so it looks like you'll be on your own up in Talon. You think you can handle it? Seriously now, Annie."

"Mark, please, don't underestimate me."

"You'll have a list of contacts, people you'll have to see. I'll make sure you get the protocol. I've gotta run. We have some reps from the West African Economic Community in town."

"Okay. I'll wait for the contracts. And Mark? Thanks a lot."

It's been a long haul from the pink bungalow on Reed Street. Right now, as she is absorbing the plush comforts of the executive lounge, her mother and father are probably just heading off in their slippers to bed, now that the midnight prayer session on Cable 10 is over. Mom will have laid out the breakfast things on the kitchen table, checked the locks for the third time, and might be checking on Polly, the youngest of the brood and the only one still at home and subject to the strict rules governing evenings out.

Annie uncrosses her legs, then crosses them again, enjoying the feel of one smooth silk stocking on the other. She pictures herself in a video clip, part of an advertisement for pantyhose or the new line of Fleur de Lis fragrances. Another glance at her neighbour still engrossed in *The Economist* suggests that so far he hasn't imagined any of these scenarios in which she stars. Damn him anyway.

She hasn't come all this way to let an African man make her feel inadequate. She has worked her way through university and secured an MA without a word of congratulations from her parents, who don't even know what sociology is, let alone the sociology of development. They had always expected her to marry a preacher in their miserable church. She wishes she could stop thinking about them shuffling about in their slippers on the linoleum floors.

It wasn't easy, extricating herself from the trap they laid in that sheep's paddock they inhabit, where the *Church Weekly Digest is* considered sufficient intellectual stimulation and fluffy slippers are all that's needed in the way of comfort. She eventually succeeded but only by moving away to Ottawa. There, she struggled to worm her way into the development establishment. She was the brains — but not the money — behind the consulting firm she and four of her fellow graduate students formed, to "monitor and evaluate the social dimension of CDO development projects on vulnerable groups and ameliorate their negative effects on women and children". She even authored that phrase.

She spent months developing contacts within the CDO ranks and now they have won a contract. A nice fat contract that will help pay for the condominium she intends to buy, which will afford her access to the Rideau Canal and a view of Parliament Hill.

"May I get you something to drink?"

She starts, then turns to stare at the man who is talking to her. "I'm going to get something to drink. Can I bring you something too?"

"Oh sorry, I didn't realize you were addressing me. Yes, please," she says.

His smile is frozen on his face; his teeth dangling in front of her like ice cubes. "Maybe an orange juice or sparkling water, something like that?" He moves — nicely she thinks — towards the bar.

She pretends to read, but her eyes stray about the lounge. The rest of the passengers suddenly look like bored accountants, each as grey and dull as the other, all immersed in spreadsheets or the *Herald Tribune* or other such drudgery. She thinks they are probably all businessmen, multinational corporate managers or executives going out to rape and pillage the third world. The flying probably bores them. None is on a mission of goodwill, to an impoverished African country to safeguard the interests of the women and children.

She extends her right hand and examines her fingernails, gleaming red. Her silver rings are polished to perfection. "Thank you ever so much," she says, as the man hands her a tall glass of orange juice.

He has a mug of golden beer. She thinks him very well travelled to be drinking beer at this time of day. Perhaps he has been flying for days and can no longer tell whether it is night or day.

"You're not British?" he asks, settling into his chair, giving her another show of his beautiful teeth. The only person she has ever seen with teeth that regular and white is her mother — but hers are dentures.

She titters. "No, do I sound British?"

"Yes, somewhat, although there's a slight twang there I can't seem to place."

"I'm Canadian," she says, sipping the orange juice. Then she places it carefully on the glass-topped table between the two chairs. "And you?"

"I like to think of myself as simply African," he says. "Where are you off to?"

"Africa," she says, beaming.

"Africa's a big place."

"Well, my contract will eventually cover several countries in West Africa. But this first mission trip is to a town called Talon. Have you heard of it?"

"Have I heard of it? I should think so. My mother's from Talon. I expect I had better introduce myself because we're probably on the same flight. My name is Chris Ansah."

"Annie Minski. Pleased to meet you, Mr. Ansah."

He is fingering his magazine and she is afraid that he will start reading it again. "What's your profession, Mr. Ansah?"

"I'm a professor of African Studies. What about you, Miss Minski? Or should I call you *Ms* Minski? I know European women are terribly sensitive about these things."

She laughs. "Not this European woman. Or maybe that's the difference between Europe and North America. I don't really care one way or the other. You can call me Annie, if you like, and make it simpler, by far."

He smiles and empties his mug of beer. "Yes, one does forget how informal are the Americans."

She reaches for her juice. Should she correct him? Remind him that she just told him she was Canadian? She wonders how to do this without being impolite. She hates to be rude, because that is what they all say Americans are. Canadians aren't supposed to be rude. She can feel herself blushing in her confusion.

He rescues her by asking, "And you, Annie? What do you do? What takes you out to my dear country?" His accent is beautiful, attached to each of his words, like a curlicue. The row of spotlights overhead is reflected in his eyes.

"I'm a consultant for CDO. Canadian Development Overseas. Do you know it?"

"Of course, yes. They're very active in my part of the world."

"I'm part of a monitoring team, sent out to ensure that development is not at the expense of the poorest members of society, the rural women and children. I will be putting together a proposal for a special program directed at alleviating the hardship of structural adjustment on those target groups."

He nods and his smile is pleasant. "That is sound planning," he says. "You've been to Africa before?"

She pauses, contemplates lying, then decides against it. "No," she says. "I know, you're probably wondering what I have to offer. It does seem presumptuous, doesn't it? But imagine, if I weren't doing this, then it could be a whole lot worse — a bunch of male bureaucrats in Ottawa making plans for development projects and ignoring the women altogether."

He doesn't answer. She notices that he wears a gold band on his right hand. She wonders whether wedding rings in Africa are worn on the right or the left hand. She blushes when she realizes he has caught her looking at his ring.

"What does your husband think of you coming out all alone? He's not a little afraid that some tall, handsome African man will steal your heart?" he asks. This time she can't see his teeth through his smile.

"Oh, I'm not married," she says. "I've got to launch my career before I can take on the responsibilities that a family entails."

"A beautiful woman like you should never tell a man in my country that you're not married. My brothers will never let you out of the country again. I'm sure you've heard all sorts of terrible stories about African men."

"I'm not the kind of person who listens much to stories, Mr. Ansah."

"Please, you're being unfair now. You asked me to call you Annie, and you're treating me like I'm your professor. I'm C.A. to my friends. You may call me Chris, if you wish."

"Thank you, Chris," she says, blushing again.

"I'd be interested in hearing what you expect to find in Talon, Annie," he says. "And in hearing how people in Canada picture my country. Canada is one place I haven't been, although I have a brother there and he tells me it's full of opportunities."

"Oh, it is. Canada is very enlightened when it comes to multiculturalism and questions of equal opportunity." She turns to face him and adds, "Mind you, I've heard so many good things about your country, I'm sure it's much the same." Because she can't seem to meet his eyes without reddening, she glances at her watch. "Should we be thinking of boarding soon? It's almost ten."

"Oh, there's no hurry in life. That's a favourite proverb where I come from. Let us have one more drink. I find it gets very dry in the aircraft. And there'll be no more Dutch beer for me for a long time."

Over their second round of drinks, she tells him more about the development project she will be monitoring and evaluating in the north. He says very little but makes enough of the right noises to make her confident that she is saying the right things.

They move into the jumbo together, and she notices when he shows his passport at the pass control that he is Doctor Ansah. It impresses her that he hasn't used his title. She is proud to be walking beside such a tall, well-turned-out *African* man. She wonders if people around them assume they are married. They are chatting to each other as though they're very very good friends, at least. She laughs along with him at the enormous pieces of hand luggage — ghetto blasters and televisions — that African passengers are trying to slip past the KLM agents and onto the plane. "Everyone has to take a gift to everyone," he says quietly, as they move into the airliner.

When the cabin doors have been closed, she asks the flight attendant if she can move to the empty seat beside her friend at the back of the business-class cabin. Although he acts pleased to have her there, she would have liked it better if he had taken the initiative himself. She settles herself in the aisle seat and flips through the in-flight magazine as the steward passes out glasses of orange juice and champagne. Once again, Chris has stuck *The Economist* in front of his nose.

After take-off, he puts on his headphones and she does the same, secure that they are comfortable enough with each other not to feel obliged to talk the whole way. She is thrilled to be inside the womb of that jumbo lunging through the heavens, southwards towards Africa. She chooses the classical channel, hoping he notices. He strikes her as someone who appreciates the finer things in life.

She reclines her seat and closes her eyes, savouring the ecstasy of flying to Africa in the company of this attractive man. She imagines that his hand brushes against hers, and shivers race down her legs and out through her toes. When she opens her eyes and gazes dreamily at him to show him that she enjoys the physical contact, she finds he has removed his tie and an end of it is draped over the armrest separating them so that it has been brushing on her hand. He appears to be sound asleep. She studies the brown sheen of his face, the curled eyelashes, the immaculate black hair.

She slips off her headphones and the seat-belt and goes to the washroom. There she outlines her eyes with a pencil the same silvery grey as the silk blouse, combs her hair back into shape and applies a faintly metallic pink lipstick. She studies her face in the mirror, pursing her lips and practising a seductive pout. In the sickly light of the washroom, she decides she looks pale and jaundiced. She adds two spots of colour to her cheeks. When she flushes, she notes that the toilets in this aircraft doesn't fill with blue disinfectant.

Intercontinental business class provides liquid soap in ornate bottles and a choice of French perfumes. She dabs some of the complimentary Opium onto her wrists and struggles against the urge to pack all the bottles into her handbag. It is only the thought of being searched at the airport, with Chris looking on as the pilfered perfume is pulled out of her purse, that finally decides the issue. She reluctantly takes even the Opium out of her purse and places it back onto the shelf.

She is still feeling soiled by that powerful temptation to steal when she walks down the aisle. She avoids row after row of eyes. She feels they are all looking at her, that they know she doesn't belong here with them in executive class. She tells herself they are just crocodiles lined up in a swamp with only their eyes and noses visible, and walks with her head high.

She wishes she had left off the blush — more so when she sees that Chris is now awake and smiling at her as she approaches. She rubs at her cheeks. "I find it very warm in here," she says, flushing more, then feigning interest in the menu that has been deposited on her seat during her absence.

"Shall we drink a little champagne?" he asks. "To celebrate your first trip to Africa, and my home-coming."

"That would be lovely," she says.

The hostess pours them each a glass. "Where will you be staying in the capital, Annie?"

"In the Shangri-La," she says.

He nods. "Yes, that's about right. Fine restaurant, dancers every night. Nice ambience. You'll like it. All the expats do."

"I've heard it's very good," she says.

"Will you be around for a few days, or are you going to take off immediately for the hot north?"

"Oh, I'll stay in the capital for a couple of days," she says quickly. Should she ask him to drop by the hotel? Or would that seem too forward?

"That's good, you'll be able to get your feet on the ground at least."

"Do you mean that you don't think my feet are on the ground, Chris?"

"Touché. What I meant was that you'll be able to get the feel of the place. Sample some of our delicious palaver sauce and *fufu* and plantains and look around at some of the people you're so interested in helping."

She glances at him to see whether that is irony she detects, but he looks as gracious as ever. "I'll be very busy, Chris. I have appointments at my embassy. I'm afraid I'll spend most of my time in front of a computer screen. This work is really quite dull, in spite of what some people may think."

He chuckles. "Yes, that's the problem these days. We spend too much time trying to do our problem solving on computers and have no time left to examine the human variable first hand."

"Well, I *will* be doing interviews." She hears her own petulance and forces herself to smile and soften her voice. "I have a whole long list of people I have to meet in the north, Chris."

"A computer list, no doubt." He laughs loudly. "Cheers, Annie. To our arrival in Africa."

She isn't sure what tingles more, the champagne or the sound of her name in his mouth and the twinkle in his eyes. She pictures him coming to meet her at a poolside restaurant — the Shangri-La has a lovely kidney-shaped pool. The pamphlets make it look like a tropical dream. She is fortunate to have run into such a charming man even before landing in Africa.

The plane touches down on schedule in the capital. She stands but doesn't rush to get her computer from the overhead compartment, taking her cue from Chris who sits quietly with his hands folded, while their fellow passengers grapple with each other to be the first to the aisle and the exit. She expects Chris will assist her when he is ready to move.

"Brace yourself for the heat, Annie. It's warmer out there than it is in here," he says, as he moves past her into the aisle and heads towards the exit. She has forgotten he has no luggage in the overhead compartment. His briefcase hasn't left his lap the whole trip.

She is unable in the press of bodies to get her computer from the bin above her. Passengers from the economy section are already flooding forward. Something is going terribly wrong. She pushes them back, "Hey, this is business class here. You people wait until we're out." She swings into the aisle, not caring that she has clobbered a child with her powerbook PC as she rushes towards the exit. "You should keep the tourists back until your executive class is out," she snaps at the flight attendants standing at the doorway.

As she runs across the tarmac towards the terminal she is glad of the low-heeled shoes. The heat takes her breath away. She is sure Chris has not intended to let her get separated from him this way. She wishes she had given him her business card — or asked for his.

She pushes her way through the mob of passengers inside the long reception hall. "Excuse me, please. I'm in a hurry."

"You're in Africa, Madam. There's no hurry in life." She turns around, her smile wide for Chris. But a sea of black faces looks back at her. It is impossible to tell who has spoken but not difficult to tell that they all find her amusing.

"Madam, please. Can you not see this is the queue for immigration? Take your place, please." The man in uniform blocks her path and points over her shoulder.

"But, I'm travelling with somebody . . ."

"Please, Madam, don't cause trouble. Everybody has to go through immigration together. Now go back to the end of the queue, I beg you. This is for foreigners," he says, indicating the long line of white people.

She thinks about arguing but realizes that the lines are growing longer by the second as the airliner empties into the terminal as the economy section spews out its cargo. Many people are watching her. There is laughter and murmuring.

Standing on her tiptoes at the end of a long line, she thinks she sees Chris Ansah at the front of the shorter line for nationals. He is embracing a very tall and stunning African woman in a bright yellow turban and robe. Annie looks away quickly.

She thinks she will die of thirst before the line in front of her clears. Her grey suit is soaked and she knows from the black smudges on her hands when she wipes at the sweat on her face that her mascara has run.

In the baggage hall, the CDO in-country representative meets her with a soggy smile and a sign bearing her name. "Annie Minski? Welcome to hell. How was your flight?"

"Long," she says, thinking how nice he looks with his red, curly hair. She can see that he is lean and fit under the baggy Blue Jays t-shirt and jeans.

As they stand waiting for her luggage to appear he introduces himself as Jay Sutherland. He says he has been in the country for four years. It is difficult to be heard over the boisterous shouting as people collect suitcases and crates from the carousel. She has to dodge and leap out of the way to avoid being knocked over by speeding luggage carts and mobs of Africans. Once he has retrieved her bags and waved his way through customs where a world war appears to be taking place, he smiles at her. "How do you like Africa so far?"

"Not much," she says. "Considering all we're doing to help them, they're pretty arrogant. And ungrateful."

"Tell me about it," Jay says, laughing as he ushers her out the door towards a waiting vehicle in the VIP parking zone. The Land Cruiser is white, emblazoned with maple leaves and CDO stickers. The engine and air-conditioner are running. The driver sits silently, waiting for instructions. After the heat outside, the vehicle is almost freezing. Jay sits beside her in the back and they roar down an impressive boulevard, overtaking every vehicle on the road. Annie begins to feel better. By the time she has checked into her suite at the Shangri-La, changed into an elegant ankle-length skirt and sleeveless silk tunic and downed half a pint of beer with an attractive man from Toronto in the tropical setting she's been dreaming of her whole life, she feels euphoric — as though she's flying again.

Strangers are like children

The walls in this house are pink and green. The accumulated grime has all but obliterated the pink that encircles the lower half of this mud-walled structure that used to be a chief's palace. I have a warped table, a three-legged chair and a pan latrine — a chipped enamelled bowl that Mathia empties for me at regular intervals during the day. There is a straw mat on the floor where I sleep, while rats and cockroaches explore the crevices of my body like men hungry for a woman. I have learned to break the necks of the rats and am no longer squeamish about squashing a cockroach with my bare palm. I throw the dead rats out the door and in the morning children collect them and put them in cooking pots.

The words they use to describe me translate as "woman pig," since I have such pink skin and blond hair on my arms and legs. This no longer bothers me. Alhassan told me the first day that this was what his people called us. He said it was not an insult. "It's just that we tend to give names that describe what we see. Your skin is pink and a little bit hairy, like a pig's. There's nothing wrong with that. How many times have you heard your people say we look like apes?"

Trust Alhassan to leave me at the mercy of tit-for-tat logic.

Alhassan must be in no man's land. I want him more, I think, than I've ever wanted anything or anyone. But they'll surely kill him if he comes back. They killed twenty-one of his supporters during the attack. They have weapons. The politicians in the capital far to the south have been playing sides in this dispute that they try to pass off as a dispute over chieftaincy — ancient Goroni politics that they say have nothing to do with them. But they won their election by paying off chiefs and traditional kings. They corrupted ancient politics with their own corrupted, modern politics. Alhassan's words.

Good thing none of the international election observers stayed long enough to find out how that works. Or maybe that's why they stayed only two days. Because they know. Alhassan says they should. After all, they helped orchestrate it all.

And now the government wants Alhassan's uncle to be chief because he's a member of the ruling party that controls the new parliament. But Alhassan is the regent, the man who is in line to inherit the chieftaincy. Alas, Alhassan doesn't play politics. He speaks about people's needs: about the school he wants to build and run, the health post, the wells, the dam, the forestry plot. Alhassan, you call me naive and innocent?

Where is he? I hear people whispering outside. They don't think I can understand them but Alhassan's time was not completely wasted on me. They are saying he is invincible, that he alone of his force was not injured or killed. They say he has very powerful *juju* and that he will return to fetch his white woman. They say they will get him then. I seem to be the chink in his African armour, his juju, his good luck, his strength. They are using me as bait to bring him back. I came to find out his fate and now I may be what decides it.

Am I a prisoner? No one is stopping me from walking out that door. I am fed *tuo* with fish twice a day and I have been given a brightly coloured wrapper that I wear like a bath towel after a shower. I put it on to sleep and when Mathia comes to wash my skirt and blouse — the only clothing I have with me. The denim of that skirt is now very thin and pale after so many washings. There is a frayed hole growing over the right knee.

My legs are covered with mosquito bites and oozing sores that attract flies. I may have malaria but I can't remember what it was like not to feel weak and dizzy.

I have lost count of the number of days I have been in this hut. I have no paper to write on now. My camera, tape recorder and notebooks have all been taken from me. So far the only person who has been permitted into this house (I almost wrote "my" house) is Mathia. She is sweet but she would not understand my need for a pen and paper. She cannot read or write.

The walls of this house are circular, plastered with screed and those awful shades of green and pink paint. My story encircles me. I can read it there. Every day I write more with my eyes. Maybe Africa has turned me into a wizard too. Maybe that's what deprivation does.

If only he would come. Stay away, Alhassan.

I begin to write again. It keeps my mind active. Marching my thoughts around and around the walls that enclose me.

I *did* come here looking for a story. I did not count on being in the story. Most journalists don't or they wouldn't do what they do. I am a writer and photographer and last year I had a series of photographs published in *Wonder Magazine*, along with an article about African healers and rulers who are living in North America. The series was called *African Transplants.* I had met and talked to many of these men. I realized even back in New York that to be a chief or king in much of Africa was to be a deity. What could be more exciting — I finally convinced the editors — than a story about kings and chiefs from the source, from some of the poorest and most remote parts of Africa? Talon was my third stop. I was cocky. I thought I had it all figured out. Don't laugh, Alhassan.

The development people in Talon told me Alhassan was a great source of information. Officially, he was a French and English teacher in the Talon Senior Secondary School. But the paltry income he received from that barely kept him fed, so he took on part-time work teaching foreigners any one of the five local languages that he spoke fluently. He was in great demand but he agreed to give me two hours each evening. I told him I wanted a crash course in Goroni, the language and the customs.

We held these sessions in my living room. I was staying in a tiny bungalow that I rented for a month on the outskirts of town in a subdivision they called the Estates — ironically, I assume. The place had crumbling walls and furniture and no amenities. It rained through.

At first I had the impression that Alhassan didn't much like me. He was extremely reserved, even distant with his exaggerated good manners and formality. It took him two weeks to switch from calling me Madam to Alison, despite my request that he call me by my first name right at the beginning of our third lesson.

Sometimes he drifted into silence in the middle of a session. His voice would slowly fade, as though snuffed out by the sounds of night insects outside. Then he would sit and stare at his hands which were always entwining themselves around some object — the cap from a bottle of Coke, the bottle-opener, the candle on the table, anything. They were beautiful hands. Very slim fingers. Their movements were fluid. Gentle. I wonder where his pensiveness took him.

On the final evening of our lessons, I asked him how old he was. He smiled, one of those cagey African smiles that give absolutely nothing away and deflect the question back at you, making your impertinence echo around the room like a bad joke or an out-of-tune piano.

I assumed he had not heard me, and asked again, "Alhassan, how old are you?"

"I think we have finished our lessons," he said, in Goroni.

"Yes, I'm sorry for that. I've enjoyed them," I answered, in Goroni.

"But you have not been listening very well, I fear," he said.

"Why do you say that?"

"Because, Alison, you will get nothing if you march into a village and ask someone how old they are. We have ways of posing questions without asking and of offering replies without answering. I suppose we are also a little short of trust in strangers. Information is not easily given out here."

"I know that. But I wasn't interviewing you. And I'm not in a village. I was asking you a personal question because I'm interested. In you as a person and not as a representative of the Goroni people, Alhassan."

"A-haa," he said, a wonderful sound they use in Talon that means so much more than a simple "I see".

"Anyway, I have told you everything about myself. You asked me questions as part of the lessons and I answered. You know my age, my profession, my business here in Africa, all about my family, my life. And I know nothing about you."

"I don't want to be one of the people quoted — or misquoted — in your newspaper articles, which I can imagine people in your country reading over their breakfasts." He grinned. "Or while they're perched on their porcelain thrones."

I considered this. "Okay, I promise never to quote you on anything. Anyway, I'm not writing for newspapers. And really, I'm only asking because I am curious about you."

He smiled again, and laughed. Alhassan laughed when I was being most serious.

I sighed with exasperation and he laughed again. He was still laughing when he laid his hand — that beautiful appendage with five long and inquisitive fingers — on my shoulder.

The current that went through me could have lit the entire town of Talon. The town had been in darkness since a flood had swept through the building housing the thirty-five-year-old diesel engine which had been used as a generator for that many years. The flood had been caused by a broken dam, which was also thirty-five years old — my age. All these local tragedies, linked only by the vagaries of cause and effect, seemed to snare me, entwine me, involve me, when he touched me that first time. The forces of nature, playing with the fragile organisms created by them. Forces we in the west think we can control. *Understand.* I picture Alhassan throwing back his head and laughing at that. It makes me smile, even now.

I glanced at his face, immediately suspicious that he was patronizing or humouring me with that touch. There was no laughter in his eyes. In the dim light of the storm lantern and a single candle on the small table in front of us, his eyes looked moist, as though he might be weeping. Or perhaps it was just the light playing on the dark, smooth pupils.

"I am thirty-nine years old," he said then. "I had a wife and two children in Zoggu. But she left two years ago for the capital. She didn't want to stay in the bush. She is the daughter of a chief, with a college education. She now works at the Ministry of Finance. I am alone now, but if I get the chieftaincy of Zoggu, as is my right, I will inherit five wives from my father. My father passed away last year. If they choose my uncle to fill that post, then the wives will go to him and I will be free. But the people in the village are demanding that I be *enskinned* as chief. I have promised them a school and wells."

I said nothing then, because I realized how full my head was of his smell. There was the lingering scent of soap, a dusting of wood smoke that imbued the entire countryside, and an earthy smell of heat and strength that weakened me. It was probably at that moment that I began to grasp what I had been taught: silence in Africa can say much, much more than words. Alhassan had told me before that among his people the words for smell and sound are the same. That people can hear through their noses. A scent is, for an illiterate farmer in the bush, an entire encyclopedia.

I nodded very slowly. He released his grip on my shoulder and stood up. He extended a hand, smiled a goodnight. He said he would come back to visit me, but not as my teacher. "As your friend," he said, with his lips forming that cagey smile. "Because I am interested in you, Alison."

I waited three weeks. How I waited. I tried to summon the patience that Alhassan told me was the greatest balm on earth. I didn't want to look as though I were chasing him, but I did walk past his house at the school a few times. It looked deserted. Eventually I went to see his brother, Yakubu, to ask him about Alhassan. Yakubu said he was sure Alhassan would come to me when he could, if that was my wish. I said it was.

"Then I will tell him and he will come," Yakubu said.

The day of my planned departure came and went. I had contacted my editor, told him I would be delayed. He didn't mind. Extra time would be charged to me not to him.

As time passed I decided Alhassan was testing me and almost convinced myself that I was rising to the challenge. In his absence I felt I was getting to know him much better. It had always been hard for me to think clearly with him in the same room. Perhaps that was why I didn't notice during the weeks he tutored me in language and culture the effect that he was having on me. He had an overpowering presence, exuding something that made it hard for me to put all the pieces together. I could focus on his hands, or his eyes, or the broken linoleum on the floor by his feet, but I could not fit the whole picture into my mind.

Then, without warning, he was back late one night. I was transcribing taped interviews with chiefs and fetish priests onto paper, wondering how to make sense of any of it. The first draft of the article — and the second and third — had gone into the waste basket. There was no way to lay the chiefs flat, to fit all that they were and represented onto a piece of paper with strings of miserable and feeble words.

He entered so quietly that I wasn't aware he was there until he touched my shoulder. It was awkward, my pretending he was just an ordinary friend, a visitor come for tea while the concrete floor under me tilted and allowed me to fall away into a bottomless pit. He waited for me to offer him a seat before he sat down then asked me how I was, how my work was going. When I had answered all his ritual greetings, he stopped talking. He stared at a calendar on the wall, one a German volunteer had given to me, which showed a large stone castle somewhere in that northern empire, surrounded by still clear water. The stark silence of that absurd photograph in that dark room made me wonder if Alhassan could make time stand still. With his silence.

When he finally looked at me, I moved towards him, but slowly. He didn't use words to draw me to him that way. I didn't take a seat on the sofa beside him because the under-strapping had recently broken, spilling me to the floor, and I knew it would spill both of us if I added my weight. Those were the kinds of things that often helped release social tension at a stiff party back home but it would have been wrong there, then.

I knelt beside him, my head bowed. He put a hand on my head, pulling my face onto his thighs. He began to rub his fingers through my hair. I rubbed my arms to still the goose-bumps. That was no cure.

The cure was so simple, as old as nature itself and just as wonderful, natural as night and day. No promises. No vows. Just taking hold of something that was there, while it was there. We talked a lot, in whispers. No specifics, just the wonder of man and woman, and how they could fit so perfectly together despite, *because* of all their differences. "Like pigs and apes," he said, making me roll away from him in laughter. Then we slept, entwined, until he woke me gently just before dawn. He told me he would come back to me when he could and left on foot, in the darkness.

He did not tell me he was going to war that day.

Yakubu told me, twenty-four hours later, when he slipped quietly in through the back, materializing out of nowhere at my rear door. "There's trouble in Zoggu," he said. "The police vehicle carried bodies through town last night, to the morgue. They say twenty-one. My uncle has taken the village and is sitting on the skins, being chief. The people of Zoggu want Alhassan as their chief. They are all fleeing to Mamton. Alhassan has disappeared. I think he will go to Mamton. But I cannot go myself. They are looking for me too."

"What are you saying? I don't understand. Alhassan was here yesterday. How could he have gone to Zoggu? When?"

Yakubu stilled my questions with a look I had finally come to recognize. It meant I was behaving like a stranger. "Strangers are like children," Alhassan had told me more than once, when I began to think out loud. When I asked him what that meant, he smiled and told me to think about it, with an affectionate look a parent might give an inquisitive child who had to be schooled in the ways of the world and the correct forms of behaviour. It was his look that made me understand.

"Do you think I should go?" I asked Yakubu, finally.

"I cannot say. It is dangerous. But I think no one knows who you are, that you are now Alhassan's woman. You can take your equipment. Say you want to do interviews. I need to know what has happened. Alhassan, if he is there, will hear there is a stranger asking for interviews. He will find you."

"Do you think I can find him in Mamton?"

"I do not know. I hope so," he said. "Do not tell anyone I spoke to you." He backed away and I had the impression he vaporized in the teak woodlot behind the estates. I remained in the doorway, trying to stop my knees from shaking by focusing on practical, rational thoughts.

It was impossible for me to take my bicycle all the way to Mamton. I needed to get there fast, and alone on a bicycle I would probably get lost. By car, it was about twenty minutes out of town, one of hundreds of villages that all looked the same to me. I needed a taxi.

I gathered my notebooks, camera and tape recorder along with a bundle of rumpled coni notes. I walked numbly out of the house as the sun rose over the teak trees and put a burning end to my happy-ever-after dreams for Alhassan and me. The thought of Alhassan in arm-to-arm, cutlass-to-cutlass combat in the bush was so absurd, unimaginable, that I could almost pretend I really was on the way to do some more dispassionate interviews about de-witching shrines and fetishes and ancient conquests.

Two chickens squabbled over a dead rat in front of the neighbour's house, and a goat chewed enthusiastically on a plastic bag. It had rained a lot during the night, my night with Alhassan that already seemed like something from another life. The road in front of my house was a brown lake. I walked past hovels and ramshackle government offices. Along the path through the forestry department's plantation of teak trees where cattle and goats were browsing with all the time in the world. The boy herders shouted greetings but I ignored them. Past the slaughterhouse, the last stop for straggly cattle. There was bellowing and shouting inside the filthy grey structure. It sounded like the trading floor in a stock market.

On the main road, I flagged down a rusty taxi that ground to a wobbly stop beside me.

"I want to go to Mamton, or Zoggu," I said to the driver.

"No go, Madam. I no do go there. Trouble-o." He sped off.

I yelled at him to come back, waving my arms with a bundle of conies clutched in my hands, showing him how handsomely I would pay him. But he was already gone and I realized I was behaving like one of the town lunatics.

"I can give you a drive, Madam?" I turned to see a man with a pleasant face, distinguished by the scarred gashes of tribal marks the length of his cheeks, behind the wheel of a silver Nissan Patrol that had pulled up beside me.

A lot of conflicting thoughts and fears silenced me. I backed away. He opened his door, came around to me and said in a conspiratorial whisper, "I know you are a dear friend of Alhassan's," he said. "I am to take you to him."

"Oh thank God. Yakubu sent you?"

He nodded.

"Do you know if Alhassan is okay? He hasn't been hurt? Or killed?"

He was ushering me into the front of the Patrol, climbing in himself.

"You're sure he's all right?" I said as we sped through town, splashing waves of brown mud water like a hippopotamus taking dives.

"He is not hurt. He cannot be hurt, Madam Alison."

"I've been frantic," I said. "I heard that his supporters attacked Zoggu. I was intending to make my way to Mamton to try to find Alhassan. You don't know how happy I am to run into you. Or have you run into me?"

He smiled, but said nothing.

I fastened my seatbelt. It left a long muddy scar across my chest — over the flowers on my shirt and across the lap of my denim skirt. My shoes were covered with the red mud of Talon, my legs splattered with it.

The police officers moved back and saluted as we passed the police control marking the edge of the town. "Can you tell me more of what happened?" I asked.

"I wasn't there. It is difficult to say what happened," he said. "But twenty-one of his people were killed in the attack."

"Yes, I heard that. You are not a brother of Alhassan's, are you?"

He paused. "Yes, I am also his brother." I almost relaxed then, knowing I was with a friend.

Alhassan, I'm sorry. I remember now what you told me about words and their many meanings. Brother, for example. That I shouldn't reduce words to their most literal, dictionary meanings. But I wasn't thinking. In fact I was trying not to think.

I had been through Mamton three weeks earlier to do an interview with the chief there. The driver who took me there was someone Alhassan found, a personable man who also interpreted for me. He told me stories of Talon and government corruption and ethnic feuds stirred up by chiefs, governments and arms dealers. I had taken notes and not concentrated at all on the road we took. The landscape in the region is flat — lush and green during the rainy season, dry and brown during the dry season. There are few landmarks at all. Villages, to my foreign eye, looked much the same. I recalled Fusheini, the driver, pulling up to the Mamton chief's palace and emphasizing that the chief was a powerful figure in the Goroni hierarchy.

But mostly I remembered his stories of Talon, and how much everyone knew about everyone else. And how incredible the stories were. I was still thinking about that when I began to wonder if we were on the right road. I had never had reason not to trust anyone in Talon. Rape, theft and treachery were common among the people here as they were everywhere, Alhassan had told me, but as a white I could count on not experiencing either the first or the last of these three social evils. But if it were true that everyone knew everyone else's business in Talon, then everyone would know that I was a friend of Alhassan's — even if *they were not.* It stood to reason — even mine, hindered as it was by a night of love and the fear of its loss — that Alhassan would have many enemies in this chieftaincy dispute, and in the regional administration, which he opposed heartily.

"Alhassan was not captured during the attack, was he?" I asked. "He's not in any danger, is he?"

"No, no. He's gone into hiding."

"I see. And he really asked for me, a stranger?"

"Yes. You're not really a stranger to us." He smiled then.

The heat increased as we drove. The sun, after an early morning rain on the savanna, penetrates the rarefied air like a laser show. The sodden air begins to shimmer, and the leaves of the newly washed and watered bushes lace the air with perfumed moisture.

"Are we getting close to Mamton?" I asked, wiping my face with the back of my hand. "It is not far, I think. Maybe fifteen kilometres from Talon?"

He nodded agreement, then glanced at a shiny watch, studded with rhinestones that caught the sun and splintered it into tiny blinding beams. It was the wrong watch for a brother of Alhassan's. Neither Alhassan nor his brother could afford a car. Whose Nissan Patrol, then, was this? I cannot believe I was so foolish not to have asked these questions before. Alhassan's training had made me reluctant to ask anyone anything.

When he stopped the vehicle in front of the village, silence enveloped us. "This doesn't look like Mamton," I said, fear shaking in my voice.

"It is here," he said, getting out of the car.

"You bring Alhassan to me," I said. "I will wait here for him."

He smiled and headed off. A narrow path winding its way through man-sized maize plants swallowed him up. It was oddly quiet. Where were the children who always flocked out of villages to stare at newcomers? Someone was pounding *fufu* in a wooden mortar, and the solid rhythmic clunking of the pestle reminded me of the pounding of a drum, the African heartbeat. I opened the door and stepped out. I wondered if everyone in the village was out in their fields. It seemed deserted.

I glanced impatiently towards the mud houses; thatched roofs were just visible above the maize.

They wore white woven smocks, and their upper arms were ringed with amulets, leather bracelets. They were on me before I had the presence of mind to run. One man on each side, firmly clasping my arms and pulling me. I had trouble making my feet move at all. My legs buckled and I pitched forward trying to escape on hands and knees before they picked me up — hence this jagged tear on my skirt. I struggled for a second, before giving up and in. Still, I cried and begged them to let me go.

There was no sense asking them where they were taking me. They appeared to speak no English, and I was not self-possessed enough to attempt to communicate with them in my fledgling Goroni.

That was a blessing. They assumed that I neither spoke nor understood their language. It is because of this that I know how I came to be captive in this awful hut in Zoggu, waiting in vain to see the man I think I may love — or waiting to see the man who may love me — come to get me and be killed.

They are deathly afraid of Alhassan, that I do know. They think he is endowed with invulnerability. I have heard them relate how, on the morning of the attack, bullets from an AK-47 bounced off his arms, his chest. They seem to think I have something to do with his invincibility. They think by holding me they will cripple his prowess, perhaps even destroy his powers.

If he comes for me, it is certain they will destroy him. They are prepared. I hear them. There are men encircling Zoggu, camped out there day and night, their guns ready. I am not his power, I am his Achilles heel. If he cares for me enough to come for me, then he will die.

I will never be used to the heat. Drops of sweat are trickling down my temples, between my breasts, down the backs of my legs. I am finally used to the dirt. Mathia will bring me a calabash of water for washing soon. It's almost night now. Night falls promptly at six here. Then the darkness encases this village in the magic secretions of the Africa bush. There are crickets and night creatures out there. No one ventures far from their compound in the darkness. Smoke infiltrates my house, and there are the sounds of pots banging, thick steaming porridge being stirred, heavy wooden spoons thumping against the thick walls of aluminum cauldrons.

I now understand why people confuse senses here. There is no smell without sound, no silence without meaning. Villagers' senses are so finely honed, so in tune with each other, that they can read with all five senses. Words on a page become meaningless. Flat. The people here read people. That is why we are so helpless once we have moved out of our own world into theirs. Strangers are like children. Yes, Alhassan, we are.

Mathia brings me a bowl of maize porridge and my washing water. It is good I have almost finished my story because there is no more space on the walls. I am leaving a space near the door for the end, by which time the story will have come full circle, wrapped itself around the wall of this prison. But now it is night and I will try to sleep.

Perhaps I can escape my confinement while I am sleeping, call on my mental energy to spirit me out of here and away.

Alhassan has been and gone. He came so close to my ear during the night that I could feel his warm breath, smell the wild fragrance of hiding on him. I could not see him, but he told me that is the least important of the senses. He told me he could not come for me, but that I will soon be free. He said he will see me again. Not to worry. He said he will take me as his wife, in a life yet to come. I believe this is true. I am waiting, Alhassan.

Fatimata's story

There is another woman in the cell. Lucy doesn't look at her, not at first. She is trying too hard to get used to the fact that she is a prisoner in Africa. She wonders how long it will take BBC to find out that their stringer has offended the authorities — seriously this time — and wound up in prison. And then how long it will take the BBC to let her embassy know she is here and how long it will take to negotiate a deal to get her out of prison, out of the country.

Lucy doesn't want to touch anything in the cell. The only light comes from a single light bulb dangling overhead. The wall looks like it's covered with dried blood or shit. The floor is worse. There's a hole in the middle of it. She can't picture herself squatting there. No, she'll explode first. If she can look at this as another story, perhaps, she can keep a grip on herself. She can use this to prove her point about authoritarian, despotic regimes. She can write about her suffering in this cell. But for now, she has to concentrate on keeping the humiliation at bay.

"Welcome to Talon Regional Prison," says the woman.

"Thanks," says Lucy, swallowing hard.

"My name is Fatimata. But most people call me Candy."

"I'm Lucy."

"Pleased to meet you, Lucy," Candy says. Then after a polite pause, "The whole of Talon knows why I am here. But I am very surprised that you, a *white* woman, could do something to get put into prison in Talon."

"I seem to have said the wrong thing on the radio," Lucy says, glancing for the first time at her companion. Candy's lips are painted the colour of a blood-orange. She's sitting on a small wooden stool, the only one in the room. She gets up and offers it to Lucy.

"Here. You sit for a while. I spend all my time sitting. Sitting can get tiring. You know?"

Lucy shakes her head. Candy's kindness, after the nastiness of the Special Branch man who interrogated her and frog-marched her from her house, makes tears seep down her cheeks. He knew so much about her. As though *they'd* been watching her for years, playing her along. *They* knew more about her than her own mother knew. She knows she shouldn't believe the stories that the man told her about her husband and the housegirl. That would have been even before he admitted he had fallen in love with an English woman and said he was leaving. But she does. She believes all of it and can even picture it clearly. Not even a fiction writer could make up details that rang so true. Maybe the housegirl had been working for the Special Branch. How else would they know about all her husband's bedroom idiosyncrasies and those pet names he used only in the throes of passion? The mortification turns her eyes into faucets.

Candy moves closer, puts her arms around Lucy and pats her back, gently, as if she's burping a baby. This makes Lucy cry harder. "It's okay. They won't keep you here long. You'll be fine."

The girl smells edible, like a coconut. It reminds Lucy of suntan oils and beaches. Palm trees and ocean breezes. Freedom.

Candy maneuvers Lucy onto the stool and then backs up so she's leaning against the wall, gazing upwards. Lucy wipes her eyes, sniffs, looks at her cell-mate. She's a beauty. Small waist and a rounded belly, lots of curves under her striped t-shirt and cotton wrapper. Her arms and legs are too round to belong to this diminutive woman.

"What are you doing in here, Candy?" she asks, when she has control of her voice and has subdued the convulsive shudders.

"Oh, that one. It's too complicated," she replies. "I don't sleep in here. I'm here from six to six every day. Don't worry. If they were planning to keep you here long, they would have brought you a mat to sleep on, you being white. Maybe they will let you out today."

"I hope so," Lucy says, wondering how she would last through a night, alone, on a mat, a feast for mosquitoes carrying deadly strains of malaria. "You spend days in here. But not nights. That's a strange prison term."

"Mmm," Candy purrs, through a smile.

"So tell me, why are you in here?" Lucy persists.

"It's a long story," she says. "I could tell you. But only if you don't have other things to do."

Candy laughs when she sees she has made Lucy smile.

"You see," Candy begins, "My husband, Maximus, was a contractor. You know contractors?"

Lucy nods. She knows a few contractors. They're swank rich men who dress like a Broadway musical, with lots of gold draped in conspicuous places. They do things like tar roads and grease palms for their lavish living.

"You've probably seen my husband in Talon. Have you been here long?"

Lucy shakes her head. "No, I'm based in the capital. This was supposed to be just a short trip to do a story on the ethnic trouble."

Candy looks incredulous. "The ethnic trouble? You're lucky you're in here and not dead."

"Yeah, well. I suppose some people might think being in this prison a kind of death. But it's all your perspective, right? Here, you take the stool. I'll sit on the floor."

Candy refuses, with a smile and a shake of her head.

"My husband, Maximus, drives a market mammie. Sorry, you probably don't know what a market mammie is. It's one of those new Mercedes with the wide back ends that ride higher than the rest of the car. They're shaped just like market mammies, you know? The market women?"

Lucy nods.

"Why am I'm telling you about market mammies and my husband? I should start with my father. He's not a contractor. He worked for the government. But there was a big retrenchment a few years ago and so he got some money to retire from the civil service and decided to go into business and build a hotel. My father is a dreamer, with big ambitions." Candy pauses. A frown creases her fine forehead, making her look more like a sophisticated young woman and less like a hapless teenager.

"His ambitions were big. Too big for the rest of him. He wanted a *modern* hotel. Just like the Atlanta in Kumali. You know Kumali? The Atlanta?"

Lucy nods. A week ago she drove past the Atlanta Hotel, a monstrous piece of opulence on the Ring Road that encircles the busy market city to the south. She wonders that her sixth sense didn't warn her then that this trip would end in disaster. But her sixth sense seems impotent in this country. Probably because she has ignored all sense. She should have known she was losing her husband long before he told her. She should have stopped reporting from here the first time a man with daggers for fingernails followed her one whole day. But she had ignored the signals, the warnings, put all her passing fears down as paranoia. She hadn't wanted to be cowed into silence by her fear of the authorities; they counted on instilling silence that way.

"Maximus built the Atlanta and my father contracted him to build another one just like it here in Talon. Maximus ordered the marble from Italy, chandeliers from France and tiles from Germany. My father ran out of money before the inside of the main lobby was finished. So then Maximus came around to our house."

She is pressing her palms together as she talks. Staring at them. It looks like she's praying. Lucy thinks Candy has forgotten she's no longer alone in the cell.

"I'd never seen him so close before. He comes from Kumali and you know how the people there are rich. When we were little, my mother used to tell us that they were rich because they sold their souls to the Devil and vomited money. So I looked at him carefully when he came into our house. He was wearing a blue and white striped jacket down to his waist in front but in the back it reached his knees. The jacket was open, so I could see how big his belly was. He wore a black t-shirt with a sparkly green bird on it. I checked to see if there was any vomit on it. The striped pants were so long they dragged on the floor." She chuckles, but she's not smiling.

"Knowing Maximus, it was probably the latest style somewhere, London or Frankfurt or someplace. He did a lot of business with foreigners from those places. His shoes were crocodile skin. I know because I asked him. They scared me because they looked like crocodiles poking their noses out from under the cuffs. He looked out of place in our family house. Our walls were painted green but I never noticed how dirty they were. Not until that night when Maximus came to talk to my father. We had one room in the family house for receiving visitors. All of the children slept in one sleeping room and my parents slept in the other one. But the visitor's room was special. We had a pink sofa that was only for important visitors. I got caned once when my father found me lying on it to feel how soft it was. When Maximus came in, my father offered him a seat on the pink sofa and he sat just on the edge of it. It looked like he thought it might make his trousers dirty."

Candy closes her eyes and Lucy sees that there are dark blue outlines drawn with kohl around each of her eyes.

"The discussion went on a long time. I was tired, and I had classes the next day. My father sent my mother to bed with my brothers and sisters. But I had to stay and serve Maximus and my father whisky all night. Maximus wanted only Black Label and so I had to go two times to the Bush House Bar at the end of the road. I had to beg Benjamin to give me the Johnny Walker and cokes on credit. The Bush House had a sign painted on the wall with a shoeless beggar, saying 'I gave credit.' Ben had printed 'I don't' in big black letters. But Ben gave me the whisky and cokes because he said I was a good girl. But really it was because my father had promised him he could serve in the bar in the hotel."

Candy licks her lips. "I wish I had a coka now. Are you hungry? My small sister usually comes at midday and brings water and *tuo*," she says. "So I don't get too hungry in here."

Lucy says she's thirsty but that she can't imagine eating anything in this cell. She urges Candy to continue.

"I was feeling tired that night. My father didn't mind me. Even when I yawned so he could see that I was tired. Business, you know. Anyway, he never thought girls needed to go to school. It was only because of my mother that I was in senior secondary school. My mother paid my school fees." She falls silent, concentrates on her short fingernails which are dyed deep red with henna.

"How did she earn her money? Your mother, I mean," Lucy asks gently, not wanting to sound like the insatiably curious scrounger of stories that she is.

"She sold second-hand clothes in the market. She sent all of us to school. I'm the firstborn. We are six children. I kept thinking that I had to be at school by six in the morning. We swept the school grounds from six to eight and if you got there later than six you missed getting a number and got caned at eight when the headmistress arrived." Candy sighs.

"I was wiping off the glass top of the coffee table, lifting glasses and removing cola bottles and arranging things nicely. I thought that maybe Mr. Maximus Mensah would notice that it was closing time. There wasn't anything more for them to discuss. My father didn't have the money. Maximus would just take over the whole hotel project. Even I could see that. But they weren't saying it. Then I noticed that Maximus was looking at me. And he started to smile. Slowly. You know, it was just like someone was drawing it on his mouth, starting at one corner and moving across." Candy uses an imaginary pencil to demonstrate this in the air.

Lucy wishes she had her tape recorder now. Candy's voice is low and deadpan. As if she is reciting a poem she has memorized for a teacher. She looks impossibly young again.

"You could see the idea moving from down there, you know, up into his eyes. He began to nod his head. Then he stood up and told my father that they would just leave it for now. He said maybe they could find a way to wipe out the debt. He shook hands with my father and didn't look back at me."

Lucy exhales, pretends she wasn't about to ask the question that sits on her tongue like an itch. She feels she has to know how old Candy is but doesn't want to interrupt.

"A week later, I know the day because it was the thirtieth anniversary of our Independence Day, my father called me to the visitor's room. He told me to sit beside my mother on the pink sofa. My mother looked like she had already died and gone stiff and her hands were ready for praying like the plaster ones in the front of the church. I guessed what it was about so I wasn't even surprised when my father told me that I was to marry Maximus Mensah. He didn't need to tell me that this was the deal for the broken contract, so he didn't. That would have made him feel bad. He said I wasn't to go out that day to march in the Independence Day parade. I wanted to go. We had been training for it all year at school. My father said it wouldn't be good for the future wife of Maximus Mensah to march on the streets of Talon with all those schoolgirls and boys. He told me to stay in my room until Maximus came for me. My mother was angry about my father taking me out of school. I was a good student, you know. Especially in maths and English. So that same day my mother moved back to her village and took the children. My father took a second wife and she had a baby not long ago. But his life isn't easy because his new wife is lazy. She doesn't even know how to prepare pepper soup. But Maximus finished the hotel for him, so my father can go there to get away from her. Are you married, Lucy?"

Lucy is caught off guard by this question. Doesn't want to answer. But Candy is waiting, her mouth open slightly.

"Yes, well I was. I'm separated now."

"You weren't happy with your husband?"

"No, it wasn't that, really. We lived in the capital and I travelled a lot. You know. Reporting. He found someone else and now he's got a job in East Africa. Anyway, I don't mind." That's not true. She minds terribly. Every time she tells this untruth about her husband, her nose itches. She scratches it. Sneezes.

"Do you have a new boyfriend?"

Lucy shakes her head, too emphatically. Her husband said that her only love was her work. That wasn't true. She still loves him but he's asked for a divorce to marry that English woman with all the teeth and blond hair who claims to do conservation work in Kenya. She doesn't want to think about this. She hates answering questions, like most journalists. "Please, Candy, I'd rather hear your story. Mine is dull."

Candy glances at her, squints as though she's trying to make out the words on a distant signboard. "Sorry," she says, pausing a little before she starts again.

"I really wasn't as unhappy about marrying Maximus as my mother was. But I was very young."

"How young?"

"Fifteen. It wasn't so bad. Not at first. We had a green storey house on Hilltop. Maximus has two brothers and each brother had a storey of the house. Maximus is the youngest but the most clever and the richest, and we lived on the top floor. For a while it was nice. My two sisters-in-law were nice to me, then. They helped me plan my wardrobe and showed me how to do my hair and use bleaching cream. They're from the south and they know all those things. We had maids to do all the work in the house and the shopping at the market. We never had to walk. Only people who are poor walk. We didn't go out much. Sometimes our husbands took us out to a party. But they took their girlfriends to the Talon Country Club, where the real high life is. Have you been there?"

Lucy shakes her head. She stands and passes the stool to Candy. Candy refuses, insists she's fine on the floor. So Lucy pushes the stool aside and sits cross-legged on the filthy floor next to Candy. She leans her head back against the wall that smells like a root cellar and latrine at the same time. She hugs her knees and stares up at the grey concrete of the ceiling. It is hung with cobwebs that are full of dead flies. She wonders how the flies got into this airless cell. Perhaps every time they open the steel door. The door has a tiny opening at eye level that looks like a slot for mail. She wonders if some of the flies have been there since the prison was built. Whenever that was.

"It's nice," Candy says.

"What's nice?" Lucy asks, wondering for a second if Candy means the prison.

"The Country Club. I was inside once. That's where we had our wedding reception. But Maximus didn't take me there again. I watched a lot of videos with my sisters-in-law. We practised sitting and talking and being sophisticated like the white women in *Dallas*. I started to get fat like my sisters-in-law. Maximus started coming home later and later and gradually, so I didn't even notice it happening, he stopped taking me out. Not even to parties. At the beginning he called me to his bedroom every day. After two years, I could wait a month for him to call me to his room. I asked him why he didn't call on me more and he said it was because I wasn't bearing him any children. He said I was sterile."

She looks at Lucy with half-closed eyes as though she has fallen into a trance. Then she glances down at her feet in shiny black pumps with dainty silver bows on the heels. With great care she removes one of the shoes and uses it to stalk a scuttling cockroach. She waits until the insect approaches her bare foot and then strikes with force. The sound of the shoe on the concrete ricochets about them like a gun shot. She uses the shoe to deftly flick the squashed bug into the hole in the centre of the cell. Then she slips it back on and continues, as though Lucy weren't there.

"I know I was unhappy. I spent a lot of time in bed eating English biscuits and reading romance books. Maximus was more clever than his brothers and he was taking over Mensah & Sons. There was a lot of jealousy. My sisters-in-law and I fell out over it and they stopped talking to me when Maximus bought himself a new market mammie. You know, a Mercedes."

Lucy nods.

"His brothers were still driving '82 saloon cars and they said that Maximus got his new Benz as a gift from a minister who had connections to the African Development Bank or something like that. They thought he should split everything three ways. So we weren't talking to each other but we all lived in the same storey building. Just like those flies up there." She glances up, then around her as though seeing the cell for the first time.

"I lived just like this. Except that there was lots of food and that was all, except videos. So I got fatter and fatter and I could hardly walk down the stairs of our house. I kept hoping that it was because I was going to have a baby. But Maximus said I was sterile. And anyway, he was only with his girlfriends and never with me so I couldn't get pregnant. Then about two years ago, I got sick. Malaria. I was three months in bed. I couldn't stand up so I had to crawl to the toilet to relieve myself. Have you had malaria?"

Lucy shakes her head.

"You go through these spells like you've been cursed and you don't know who you are. Sometimes I thought I was an angel sitting on a cloud. Once I thought I was a chicken." She giggles. "Although I was too weak to walk, I started to run about and tear off my clothes. I couldn't breathe and it was so very hot. My mother must have seen me even from the village, because she came that same day. She found me lying on the floor. She went out to the forest and came back with some herbs and bark that she boiled to make medicines. She made me drink them until I stopped vomiting and the fever left me. She stayed a week with me. Then one morning I woke up and saw her and knew I was myself again. I had been reborn. My mother wanted me to come back to the village with her. But I told her I was going to stay in town because if I went to the village I knew how my life would be. She didn't understand but she said she would pray for me, because she could see things I couldn't. I wanted to be free, you know, happy in Talon. I wanted to see my school friends again. I got up, got dressed in a black and white polka-dot dress I had from early days of being Mrs. Mensah. It fitted me again and it had a pretty skirt with ruffles to my knees. I walked into town and went to my school and watched the new students and met my former teachers and they said they didn't have any good students of maths and English now that I was no longer there. Then I walked to the Point Ten with my former maths teacher."

"I know that bar," Lucy says. "That's where I met the guys I interviewed about the ethnic thing. That's why I'm here."

Candy smiles, a full toothy smile that makes her look as if she has found the happiness she was looking for that day she was reborn. "That's why I'm here too. Because that's where . . ."

"No, don't jump ahead, Candy. I want to hear the whole story. Step by step."

"All of it. Okay. Well, you know how the Point Ten is. I met all sorts of old classmates that day and we drank coka and talked about everything. Most of my girl classmates were married and of course they couldn't go to the Point Ten. But the boys could and they told me all the news. Most of them were still looking for work and just hanging about. They talked a lot about the government and they were just starting to talk about having multiparty elections. I didn't know what that meant so they told me. I tell you, it opened up a new world for me, hanging about even though I knew it was a terrible thing I was doing, being there and talking to men. They played Dolly Parton and high-life tapes all day in the Point Ten and I had to keep really still in my chair because I wanted to dance because I was just so . . . so *happy*."

Candy pauses, scratches her ankles, tucks her wrapper modestly between her legs. The printed cloth shows neat rows of blue and white guinea-fowl marching around Candy's thighs. "Every time Maximus had to travel I went to the Point Ten. I was careful to sit in the back in case someone who knew Maximus drove by. It didn't make any difference, though. Because everyone in town knew I was being bad and going out alone. But everyone feared Maximus too much to tell him. Apart from that, he was away a lot. You know. Travelling. I heard people say he took girlfriends with him when he travelled. People feared him a lot. So they didn't want to be seen talking to me."

A few live flies struggle to free themselves from the webs overhead. Lucy can't imagine where they have come from. Can they breed in concrete? Or have they flown out of the dark and stinking hole in the centre of the cell? Their buzzing is loud against the silence of that concrete cubicle. Candy takes a deep breath.

"Then one day I met Wayne Brooks." She looks at Lucy. "You may not believe it, but before that no white person had ever talked to me. I had seen them and heard about them but I had never talked to one before. He came into the Point Ten and sat down at the table where I was sitting. I always sat next to the bar so I could talk to Ruby while she served drinks. 'Hi there,' he said. I didn't answer and Ruby started to laugh and then he asked her about me and she told him a few things. Nice things but foolish. How all the men in town liked me. But how I was shy and a schoolgirl. I was looking at him because his face was so red. Now I know that his face was always sunburned because he had to stand in the sun all day on the new road they're building. But I didn't know that then. I didn't know anything. I couldn't stop looking at his blond hair and wondering what it felt like and if he ever combed it. I remember thinking that his eyes looked slippery, like there was oil in the sockets so he could slide them around in any direction. He was laughing at what Ruby told him about me and I kept telling her to stop telling lies. He was wearing a white t-shirt and I remember being surprised that he would go out wearing a shirt that dirty. He had a belly just like Maximus. I smiled at him because I was feeling embarrassed by the things Ruby was telling him. He asked me if I'd care for a cigarette. I told him I didn't smoke. Then he asked if I smoked after sex. I didn't even look at him. I was too embarrassed and thinking he must be crazy to say things like that out loud. He said it was a joke and that I had better learn my lines and that the right answer was that I had never looked. I was still feeling confused and he was laughing so hard that all the people in the Point Ten were staring at us."

Lucy feels suddenly nauseated. She decides it's the smell of the hole in the middle of the floor. She wonders what prisoners are supposed to use to clean themselves. There's not even a bucket of water in the cell. "Go on," she says, touching Candy's arm gently. "Please, continue."

"He said 'What's your name, Sugar?' I said 'Candy', making it up. He laughed some more. But after a while he stopped laughing all the time and he told me how pretty I was and how lonely he was. And so he decided that I was his girl. And he was usually nice to me and I didn't tell him that I was sterile because I had listened to people talking and read some of his magazines and I learned that sometimes it's the man who is sterile and not the wife."

Candy swallows and Lucy glances away, at the steel door that keeps them both prisoners in this cell. She wonders who would stop them if they could get out that door. If they could break it down. Would they be shot? No, probably just beaten and dragged back inside.

"I liked Wayne very much. I could only see him when Maximus wasn't around. I stopped going to the Point Ten but I was afraid all the time that someone would see me in Wayne's pick-up when he came to get me at the taxi-rank. I always telephoned him when Maximus went out of town and then I walked to the taxi-rank with a basket like I was just going to market to buy cloth or something. He always took me to his trailer in the work camp outside town on the Sala road. They were just getting everything set up in the camp, you know, a generator and water and a clubhouse. There were ten white men there. They worked for Manley West Africa. Manley was building the new road." She turns suddenly to face Lucy who has been studying Candy's profile, fascinated by the sparkle of the one light bulb reflecting on her eyes.

"You really want to know why I'm here?" she asks, her huge dark eyes on Lucy. "*All* of it. I mean, everything?"

Lucy nods.

"It was the party. Wayne said he wanted to have a house-warming party for the Manley men at the camp. He asked me to get ten of my friends. He said I should get the best-looking girls in town and bring them over to the camp canteen on Saturday night. You see, he thought I was one of *those* kinds of girls that go to the Point Ten on Saturday nights. So I had to ask Ruby to help me. And she could only get six girls. She had nine but three didn't come because they were having their days and we don't associate with men during our dirty days. When we came in the men were already boozed and then Wayne shouted, 'Hey guys, the Miss Africa pageant!'"

Lucy is amazed at how well Candy imitates an American man.

"While he shouted this Freddie was taking a video. So that was the opening of the video. Wayne and all of us girls were supposed to stand and smile for Freddie who was filming. He said we should all pretend we were on an airplane and act like stewardesses. But none of us had ever been on an airplane, so we didn't know what to do except just stand there. I told them we should pretend we were flying, like birds. So we flapped our arms. Wayne laughed and then he made a speech. Like this."

Candy stands up, thrusts her little curved hip out like she's a country singer playing a rancher in a western. She speaks in a baritone that doesn't live inside her small frame. From the accent that she has mastered so well, Lucy guesses that Wayne comes from the south. Or maybe it's an accent she picked up watching *Dallas*.

"Gentlemen, your attention please. This is your captain speaking. We wanna welcome you to Candy's Airline with its beautiful line-up of air-head hostesses. We will be flying at an altitude of ten inches."

Candy holds up her hands, fingers splayed. "He held up his hands and on each finger he had a different colour condom. 'These little guys will ensure you a safe flight to places where no man has dared to go before. And just in case he has, these little rubber men will be here to make sure that the flight is smooth. AIDS free.' We were trying hard to laugh along with the men because we were supposed to be having a party."

Candy clucks her tongue.

"Freddie kept on filming. Wayne gave the girls to the men like prizes. 'And to Dave Evans, the hardest working man among us, we would like to award Abiba.' I can't remember it all. Then Freddie moved in close to film while Dave undressed Abiba and told her to put on some red lacy panties that had a hole in them, just where you need panties and no hole. If you could see the video I wouldn't have to tell you all this. It's embarrassing to talk about things like that."

"I don't want to see the video," Lucy says.

Candy sits heavily on the floor, tucks her wrapper around herself, hugs her knees and rocks back and forth on her haunches.

Lucy tastes salt. "Go on," she says.

"Then Wayne grabbed my arm hard so it hurt. He pulled me into the middle of the room and he had a lion skin he got when he was working somewhere, I can't remember where. He said I was supposed to crawl around on it without my clothes on. 'Act like a lioness,' he said. I didn't know what a lion looked like so I just stayed there naked on the skin and he came up to me on his hands and knees. Then he got on top of me, from behind, just like an animal! And he bit me really hard on the shoulder. It pained me a lot. He never hurt me before that night."

Candy's chest is heaving as though she is having trouble getting air into her lungs, or as though her chest is too small for all the air she is gulping.

"After that I got up and drank a whole glass of whisky. I don't drink so I didn't know what happens when you do. I heard Wayne making loud noises when he was holding the video camera and Freddie had one girl under him and one on top. Then I fell down."

Candy looks quickly at Lucy, then away. She tilts her head back so the tears that have gathered in her eyes don't spill.

"What started the real trouble was that Freddie made copies of the video because Wayne said they wanted to send it to his friends in America. And someone, I still don't know who, stole a copy. Probably one of the workers at the Manley camp. Lord, forgive me." She is almost whispering now but the words come fast, falling into the silence like torrential rain dripping through a forest canopy.

"It got shown at the Talon Country Club. Maximus was there. But I wasn't the only wife of a Big Man who was in it. Abiba is the third wife of the Deputy Regional Secretary, who's a Party man. I mean Party. The *President's Party*. It was awful. The military raided the camp. They took Wayne and the others to the high security prison. If their ambassador hadn't come they would have been shot. That's how mad the men in Talon were. But their ambassador got them out of prison and out of the country. Abiba told me that Manley gave about a million dollars to the government. They said it was for the victims. Our husbands. They said I organized it and they brought me here. I've been here since," she counts on her fingers, "ten months."

Lucy's hands are clenched into fists. Candy is erasing the tiny tears that keep dripping from her eyes. "I was wicked. So bad. But I never meant to be a wicked woman, one of *those* kinds of women. I pray all the time, you know." She freezes when she hears the footsteps approaching. Scuffing of heavy boots on gritty concrete. The door opens. Lucy glances quickly at Candy who has manufactured a smile from the tragedy of her face.

The prison guard is actually smiling and Lucy notices that he's young and not at all thuggish. "Looks like you're free to go," he says, speaking to Lucy but looking at a spot on the far wall. "There's a car here. They are taking you to the airport. They say you're to go back to your country."

"No, wait," Lucy says. "I'm not ready. I don't want to leave quite yet."

He stiffens. "The car is waiting. They have come for you."

"Joseph," Candy says, quietly, "let her stay some minutes."

He looks surprised, but Lucy notes the softening of his features. "Please, Joseph, for me."

He shuffles his boots on the floor, like an awkward schoolboy. Looks at the floor so Lucy can't see his face. "Okay. Five, Cand . . . Fatimata. Five minutes."

"Joseph," Candy says. "We don't have our watches in here. We don't know what time it is."

"A few minutes, then. I'll come. I can't make the foreigners wait." He turns and goes out the door without a backward glance.

They both listen to his footsteps retreating.

Then they wait a little longer, waiting for the silence to settle.

Lucy can't decipher the look on Candy's face. Her eyes are alight now, as though she has already escaped.

"Candy, I have an idea. If you know where I can find Wayne in America, maybe when I go home I can . . ."

Candy is shaking her head.

". . . what he did is wrong. I can find him and make him pay."

"No, you don't understand. Wayne is finished. God will take care of him. He is not important. You don't understand." She rubs her small rounded belly under the wrapper. "I'm going to be a mother. Joseph is the father. He was my classmate. He works here but he is a good man. He takes me to his quarters at night. He loves me. I love him too. We are happy together. All we have to do is wait until the baby is born and then they will let me out of prison. We have time. I'm lucky, don't you think?"

Lucy wants to say no, she doesn't think Candy is lucky at all. But Candy is now beaming at her and there is the after-image of Joseph's face and suddenly she recognizes the look he wore when he looked at Candy. And it matches the happiness that shines now from Candy's young face.

"Joseph thinks it's going to be a boy," Candy says. "But I think it's a girl. I have plans for her. *My* daughter is going to finish school and be an important person."

The footsteps are returning. They only have another few seconds alone together. Lucy stands, pulls Candy to her feet and embraces her. "Candy, you're . . ." she says, but suddenly she is crying again and nothing intelligible comes out.

Candy hugs her tightly, pats her on the back, misinterpreting the tears. "You'll be okay, Lucy," she says. "They'll send you to your country so you'll be okay. I will pray for God to be kind to you because He has blessed me, you see."

Lucy musters a smile and waves to Candy, who is sinking onto the stool as the door shuts. Through Lucy's tears, Candy looks like she's dissolving. Joseph smiles at Candy as he gently closes the door on her. He doesn't lock the door, and it occurs to Lucy that it's been unlocked the whole time she's been inside the cell.

Joseph leads her down the corridor, past all those closed steel doors. He is formal and correct as he solemnly returns her rings and her watch to her. He asks her to sign for them, please. To show she got all her things back. She wants to ask him to be good to Candy but she feels this would be presumptuous. She leans over to sign the form, then glances up.

"Candy's a very special woman," she says, wiping her eyes with the back of her hand. All she does is mix sweat with tears and smear them all over her face.

Joseph looks embarrassed, then bashful. "Thank you, Madam," he says, with a smile that melts into her. He looks like he's about to say something more when four Big Men troop in. She notes the paramilitary uniforms and all the stars and badges that spell power. Her tears evaporate. They are shouting at him to hurry up because the ambassador is waiting for the white woman. She shrugs, glances at Joseph and leaves her plain gold wedding band on the desk.

"For Candy," she whispers.

Little Comfort

Comfort was the only real friend I had in Talon. She had a very round face on a big round body. She jiggled all over when she laughed and she laughed a lot. I usually laughed with her, not always because I understood her subtle humour but because just being around her made me happy. Her name said it all.

Talon was the regional capital in the far north of the country where the savanna was rapidly turning into desert. My bungalow was comfortable and spacious. It didn't fit in that part of town which was still really a village of mud-walled houses that had been surrounded by the town and overwhelmed by rural people flocking in to find sustenance — mostly in vain.

My house was separated from Comfort's by a formidable wall of decorative bricks. In the beginning, Comfort's kids spied on me and my house through the ornate openings in the bricks. After a while they just climbed over the wall and filled my home with the happy sounds of children at play.

Comfort and her children lived in a bright blue clapboard house with one bedroom, one living room that she called the "hall", and an outdoor kitchen. The chicken coops in her compound were much bigger than her house. She made her money raising chickens and selling eggs. I sent food from my table to help feed her six growing girls; she gave it to her chickens. She said her egg production doubled and that now she could afford to feed and school her own children.

Comfort's husband worked in the gold mines in the south of the country and came only once a year when he got two weeks off for Christmas. That's why all her daughters were September babies. She told me she would have to make a son for her husband eventually or there would be trouble. She laughed when she said that.

I noticed she was pregnant just before Christmas that second year. She didn't say anything about her swelling belly to me; no one talked about due dates or pregnancies in case it invoked evil spirits or incited *juju*. Besides, the pregnancy was awkward. Her husband hadn't been around for almost a year.

When he came on Christmas Eve I heard the fighting and I learned something about Comfort — she could cry and wail as loudly as she could laugh. When he left, on Christmas Day, he took several cardboard boxes with him. I went over later to deliver the turkey I had roasted for Christmas dinner and noticed that Comfort's prize possessions — a black and white television and a radio — were gone.

Comfort saw me looking at the empty places on her shelves but didn't say anything. She clapped her hands and swatted her children about, telling them to get themselves washed and ready for a feast that Auntie Doris, as they called me, had brought them. I placed the wrapped gifts — six boxes of crayons and six colouring books — on the table. Comfort refused to allow the children to play with them, saying they would only spoil the nice crayons and the books. She put them on display on a top shelf beside the precious enamel bowls she hoarded. She called the things on those shelves her "bank account and insurance policy".

The kids devoured the turkey, laughing and smacking, and Comfort provided a huge bowl of *tuo* with chicken stew which we ate with our hands. I couldn't decide whether I had seen those dark patches around Comfort's eyes before. Her cheeks were deeply marked with the long dark scars of the Goroni people but the gashes of scar tissue were angled away from her mouth and added to the impression I had that she was usually smiling. Or laughing deep inside.

Afterwards I invited them back to my house to watch Stephen Spielberg's Christmas video. We ate popcorn and drank bottles of sugary soft drinks; the three younger children fell asleep on my floor. At ten, she stood them all up and marched them out the door, much as she would her chickens.

When they were gone I felt very lonely as I often did in that town where, except for Comfort, I was very much on my own. I had not managed to nudge my way into the expatriate community, mostly experts and advisors who occupied air-conditioned offices and impressive homes in residential camps built especially for them. I was a so-called volunteer of progress and I worked mostly in the villages on agroforestry projects. I felt very shy around the other expatriates — who seemed so knowledgeable and insular. I think they interpreted my reticence to accept their invitations to their clubhouses as a snub, which it wasn't. In any case I seldom went and they seldom invited me. So I got the company I needed from my neighbour and friend Comfort and her six children.

After they had gone home that night I turned off the lights, lit some candles and poured myself a glass of wine I had bought at United Trading Company as a Christmas gift to myself. But it tasted off and left a bitter taste in the back of my throat. I fingered the wine glass, admiring the play of the flickering candlelight on the red liquid inside. A breeze had come up and it was cool in the porch. I thought about Comfort and admired her discretion; she had made no mention of her husband or his sudden departure. I wondered who the father of that new baby could be. Except for the hours she spent during the days on the roadside selling her flats of eggs she never went out to socialize. I had never seen anyone but her own family members from the village in her house. In any case, adulterous coupling in that tiny house of hers struck me as impossible. Despite her earthy humour Comfort was strict on moral questions of correct behaviour for mothers, wives and her daughters.

Then it occurred to me how little I knew her after almost two years. I stood up and dumped the red wine into a potted palm.

At Easter, when Comfort was as swollen as a southern market mammie, she finally brought up the subject. We were sitting on her front step, drinking sweet icy hibiscus tea I had brewed up earlier as we watched the sun setting over the locust bean trees that towered over the west side of my house. We were both steeped in sweat. The rains had not started but the humid winds from the south had blanketed us with the hot, sultry air that heralded the onset of the rainy season which would bring life back to the northern savanna.

I swirled my tea, enjoying the tinkling sound of the ice cubes against the glass, thinking how much the deep red tea resembled the wine I had thrown away at Christmas.

From over the wall I could hear Comfort's daughters whooping and laughing. I had put the television out on my front porch and they were watching cartoons I rented at Video 2000 in town, a shop in Talon that offered the best selection of illegally dubbed videos.

"This one I'm making for you," she said suddenly. I glanced at her, not comprehending, not at first. She was rubbing her big belly as though she could remove the baby like a genie from the bottle.

I laughed, embarrassed. "Comfort, what would I do with a child? I don't have a husband."

"And neither do I," she replied. She was smiling. I didn't know how to respond. I had never really considered the possibility of having children, although sometimes I had a deep feeling of envy or emptiness when I saw young, devoted mothers with toddlers in their arms — but this happened only when the child was sleeping. Something about a sleeping child brought out a tenderness, a visceral need with which I was not familiar and which I dismissed as quickly as possible.

Since my divorce five years earlier I had not even considered the possibility of a regular man in my life, let alone children. I liked working abroad, I liked the freedom I had. I liked to move about, plant trees and let them put down roots while I up and left for another part of the world. I had come to Talon from Costa Rica and was hoping to move next to Nepal.

I liked Comfort's girls — in a way I had become like a parent to them, a bit like a father figure, I suppose. I provided treats from time to time and I enjoyed their company in small doses but I was happy to hand them back to their mother when they began to tire me out with their energy and noise.

"But what if it's a boy?" I asked. "You said you were waiting for a boy."

"Mr. Abilbo needed a boy," she said. It took me a moment to realize she was talking about her husband. Something in her tone suggested she already viewed him as a distant stranger or a spirit figure not of her time on earth.

"Well I don't really know what to say, Comfort. It's kind of you to offer your baby to me but I'm really not the mothering type. And I'm sure there are a lot of legal obstacles to a single white woman adopting an African child."

She said nothing. The evening was settling over us like an enormous crawling insect. I scratched my neck. There was magic in the African dusk which came in Talon at shortly after six, three hundred and sixty-five days of the year. Comfort used the end of her faded wrapper to wipe the sweat from her face. She sat with her legs spread wide, to support the belly with the baby inside.

I thought I could see it moving. The chickens had begun to squawk. Egg production, I assumed. A cock crowed.

"When are you due?" I asked finally. She'd told me the year before not to ask that question, laughing and saying if I knew the date I might invoke *juju*, even unknowingly. I didn't think she really meant it but I couldn't be sure and anyway it was custom. Comfort may have gone to a Catholic school, may have attended mass each Sunday at the Sacred Heart Cathedral, but inside she was a riddle of faith, at least to me.

She grinned at me and I read her smile as an admonition she might give to her youngest daughter.

"Soon," she said.

She went into labour on May first. When I arrived home from the village my watchman told me that Comfort had gone to the hospital.

"When? How?"

"Some hours now. She do walk."

None of her girls were at home. As I sped to the hospital, a twenty-minute drive over the lunar surfaces of Talon roads, I imagined Comfort waddling her way there — it would take her hours. She had probably waited until the labour was advanced before going. I watched for her along the road, hoping I might overtake her.

At the hospital they told me she was already upstairs in the delivery room and I should "exercise patience" downstairs until a doctor came.

I sat on the low wall that flanked what had once been a garden in the centre of the courtyard that comprised the admissions room, waiting room, visiting room, storage bin and rubbish heap. It was a depressing and smelly place that had seen neither a cleaner nor a painter since it had been built shortly after independence. Three road accident victims were brought in and carried roughly into the casualty ward which I could see from where I sat. They were placed on mattresses on the floor. After that no one seemed to pay them any attention at all. The trails of blood they left on the gritty concrete floor were not wiped up before the hospital staff left shortly before midnight. By then they had darkened, and in the sickly fluorescent light they looked like the rest of the stains on the floors, the walls, the ceilings.

"You can go home and come back in the morning," said the nurse at the admissions table as she pushed the table into a corner full of broken beds. "The next shift begins at six in the morning. There will be nobody here and I doubt the doctor will come now."

"No, I'd rather wait."

"But there's no point in waiting. You will not be admitted until visiting hours. In the morning, in any case."

So I went home. Comfort's house was in darkness. I supposed her daughters had been packed off to the village. I supposed that I was being silly to fret so much about the birth. Comfort was not a novice in such matters and she *was* in the hospital, not squatting alone in the bush somewhere to bring forth her seventh child as most village woman would have been. I managed to drift off to sleep sometime in the dead of night and dreamed of Comfort's big smile as she showed me her new baby. The baby had Comfort's face and smile.

I drove straight to the hospital as a sickly sun rose behind the ruins of rain clouds that had dropped their precious water before floating northwards to Talon. At admissions, the nurse told me that the delivery was going well. I should come back later.

"Are there any medicines or materials she'll need?" I asked.

"I don't know," said the nurse.

"But can't you find out?"

She glanced about the hospital, where already hundreds of people were gathered, sprawled on the floor with crying children. She shrugged. "I'm sorry, Madam. I'm very busy."

From there I went to one of the agroforestry plots in a village on the outskirts of town to see if they had begun to sow the maize and prune the trees. They hadn't. They said they still hadn't been able to get any hybrid maize seed. I suggested they use their own local seed. They said they had been using hybrid seed for years and no longer stored their own seed. I lost my temper, not at them, at the hopelessness of what we were doing on the continent; I left feeling thoroughly dispirited.

By noon I was back at the hospital. This time the nurse at the admissions table sent me upstairs to wait outside the operation room.

The doors to the operating theatre were closed and there was no one about. I sat down on the floor and waited. Two hours later a doctor emerged. His lab coat was splattered in blood.

I rose. "Has Comfort Abilbo delivered?" I asked.

"Yes, Madam. It was a very difficult birth. The head is very large and we had to do a Caesarian. The mother is still under anaesthetic. You will have to come back tonight."

I asked him what the operation had cost and told him I would pay him when I returned. He said Comfort had already paid before admission. "We have no choice. That's the new rule here," he said. He looked like he might say more but then he turned suddenly and walked away.

The next morning I found mother and daughter sleeping on a mattress in a large ward full of amputees and living cadavers. It smelled terribly of human faeces and terminal illness. Not at all a place to bring a newborn child.

I placed the vase of flowers I had cut in my garden on the floor beside the mattress, wanting them to be the first thing Comfort saw and smelled when she opened her eyes. I sat down on the floor to wait. Two nurses were going in and out of a curtained cubicle. Whoever was inside was screaming. My stomach knotted. Someone else yelled something in Goroni and the screaming stopped.

I examined Comfort and her baby. Comfort lay on her side, her stomach still enormous, her face much older than it had been two days earlier. There was peace there, but fatigue rather than humour etched into the tribal marks around her mouth. The baby was almost entirely covered in a greyish towel. I could see a bit of her face, which was very pale. The head was indeed very large.

Comfort must have sensed my presence. She opened her eyes but did not smile. She reached for my hand, and held it, staring straight into my brain. "It did not go well," she whispered.

I feigned brightness. "Your new daughter is beautiful. Here, I've brought her a pink outfit with a hat and socks and a sleeper." Comfort hardly glanced at it.

"You've done very well, Comfort. She really is beautiful. Like her mother."
She shook her head very slowly, and closed her eyes again.

I visited Comfort every day after that, bringing her food and ice water from
home — there was neither water nor food in the hospital. She told me she had
sent her daughters to the village before coming to the hospital. She had known
there was something "not right" about this birth. I asked the doctors when she
would be released. They said they didn't know. Her blood pressure was very
low, and she wasn't responding to the medication. There were some complica-
tions. A week later there was "infection". Then they spoke of internal bleeding.

Comfort was wasting away before my eyes. Each day I took enamel bowls
full of her favourite Goroni dishes I bought from local chop bars and came back
to find them empty. Comfort could not have been eating the food or she would
not be shrinking so fast. I suspected the nurses or other patients were taking it.

They kept her on drips. Her arms were covered with small swellings where
the needles had been inserted over the weeks. The skin around her elbows and
upper arms hung loosely as though it were a size too big.

The baby, though, was growing. Comfort was giving her all she had left,
the rich milk that flowed from her swollen dark breasts.

"What is her name?" I asked, every day.

"No name yet. I have to wait."

I began to spend longer and longer with Comfort and her baby-without-a-
name. The nurses had come to know me and had found an old bent metal chair
that they brought each time I came. I would sit for hours holding that bundle
of baby in my arms while Comfort slept or simply stared at the grimy ceiling
where overhead fans sat bent and twisted and useless. The only air came
through the windows where louvres had gone missing over the years. The baby
seemed to know me even the first time I held her. Her eyes, very black and shiny
and wise in that brown face, rested on mine as though she had overheard, from
the womb, that conversation Comfort and I had had on the step at Easter, as
though she knew she belonged to me.

When she was three weeks old her body was round and soft and had caught
up with that prematurely large head and wise face of hers. Her hair was soft,
little tufts of dark curls that I rubbed with my fingertips. My breasts ached
sometimes when I held her, or in the middle of the night when I thought about
her — as though my own latent organs of motherhood were awakening.

Comfort had forgotten how to smile, but that tiny baby, one month old, was
learning. She now grinned at me when I held her and offered her my bracelets
to play with. She was very advanced for her age.

"She's yours, Doris. You must take her now," Comfort whispered to me one
afternoon as a dark mass of thunderheads amassed on the eastern horizon,

visible through the dirty louvres of the windows that lined the second floor ward.

"You hear your mother?" I asked the baby that I had begun to call Little Comfort. "She's trying to give you away. What do you think of that?" The infant gurgled and her eyes widened.

"Now hear me, Doris," whispered Comfort, struggling to sit up. She clutched her stomach and grimaced.

"Lie down, Comfort."

But she continued to struggle until she was leaning against the wall behind her mattress. I had asked for a bed, offered to pay for one — they had said there were none in the hospital. Comfort had calmed me down, insisting that she preferred the mat on the floor.

"They came from the village." Comfort spoke so quietly that I had to lean very close to hear her. "I know what they're saying about the baby. There was one man with them. I know him-o. He's wicked. How he looked at me and the baby. Her head is too big. She stares too much for her age. He said that two children in the village have died this week. He thinks my baby is a *kinkirgo*, a child of the Devil. He has always thought I was a witch. That's why I left the village."

"Oh, Comfort," I replied. I hugged Little Comfort closer. She had begun to whimper. I held her out to her mother, but she didn't take her.

"It's true, Doris. That's how it is. The man, I fear him. He's the one decides which are children of the Devil, here to bring bad luck and death. He sees I'm dying too. He's cast a . . ."

"Comfort, stop it. You're not dying. Lie down and . . ."

"They are going to kill the baby, Doris, if you don't take her. They use poison, plenty of wicked things. They bash in the baby's head. Twist the neck. No burial even. The spirit is alone, can't be with the ancestors or come back again. That's how it is." She was having trouble breathing.

Little Comfort had begun to cry louder now, and I pushed her to her mother, who offered her a breast. Most people in the ward were asleep, or staring silently at nothing.

All I could hear was Little Comfort sucking her mother's milk. Her tiny hand reached upwards then came to rest on the brown breast she was suckling.

"Comfort, I can't just take her now. I have no milk or bottles or anything. There's also Social Welfare. I don't want to be accused of kidnapping." I thought Comfort was delirious, but I couldn't be sure. I decided to go to Social Welfare, just in case, and to talk to the doctor to see what he made of Comfort's story.

"Then you go now. They will come. I know them. Maybe not today, or tomorrow. But soon."

I could find no doctor around to ask about Comfort's condition. There was no one in the office at Social Welfare although I waited until closing time. I rushed back to the hospital at dusk.

Comfort said they would come soon. What is soon? Too soon? Too late. I was too late. The nurse told me Comfort had passed away shortly after I left. When I shouted my shock and disbelief, she told me I was free to go and see her — in the morgue. They said she had tried to leave and made it as far as the lobby before she collapsed and haemorrhaged to death before they could get her into intensive care.

The baby without a name, Little Comfort? She was taken, they said, by the father from the village. They said that Comfort had been trying to steal the baby away from the father when she collapsed. I said the baby had no father in the village. I shrieked that they had allowed a stranger to kidnap the baby. They asked me if I knew the father. I was quiet then.

I went to the village, an hour's drive away. The place was in blackness; everyone seemed to be asleep. I ran from one hut to another, shouting questions and accusations at anyone who came to see what lunatic had invaded their village at night. But no one would answer my questions about Little Comfort. They acted as though they had never heard of Comfort's baby. Then one man said the baby had been born dead. I screamed that he was lying. The villagers stared at me in the darkness, in the silence they inflicted on me.

Comfort's daughters were farmed out to different families in the village; they would perform household chores until they were old enough to be married off to waiting sons. The chickens and Comfort's belongings — her dishes and bowls that were her insurance policy — simply disappeared, although I saw no one lurking about her house. The little blue house remained empty for the remaining three months of my stay there, and offered me no comfort at all.

Mother of my invention

Josephine beckoned me to come out back. It was Sunday, the day of rest and drinking for the men. The commander of the Talon Military Base had arrived and was regaling the motley collection of young army captains and a few stray development workers with irreverent tales about the President's unannounced visit to the base earlier that week. It seemed the President suspected disloyalty among the Goroni troops here in the north. The men were laughing tears. I was amazed at the commander's indiscretion, anxious to stay and find out what it meant.

But I could not ignore Josephine, who had appointed me her "daughter". As if she needed a ninth. As if I needed another mother. At thirty-four, I still could not deal with my own who was, thankfully, many thousands of miles away.

I rose and excused myself politely from the table. The men didn't notice my departure. Not even my husband.

"Cattie," she said, "I want you to make the salad like a white makes salad."

Salad. She called me out back to make salad? Josephine made great salad. I had eaten perfectly good salads that she made and served in her restaurant almost every Sunday for more than a year. Still, it would be ungracious to refuse her request.

The lettuce was swimming in a rusty barrel of brown water. The tomatoes sat in neat pyramids, four per pile, on the damp, red earth. Delila, Josephine's third daughter, was cutting onions with a knife that resembled a machete. She held the onion in her palm and hacked away at it. With each cut I pictured the butcher's knife slicing her hand neatly in two.

"Delila, I can't watch you doing that."

She started, surprised by the panic in my voice.

I reached for the knife. "You're going to cut your hand. Don't hold it . . ."

She jerked away reflexively. Then she looked down at her hand. Blood was oozing from a cut between her index and middle finger. She licked at it, frowning.

The unexpected injury silenced the compound. The chickens stopped cackling. The cock dismounted a small red fowl and stared balefully at me.

One of the girls came out of a hut with a strip of coloured cloth and Delila wound it around her two fingers.

Josephine was the first to speak. "You see, Cattie" (she couldn't get her tongue around my name, which is really Cathy), "this is not fine what you say to Delila. You call on the spirits like that, they come." She shook a plump finger at me. "I know you don't know any better. African spirits are full of mischief-o. We will teach you. You are my daughter." Then she laughed deep and hard, bringing forth merriment from a large belly. Her daughters and granddaughters took it up. The excited babble was so loud it drowned out the noise emanating from inside, from the table full of drunk men.

"Auntie Cattie, Auntie Cattie," shouted the children, clapping their hands. Josephine shooed them away, wielding a switch that whistled as it sliced through the hot afternoon air.

"Now," she said, firmly back in charge, "you make us a nice salad. So it looks like a photo. You teach us how to cook for white men and we teach you things too."

I peered into the murky depths of the barrel and began fishing lettuce leaves out with my fingertips. Josephine returned to the never-ending task of keeping her clients supplied with beer. It now sounded as if there was a full battalion, or two, in there. Every now and then I heard my husband's laugh. I was already preparing to rake him over the proverbial coals when we got home in the evening. Not that it was his fault that the women thought my place was with them, showing them how to cook for white men (as if I knew anything about cooking), but I had to vent my resentment on someone. And my husband was the most convenient target. Besides, he hadn't even noticed Josephine coercing me away from the table. He knew how much I loved stories of political intrigue, which the commander not only knew but also helped orchestrate. But my husband hadn't offered me so much as a sympathetic wink. No, he would not get off lightly.

"Delila, where did you get this water? It's not clean. I need a bucket of fresh water to wash the salad."

"That water is clean, Auntie. Francesca just fetched it this morning. You know Francesca has brought forth?"

"No, I didn't know. I didn't realize she was that far along. I'm happy for her. Boy or a girl?"

"A girl," said Delila, lowering her voice to continue. "My mother's curse is also ours. She cannot bring forth a son and we, her daughters, cannot either. Even the fetish priest can't help. When he tried to, my mother brought forth the twins, Elyse and Elsie. That's why we're all girls and why Francesca had a baby girl."

I had trouble keeping track of all the children. Josephine's last-born daughter was only three, younger than two of her granddaughters.

Delila tossed the last of the onions onto a metal tray. "We call the new one Baby Edwina."

"That's a nice name. Please, Delila, can't you get one of the girls to bring some clean water?"

"Auntie, I told you. The salad was dirty and the water was clean and now the salad is clean and the water is dirty."

"Okay, but don't blame me when everyone gets diarrhoea from parasites," I said, shaking the lettuce to dislodge as much of the water, and hopefully the resident amoeba population, as I could.

"Oh, there are no microbes here, Auntie," Delila said. "I studied microbes in biology lessons this week. We don't have any of those here."

"No? How do you know?" I looked about me. The kitchen behind Josephine's Parachute Club was a mud compound overrun with chickens and children and their respective wastes. The fireplaces consisted of three stones and the fire over which sauces in blackened cauldrons gurgled and spit red palm oil like small geysers of molten lava. Large chunks of goat meat rolled and danced in the boiling sauces.

"Because I saw them in my biology book," Delila replied.

"What do they look like?"

"They're ugly. Horns and spines and hairy legs. About this big."

I glanced over to see her holding her hands a few inches apart, indicating, I assumed, the size of a textbook photograph of a micro-organism magnified a billion times by an electron microscope. "Oh, Delila, that was a photograph." I tried to explain magnification.

She nodded wisely, but it was obvious that she was skeptical of my mysterious logic, my own magic and scientific fetishes. She waited politely until my patronizing lecture fizzled out before getting back to something that interested her. "The baby is almost white, " she announced.

"Who? Francesca's baby, Edwina?"

"Yes." She grinned. "You remember the French commandant who was here last year?"

I remembered him well. He was old, wrinkled and embalmed in whisky. How could Francesca, an eighteen-year-old with a mind sharp as a butcher knife, have borne to let him touch her, let alone . . .

"He's the father?" I asked.

"Well he's not the son," Delila said, laughing that tinkling laugh that sounded like brass wind chimes.

"But does he know? I mean, will he help Francesca support the child?"

Delila gave me a pitying look. "Auntie, he's gone back to France. To his wife and family. He showed us the pictures. The wife is very beautiful. Three sons who are almost grown men. He promised to send one of them to me."

If I had it all straight, of Josephine's eight daughters only the two eldest had an African father. He had been a captain in the army and had "gone missing" when French mercenaries came in to put down a coup a few years after independence.

The rest of the girls were the daughters of foreign military men who had passed through the Talon Military Base over the last twenty-five years. Josephine told me this herself. It was something of which she was not in the least ashamed. It made me ashamed but not on Josephine's behalf. On behalf of the rest of the world that left offspring behind them when they left Africa, just like litter left after a picnic.

"Look how she does that, Deli." Josephine swept her hand over the salad, as though it were something sacred and untouchable. "Cattie, your salad looks just like a flower." She wiped sweat from her nose with the folds of her wrapper, exposing an expanse of brown, wrinkled belly stretched loose by eight pregnancies.

"I need some avocados, and it takes time to cut the tomatoes up nicely. Are the men ready to eat yet, Josephine?"

"Those men? They wouldn't even mind if we forgot to bring the food. Just as long as we don't run out of beer. And whisky."

I smiled at Francesca, who had come out of her hut and was sitting nursing her tiny baby on the doorstep. The baby was completely hidden under layers of pink blankets. In fact, the compound was suddenly full of girls, all unnaturally subdued. Josephine must have instilled the fear of something in them to make them so quiet.

"Cattie," said Josephine, standing over me with her legs apart, arms akimbo, "we are worried for you. You need to make a baby for your husband. He will divorce you soon, if you don't."

"Oh, Josephine, no no no. We don't want any children yet. We've only been married a few years and we're not ready." Actually, my husband and I had been married for ten years and had decided not to have any children because we both had careers and wanted to keep living and working abroad. It just seemed easier without children.

Over the years, usually in airports when I was coming to or going from Africa, I watched mothers with small children. I pitied them. Not even that. I had no respect for those women, reduced to screaming children themselves, running after little brats who took obvious pleasure in terrorizing other passengers who would like to sleep between continents. Motherhood did not appeal to me, not at all. Not what it entailed in my part of the world, at least.

Besides, I had no time for children. I was working as a family planning consultant and spent most of my time helping women prevent unwanted pregnancies at a clinic in Talon. Josephine had blithely ignored my repeated offers to equip her and her daughters with contraceptive devices. It annoyed me, although I knew it shouldn't, that she would poke her nose into my own family planning. That's what I did every day here — poke my nose into other people's private lives.

"You listen to me, Cattie," said Josephine, looking twenty years older when she screwed up her eyes like that. Motherhood had added dignity, not years, to her bearing. She could still pass for a woman of thirty though I guessed she was close to fifty. She worked seven days a week in her roadside restaurant to earn the money to pay for her daughters' schooling. She didn't seem to mind when they lay with white men, something I never understood. But if they did poorly at school or mucked about with local boys to cause scandal, it was the cane for them. Francesca had even stayed in school during her pregnancy. Josephine took on the headmaster over that — and won. I couldn't fathom her determination to educate her children and then allow them to be reduced to terminal motherhood.

I sliced tomatoes on a metal tray, arranging the red quarters neatly around the perimeter of the large glass plate. Josephine squatted beside me, modestly tucking the skirt of her wrapper between her legs.

"Listen to me, Cattie. I know men. White, black, yellow. They all want children. A woman who can't produce children is no woman. She's a witch. You know why I have only daughters? Because my auntie was a witch. She was jealous of my mother because my mother had six children. My auntie couldn't bear her husband any children so he divorced her. My mother gave me to my auntie but that still didn't satisfy her. So my auntie cursed me. On her death bed she said I would bear only daughters and my daughters would produce only daughters." She sighed and gazed pensively up into the dark canopy of the mango tree shading us from the worst of the afternoon sun. "At least that's better than no children at all."

I scooped up handfuls of onion chunks and tossed them on top of the salad. They were strong, those succulent purple onions. My eyes watered.

"I have some *juju* for you, Cattie. You put it on the wall, over your bed, and you will bring forth. Your husband will be happy. You are my daughter. It makes me unhappy when you are not happy. I've been blessed. I have enough good luck to share it with you."

I wiped my nose with the back of my hand, and with stinging eyes looked at what Josephine was holding in her hands. It was a tail, a furry black and white tail. "What's that, a civet tail?"

"No, this is from the monkey, black and white monkey." She shook it. "You put this over your bed, and you will conceive. You will feel it in your womb. This black and white tail is for you. You take it. From Josephine."

The unsavoury talisman, probably from an endangered species of primate, dangled in front of me. I hid my revulsion, trying to humour her and pretend to be gracious and grateful that she cared. I would, of course, throw it away once I got home. Maybe even laugh over it with my husband. After I raked him over the coals.

"I'll take it later, Josephine. I've got to finish the salad now. Where are the avocados?" I asked of the female audience in the compound.

My eyes settled on Francesca who was nursing her infant. A tiny hand escaped from the blanket in which the baby was swathed. It clutched at air as it sucked mother's milk. So *helpless.*

Josephine thrust the furry talisman into my hand. The black and white tail hung limp from my left hand; the knife was in the other. Something stirred in my abdomen. An ache. I can't find the word. There is none. It was a feeling, not an idea.

Josephine smiled at me, rubbing her palms together. Then she turned to Delila, who was watching me with an inscrutable smile.

"*Delila, Cattie asked for avocados. You sit there like a Goroni princess. Move, you lazy girl!*"

Delila fled to fetch avocados. Avocados. What on earth did I care about avocados? My mind had tunnelled into my womb and was sitting down there, hurting like the excision of a wisdom tooth.

Nine months later I gave birth to a very beautiful baby boy. His name is Joseph. His true mother is not me, I know. Joseph is Josephine's son. She tells me so every time we go to the Parachute Club and she grabs him from me and dances with him gurgling in her arms with that smile of hers that stretches right across the swollen belly of Mother Africa.

Dark side of the moon

At a quarter to eight she walks with Jimmy to the white Land Cruiser, trying to talk to him about this and that, make everything seem normal. She asks him what he wants Baba to make for lunch, trying to delay his departure for the office. Anything to foreshorten the long day ahead of her.

Jessica cries and says, "Don't go, Daddy." Christine doesn't cry; she's got to keep everything under control. She picks up her daughter as her husband drives away.

"I want to go with Daddy. I don't want to stay with you."

"Don't kick me, honey," Christine says. The girl continues to pummel her with her feet. Jessica, at four, is getting too big for her to carry and has long since been too much for her to handle. She puts her down and together they watch Daddy's car pull out of the drive and disappear down the road to where he'll spend the day dealing with people and plans for rural water systems.

Although she knows she should, she doesn't care about rural water resources or the village women who have to walk miles for a bucket of swamp water for drinking. They've always done it, why shouldn't they continue? She would never say this out loud but she shouts it in her mind almost every day.

"Daddy will be home at lunch, sweetheart," she says to Jessica. The girl has already forgotten about her father.

"I want to go to school," she says, pulling her mother by the hand.

There are three hundred and eighty-five days left. She counted them yesterday afternoon on the Canadian Wilderness calendar while her daughter was napping. She tried not to see the glossy photographs of turquoise Rocky Mountain vistas and the wilderness lakes in early morning mist. Sometimes she has to make a conscious effort to breathe, as though her reflexes packed up while she was unpacking in this African outpost.

Now, as she walks with Jessica to the kindergarten, she forces air down her lungs, feeling her stomach muscles tighten with the effort of suppressing the anguish. She thinks she could burn herself up, extinguish herself in a pyre of despair and agony, if she allowed herself to admit that she and her life have turned out this way.

The teachers greet them with gusto and giggles, running to meet the small white child who leaps into their arms laughing, glad to be among joyful people. Christine tries to force a smile for the two attendants who wish her a good morning. Her smile is taut. She keeps her lips stiff in case they fly wide open and something terrible flies out, something winged and hairy that's crouched in the back of her throat.

The sun at eight fifteen is already powerful enough to make her dizzy as she walks back across the compound to her house. It is a large rambling house, a huge complex of rooms that have no reason to be — attached to the main body of the bungalow like unpopular sideshows.

It's July, summer at home. Mom and Dad are at the lake now, playing host to all their old friends and neighbours. She can almost feel the rough boards of the wharf on her belly, as she pulls herself out of the cool water and stretches out to dry in the summer sun. Mom and Dad are sure to be pottering about the place as they always do, even though there is nothing that needs done, trimming the hedge maybe, or arranging rose bushes over the trellis. They're wearing the old straw hats that winter on a hanger beside the fireplace in the cottage.

That's where she and Jimmy should be. She conjures the sounds, smells, the voice of her father: "Chrissie, Jimmy, we've got some fresh lemonade." Jimmy reels in his empty line. The only thing he can't do well is fish; he's never caught a thing in that lake but he laughs and says he will, one day. She stands, shaking out her towel and her sun-dried hair. Jimmy's arm encircles her waist and they walk slowly up the grassy slope to the brown cedar cabin. She can feel the firm flesh of Jimmy's lower back in her palm as though the images of the glorious summer days at the lake have leapt into the here and now. She closes her eyes and smells the hot grass, the pine and the fir trees behind the cottage. She remembers the pleasure of examining her own body, as it looked before they came here. How her tan spread like a golden sheen over her curves — she had more of them then and fewer sharp angles — and they drew Jimmy to her every night.

Her eyes open and register local scenes that do not belong in her field of dreams. Some filthy boys are fishing for mud-fish in the slimy green water of the gutters. Half-naked little girls, not much bigger than Jessica, carry metal buckets of water on their heads. She wishes they weren't always staring at her as though she were a ghost, and calling to her in unintelligible words and the

"Allo Allo Allo", which always sounds to her like the disrespectful tone of a mockingbird.

When they came, twenty days short of a year ago, Jimmy offered to hire a language teacher so she could learn one of the local languages. She is glad the subject has been dropped. When she is gone in three hundred and eighty-five days she will never have to hear the incomprehensible babble of the languages here again.

Baba is working on the living room floor, pushing a cloth round and round, working up suds to show that he's getting the floor truly clean and shining. The floors are terrazzo and Baba scrubs them every morning, waxes them once a week.

She has had curtains made for all the windows. She chose the cloth herself at the market in the early days when she put her decorating skills and energy into making the house a home. The curtains are yellow, purple and green. She thought the jungle colours in meaningless swirls were just right when she bought the cloth and spent two weeks sewing them and hanging them. Now she finds them garish, gaudy and overwhelming. She thinks about tearing them off the windows. The cloth here is never subtle — always loud and crass. This is what she secretly thinks about the people too. But she doesn't dare say that, not even to herself. Her gut is filled with forbidden thoughts. She must pretend. She is sure the other expat wives are pretending to find it all interesting — surely there is nothing to like.

She walks to the kitchen, glances out the window at the too-brilliant flowering plants that mock the barren shades of brown inside her. The tropics are too vibrant and lush and colourful. Next to the plants in the garden, planted and nurtured by her energetic predecessor, she feels like a drab female lizard. Some afternoons she sits for an hour or two in the sun, trying to recapture the feel of a healthy tan on her skin. She stays out of sight in the walled-in patio area between house and boys' quarters. She watches the lizards doing their push-ups. Their bobbing looks as dislocated as her days feel but their movements have a purpose. Jimmy says they orient themselves that way.

The boy with the flute is passing. She has half a mind to record his music but doesn't know how to go about inviting him inside. He passes the house each morning. Baba says the boy is "not normal". He laughs at him and tells Christine, "We fear him, Madam. Wicked spirits make him crazy."

She is surprised to see the boy pass through the blue gate as if his flute is leading him to her. Baba, who is bent over the tap outside refilling the wash bucket, slowly comes to attention. He fingers the slingshot, which always dangles like a fetish around his neck. Christine watches as Baba bends to pick up a handful of stones. The boy doesn't seem to see him. He is still approaching the house, playing his flute. The tune is reminiscent of a serenade to the magnificence of the Andes; it has nothing to do with Talon, this luckless town in a luckless stretch of savanna.

She wants to move, open the window, shout at Baba who is taking aim. But it is too late. The shower of gravel has struck the boy. He drops his flute as he stumbles, rushing to escape. Christine finally makes her legs move. She races outside, ignoring Baba's protests as she picks up the simple instrument, a length of cane with a few uneven holes. She follows the boy to the road where he is standing now watching her. She holds the flute out to him, like an offering. He eyes her for a long time before he suddenly grins, snatches it back and heads off up the road on the run.

She watches him go. His knees are too large, his gait pigeon-toed, and she is filled with a sadness that feels like a free-fall into a bottomless pit.

She wants to strike Baba, tear off a branch from the *dawa-dawa* tree and beat him. She is frightened by the urge. She walks silently past him and into the house.

Baba is her only company in the house all day and he's wonderful with Jessica. He irons clothes, cooks, cleans and sometimes offers to do the marketing on his bicycle when he notices that she has not mustered the energy to take the taxi ride to the market in town, to face the harrowing experience of haggling for a few pock-marked tomatoes or half-rotten bananas.

She knows she should be thankful to have him and his help in the house. It is one of the advantages of living in Africa, they say. "It's wonderful. I don't have to spend all day ironing shirts and sheets," Pat says. "I have lots of time for all my other interests. I'm thinking of enroling in a correspondence course in creative writing, and maybe getting involved in the women's weaving cooperative."

Christine thinks that when the boy passes tomorrow morning she will go and talk to him, ask him what he feels and thinks about, this boy who is "not normal". It worries her that the only person in whom she has developed any interest or curiosity is this knock-kneed and half-witted boy with the flute. She really should record his music; that's a language they might have in common. She should try to find Jimmy's pocket recorder, get it ready when the boy passes again. She doesn't feel like searching. Maybe later.

She loads the washing machine and stands wondering what to do. She thinks that the emptiness she feels must be hunger so she eats a piece of the awful white bread that is made here. It's gooey and far too sweet. Pat has given her a recipe for bread she makes herself with millet but Christine has never made bread in her life.

She has barely swallowed it when she has to run to the bathroom and vomit it up, along with the coffee and the orange juice she drank with Jimmy and Jessica earlier in the morning.

She wonders if she's getting malaria. Her head feels too light and airy as though it is struggling to float away from her body. Maybe she should lie down and just rest today. Baba can go to the market and make *jollof* rice as Jimmy requested. But Jimmy won't complain even if there's no food in the house or on the table at lunchtime. He will make a sandwich for himself and Jessica or send Baba out to the police barrier to buy plantains and beans wrapped in leaves, from the women who run chop bars there. The thought of this fly-covered food makes her retch again. But there is nothing left inside.

Later, Jimmy will ask her what's wrong, if there's anything he can do. She will tell him no, it's just a touch of flu or malaria. He doesn't say anything about her weight loss, her dark moods and her silence when he tries to evoke some laughter in the house with his slapstick tomfoolery. It has been ages since she had any appetite; she hasn't had a period in months. She has read about this syndrome in anorexic women who lose too much weight too fast. In her mind, she's already dying.

Jimmy knows how miserable she is, and she knows he knows, and talking about it will just make her cry and make him feel bad that he has brought her here. Their bed is big — so big that lately they can sleep together without running into each other. Last night Jimmy fell asleep while he was reading *The Little Train That Could* to Jessica and didn't come to their bedroom at all. She looked in on them in the night. They had their arms around each other and were breathing into each other's mouths, like a couple of lovers. She lay awake in the master bedroom, staring into the darkness, wondering what to do to relieve the boredom of the sleepless night, wondering how to find life inside her. Perhaps the headache is just due to lack of sleep.

She lies again on her back on the giant bed now, listening to Baba humming now as he works his way up the hall with the mop. She gets up and slams the bedroom door shut. She returns to the bed, covers her eyes with her right arm. It would take a whole day — just a day — to drive to the capital. There are flights from there every day, heading back to civilization.

Civilization: a place with no dust, filth and staring eyes. None of this poverty, away from the obligation to put on a brave face to meet those smiles and greetings. Always greeting each other. She wishes she knew what they found to smile about.

"Don't they understand that sometimes I just don't feel like talking to anyone at all?" She said this at the dinner table, over a plate of untouched beefsteak and boiled yams, then stood and fled before the tears started. Jimmy caught her, pulled her back. "Chrissie, it's okay." He hugged her, but tentatively as though she were dying from a contagious disease. "If you don't feel like talking, you don't have to. No one is forcing you to do anything you don't want to do. Just relax. This is just a normal phase you're going through. After that, you'll never want to go home. Believe me, this place grows on you. The people here will make that happen to you. Be patient. Soon you'll love it even more than I do!"

In the three-day orientation in Ottawa she had believed him, dismissed all the warnings about the alienation that one feels when one moves to a new continent and a new culture as something that happened only to other people. She had hoped that she would catch Jimmy's enthusiasm. She had tried, at first. She went to the market, made the curtains, fashioned tablecloths from the colourful batiks, arranged the rattan furniture in the living room, hung up traditional weavings on the walls and re-created the comfort of the cottage at the lake in this godforsaken town.

It makes it much worse that Jimmy really does love it here. He worked here five years ago as a volunteer of progress. When they arrived, he took her to the villages and showed her the wells he had dug — most of them were now boarded over and dry or caved in. They spent their first few weeks visiting all his old favourite haunts, that horrendous Point Ten bar, where he renewed old friendships. It made her feel small, as though she occupied a tiny sliver of his life and could claim only the love he had left over after the rest of the world was done with it.

She sometimes wants to tell them, all the intruders, that Jimmy belongs to her; only she has known him from childhood. They were summer neighbours at the lake. Jimmy, older, had earned a reputation at the lake as that wild Lovett boy. Dad called him the "yahoo with the motorboat." Christine was not even five when Jimmy and his gang of boys and girls were caught smoking in the boat-house at the Lakeside Club, but she remembered the uproar among the parents. She sat beside her mother when those delinquents were discussed, letting her mother stroke her hair. She had always been a good girl.

She could not remember what she had thought then about the older kids or that wild, dark-haired Lovett boy, seven years her senior, or even when she had really noticed him. She had the impression, probably helped by table talk in her own cottage, that he came every year with a new girlfriend. When she was in her teens, he didn't come to the lake. He, like most of the older ones, was off travelling somewhere. Everyone seemed to be working their way around the world by the worn-out seats of their jeans, dwarfed by knapsacks festooned with flags and mementos from far-away lands.

She had never understood why Jimmy and other kids were inclined to move away from their homes and their parents and to travel the world. She lived at home while she attended university; no summer jobs selling hamburgers or on the highway as a flag-girl for her. Summer was just not summer, away from Mom and Dad and Lake Mishiboom. The Walshes and the Armstrongs came out for evening barbecues and tennis and spoke of their own wayward offspring. "If only Tommy would write to us. Last we heard he was in Bangladesh. Can you imagine? He wanted more money to continue his travels." Mr. Walsh chuckled. "Then he called and said he wanted to go to Bali and I said where the hell is Bali?"

"Chrissie doesn't even accept money from us although we sure like to give it to her," her father said. That was the summer Dad bought her a red Ford Dasher as a highschool graduation present; he said she deserved it.

"We sent him the money," said Mr. Walsh. "But we told him it was the last and that he should come home and get himself a job."

"Yes, we consider ourselves very lucky to have a daughter like Chrissie," said her father and mother, at the end of these exchanges.

Then, five years ago, Jimmy came back to the lake. He showed up at his parents' cottage on a motorcycle, with a black woman on the back. Christine never knew her name — it was said that it was a native name and hard to pronounce, so people just called her "that Jamaican." What Christine remembered was her slippery accent and rounded thighs and how they could hug Jimmy's hips.

She hadn't meant to spy on them. She always went for a swim at dawn when loons rather than motorboats owned the lake. She loved the mist and the solitude. She had more right to the lake than did Jimmy and that black invader.

They didn't hear her open the door of the cottage and come outside, or they didn't care that there was someone watching. They didn't even pause in what they were doing. But she did, stopping and pulling her terry robe around her protectively. Two naked bodies, one white and one black. She was not shocked by their passionate gymnastics, just fascinated. She had had her share of boyfriends, young men to whom she was mildly attracted and who were sure to please her parents. She had always chosen solid, straight men with potential in banks or engineering firms. She had made love with two of them, but only by dark in their apartments, never in a car or in her own home, certainly never on a beach. It had never been anything like the love she saw exploding and writhing on the beach that morning between Jimmy Lovett and that Jamaican. They rolled over and over each other, black and white limbs intertwined. The girl threw her head back and laughed, pinning Jimmy underneath her with those round thighs.

In the days that followed she watched everything that went on at the Lovett cottage: Jimmy serving the girl a bottle of beer as she lay reading in the hammock, the girl climbing on the back of the motorcycle, wearing black leather pants. She observed them with a feeling she thought was disgust which was, she realizes only now, agonizing envy.

The girl's hair was cropped neatly, making her neck look even longer, her face more exotic. Jimmy seemed unable to stop touching her. Even as they sat on the wharf with their legs dangling in the lake, he had an arm across the girl's back, resting on her right buttock. Christine put down the cob of corn she was eating, wishing Mr. Walsh would shut up about his golf score. Mrs. Walsh was gushing over the tenderness of the corn. There was a loud splash as the girl pushed Jimmy into the water. She, her parents and the Walshes watched as Jimmy pulled the black girl into the water with him and kissed her. The two heads bobbed under and came up, still glued together, like a pair of buoys.

"Looks like someone lost a bowling ball out there and Jimmy's found it," her father said. "Must have picked up a fondness for exotic colours over there in Africa."

The pain in her head is spreading now. She wonders if she is making up the headache, to give herself a tangible reason to feel as she does. She should get up, go and see Pat. But Pat would start listing all the things Christine should be doing, reasons for her to like it here. Pat seems to have friends all over town and she often invites Christine to come out with her for coffee at their houses. She went once, listened to their plans for nursery schools, women's cooperatives, renovating the orphanage. She doesn't have their sense of purpose or their skills. Her business is aesthetics — interiors — mixing colours and patterns to create an atmosphere of exquisite taste. She sees no room for that here. When it was all still new, before she had to start pretending — even to herself — that she was doing fine, she wrote it down in letters to her mother. "It's hot, dirty, poor and backward. Some of the Canadians here claim to love it. They say the culture is "interesting" and that I should try to "get involved" in something. In what? I ask them. They say I should teach, or work in the villages. Mommy, if you could see the villages. The kids are all ridden with disease and there's just no hope. Men have three or four wives and dozens of children, whom they can't feed or clothe or school. What can I do? In fact, I think most of them will have to die. How I long for a Saturday morning at the farmers' market. Here the markets are filthy. Children do their business right underfoot, where I buy tomatoes. There are almost no fresh vegetables grown here. I'd kill for a plate of broccoli."

"Chrissie, please," wrote her mother, "if it's so awful, why don't you come home? Jimmy would understand. That's no place to bring up Jessica. We'd be so happy to have you stay with us until Jimmy's contract is up. By the way, your father has spotted a lovely Spanish-style home that's for sale on the river valley. It's not cheap, but he says he would put up the down payment for you, if Jimmy feels he can't afford it, that is, and you could set up your own real home here. We didn't bring you up for a life over there. Jimmy should know that, after all. Dad has promised him a share of the stock when he comes back. He doesn't need to go traipsing all over the world to find a job. He's got a family to consider. Please, honey, why don't you just pack your bags and hop on a plane and come home to Mother and Dad?"

She didn't answer that question and she still asks it of herself all the time. She tells herself she can't leave because she owes it to Jimmy. She will be thirty-one when they go back to Canada. Then she can have the second child. She musn't get pregnant here. There are too many dangers. No doctors or ultrasound machines or sterile operating theatres. At least she can't imagine that there are.

Jimmy always said he wanted a big happy family with loads of children. She says nothing when he reminds her of this.

The image of Jimmy and that girl on the beach haunts her now. It won't go away. It is the picture behind the headache. How could he have made love like that, caressed that other girl that way, just months before he told her he loved and wanted to marry her? Why does this come to her now, over here, so long after the fact?

She thinks Jimmy loves the act of love, or used to, the same way he loves people — any colour, any size and any shape.

She doesn't know why Jimmy fell in love with her.

Yet, he had seemed so sure of what he was doing.

To avoid seeing them at it again on the beach, just in case that kind of thing was a morning habit with the two lovers, she started taking her long swims in the evening. The water seemed smoother and more soothing in the evening. By mid-August the nights were cooler, and after her swim she would walk back to the cottage and sit by the fire, listening to Mom and Dad talk over the day — the latest news on lakeside affairs — and make plans for their annual pilgrimage to Florida. She was preparing to start a job as junior designer with Interiors in the city, and for the first time she would not be able to accompany her parents to Florida that winter. She felt vaguely relieved, but sorry too. She loved shopping in the Ports International boutiques in November with her mother, who always seemed to look chic and professional and knew what colours were right, while frumpy housewives trundled past picking out shapeless ski jackets and snow-boots in the bargain bins.

For days she didn't see Jimmy and the girl and she assumed they had gone back to the city. She suddenly felt lonely, as though summer had come to a premature end. She swam long distances, across the lake and back, trying to get rid of the itchiness in her toes and fingers. She did the crawl and breast stroke, moving blindly through the water, looking up every now and then to gauge the distance back to shore. She cried out in fear when the canoe loomed up in front of her.

"Christine, what the hell are you doing way out here?"

"Swimming." She trod water.

"You're lucky I didn't plough into you. Want a ride back to shore?"

"Okay," she said. Jimmy helped her into the boat and paddled the canoe back to her wharf, not speaking. Evening fell on the lake, and cottage lights reflected on the surface. "How about something to eat at the Club? Do you get hungry after a swim?"

"Not tonight, thanks." She stepped out of the canoe, picked up her towel and wrapped it around herself, shivering.

"Then tomorrow?" She glanced at him, at that big smile. "About seven? I'll pick you up."

"Wild Jimmy Lovett must have finally come to his senses and decided to spend some time with his own kind," said her father at dinner that night. He didn't say the right colour but Christine knew that's what he meant; she had thought it too.

"I hope he takes off that earring and does something with his hair, honey," her mother said as she brushed out Christine's long blond hair before Jimmy came for her. "Or else people will think you've come with the wrong man. Your hair is so lovely, I could brush it forever. Don't you ever cut it."

"Take care of our little girl," Dad said to Jimmy, as she climbed on the back of the motorcycle and waved goodbye.

"You have to hold me here," shouted Jimmy, reaching back with one hand and placing each of her arms around his stomach, one after the other.

"What happened to your friend from Jamaica?" Christine asked him over shrimp cocktail, allowing him to refill her wine glass, not wishing to appear prudish or dull.

"She wasn't from Jamaica. We worked together in Africa. She had to go back to work. She's working in Haiti now. We're just ships in the night." He laughed.

"Oh, I see." She smiled, waiting for him to continue and to tell her more. Instead he dazzled her with a lopsided grin and the gold stud in his left ear that twinkled in the lamplight. He reached across the table to touch first her hair and then her cheek, and knocked over his own wine glass. They both giggled. "See what you've done to me, girl-from-next-door?" he said. "I'm all jitters."

He ordered more wine and he made her laugh all evening. Nothing in her life had prepared her for the wave of emotions that swept over her as they rode back to the cottage on the back of his motorcycle. She pressed her right cheek against the cool leather of his jacket, sighing with ecstasy that she had not yet sampled.

Later, on the wharf in front of her parents' cabin, he made love to her, and when she whispered his name into his chest, he rolled with her into the cold velvet of the midnight water. Two months later, after she told him that she was pregnant, he proposed to her. He was back in school finishing up a degree in engineering. He said he had been planning to get married anyway. He didn't say to whom.

"Oh, Chrissie," said her mother, rising from the table and hugging her from behind. "That's wonderful." Her tears continued throughout the meal.

"Mom, are you happy or sad?" Christine asked her.

"Chrissie, of course I'm happy," she sobbed. She hadn't touched a bite of the roastbeef, or the creme torte she had baked for Sunday dessert. "It's just that it's come so quickly and you're so young. You're still my little girl. And Jimmy, is, well, he has been such a wild boy. He's caused his mother and father so much worry. I wonder really if that's what caused his father's, well you know, drinking problems. Going off to all those places and bringing home all those strange girlfriends in rags and beads and robes. But I'm sure he's changed now. He'll make a wonderful husband."

It was Christine's turn to get up from her place at the table and move around to hug her mother, anything to stop her from crying. Her father came in with a bottle of champagne and they drank a toast. "Here's to having a new son-in-law and all those grandchildren," he said, "and most of all, here's to the two girls in my life."

The subject of the six-month pregnancy was never mentioned. Christine was also the result of a six-month pregnancy and that had never been mentioned either.

At Christmas, when she began to spot blood, the doctor recommended that she stop working and spend the remaining months of the pregnancy "resting". Jimmy thought that was a good idea and they agreed that she would give up her job for a few years, until they had finished producing the big family and all the children were in school.

"As long as you will be happy," he said. He had cried at the birth and cut the cord himself with the scissors. "I love you, Chrissie, and I'm so happy," he said as she took the wrinkled infant to her breast in that green hospital room.

Sometimes she thought Jimmy would be happy if someone dropped him on the dark side of the moon. He would just walk over to the bright side and stand there smiling up into space thinking himself the luckiest guy in the solar system. "But I am," was his response when she told him this.

She can't leave him and go back home. There are still three hundred and eighty-five days left in his contract here. He knows that many young and beautiful African girls. She saw him with "that Jamaican." She knows he thrives on fun and laughter; and here everyone seems full of both. But not when she tries to talk with them.

The headache explodes behind her eyes, and she realizes she has groaned out loud. She covers her mouth with her hands. The sound of the mop going round and round in the hallway and banging against the door has stopped. Where is Baba? Listening to Madam cry in her bedroom. She imagines him telling the tale to everyone in his hut when he goes home after work. "Madam cry like a baby all day. I can't know what wrong with her. She rich in a big house and Mastah give her everything she want. White Madam make no sense to me-o."

The clock tells her it is already nine thirty. She should get up and take some tablets — the ones for malaria and the codeine pills in the drug cabinet. A glass of ice water. She walks unsteadily to the living room. Baba is there, dusting the shelves with their collection of pots, bronze statuettes and bowls she has picked up over the months at the arts centre. She tries to smile at him. She wishes she could have got to the kitchen without meeting him. How can she feel so lonely and still miss her privacy?

"Madam not feeling fine?" he asks.

She shakes her head. "Well, not really," she says. "Something is just not right inside me. I think it's malaria."

Baba clucks his tongue. "It do pass, Madam. You feel poorly, but it do pass." He sounds sympathetic but he seems to be grinning at her.

She looks at him sharply, wondering if he is reading more than he lets on, but he is wiping down a bronze figurine of a leggy African woman carrying a smooth gleaming water pot on her head. He rubs and rubs at the rounded bronze belly of the woman in his hands. He is definitely smiling. He continues to rub on the figurine as he speaks.

"How my wife did suffer with the last one, Madam. But that boy be most strong of all my sons." Her hand moves to her belly, that small swelling between her hip bones. She has long since forgotten to note down the dangerous days on that calendar on which she has been counting, instead, the end of her days here in Africa.

"Oh my God," she says, as the obvious hits her.

"God is good, Madam," says Baba. "Children be His gift to we mortal beings on this earth. But sometimes He make us suffer plenty before he give us something good."

She realizes that for the first time in months she is smiling. Something inside her moves, like a cloud that has been blotting out the sun. Of course there are doctors here; Jimmy will know someone who knows someone who knows a good doctor. And that doctor will be smiling and gentle and tell her how far along she is and give her good advice on how to look after herself.

She glances at her watch, calculating the minutes until Jimmy comes home and she can greet him with the news.

Gladys

Gladys heard the car grinding its way over the craters on the road, long before it reached the village. She was in the family compound, mashing groundnuts on a stone for the evening soup. She fought the impulse to go and see who was passing. It would not do for her, a young woman with full breasts, to run barefoot onto the road like one of the shoeless children of Taali.

Apart from the rare vehicle on the road the only sounds in the village were the muted voices bouncing back and forth behind thick mud walls and the occasional cry of a lost baby goat or a squawking guinea-fowl. The maize mill had been silent for a week. Diesel had run out and no one could agree on who should pay for more. It didn't really matter because there wasn't much maize left in the granaries to grind.

They were deep into the long dry season, the time of year when there was nothing much to do in Taali except wait for the first rain and planting time. Tempers flared like bush fires at this time of year. Everyone was hungry. The next harvest — the next full belly — was a whole farming season away. The air was so hot that even the blue-tailed flies seemed to have trouble taking off.

Cars and lorries passing through brought fleeting distractions. Gladys sometimes let herself imagine that she could board them and travel to places far from Taali. Just as Paul, her senior brother, had done. She wished she were still at school in Talon. Away from the chores. Away from her father's second wife who treated Gladys like a maid servant.

She had been up since well before dawn, fetching water, chopping firewood and cooking. She glanced over at her mother and her mother's rival, that lazy and annoying second wife her father had taken. They were roasting sheanuts in a corner of the compound, bickering over who had collected the best nuts.

The car seemed to have stopped but the engine still hummed. Gladys put the top back on the pot and removed the burning faggots, dousing them with drops of murky water from the bucket she had carried from the stream at dawn. She was looking for a pretext to head out to the roadside when her junior brother came running into the compound.

"Sister, you must come and see. The pick-up is blue and shiny," Ben said, "bigger than the chief's palace. White men have come." He spoke in Abule.

"So, you never saw a white man before, you foolish boy?" She feigned disinterest while curiosity knocked at her ribs like a funeral drum. A white man had come through a few months ago to look at the old stone house, left over from colonial times, and since then there had been rumours that a new missionary was coming to repair the school in Taali. There had been no teacher in the village since Father Carlos left two years earlier. During a rainstorm last year the zinc roofing sheets had blown off the unused school.

"But these ones stopped here. You have to come, sister, because you are the only one who speaks English."

She stood slowly and followed Ben to the road. The blue pick-up was parked in front of the stone house, surrounded by children. She pushed her way to the front of the mob, cuffing them and scolding them for their lack of manners, eager herself to have a long, unabashed look at the strangers.

There were two people inside the cabin: a dark-haired man with a turned-up nose like the back end of a chicken and a woman with a mass of blond curls around her face.

Gladys had trouble keeping her place at the front of the crowd. The children behind and around her pushed forward, poking and hitting each other. The man and woman sat inside the cabin of the pick-up, talking. The engine was still running, and Gladys wondered if they were lost, if they wouldn't just drive off again once they got their bearings. The woman looked frightened and sad at the same time. She didn't glance at the crowd gathering around the vehicle.

Gladys was practising a welcome address in her head when the man turned off the engine and leapt out, startling everyone. Then he leaned against the side of the pick-up with his arms folded over his chest and began to speak.

"I'm here to open the New Dawn church," he said, in a language that was just barely recognizable as Abule. It sounded to Gladys as though he had a sheep inside him somewhere helping him talk. "I am the Reverend Bilhouse and this is my wife, Pam. We're going to build you a church and repair your school. I'll be holding services right here under this baobab tree on Sunday morning, and I welcome you all."

Gladys thought it strange that this man would welcome them to their own village. By rights, he should have gone straight to the chief's palace to announce his mission and be welcomed. But he seemed very friendly, smiling like Bandi, the Taali idiot, and it looked as though he had rubbed his cheeks with sheanut butter to get them shining pink like that.

The pick-up was piled high with furniture and suitcases. When they started pulling things out of the car the onlookers grew still, dazzled by all the *things*.

Everything looked shiny and new, piled up on the dirt beside the car like mounds of pearly maize after a good harvest.

Mrs. Bilhouse stayed close to the pick-up, clutching the open door, as if undecided as to whether she would stay or leap back inside and drive away. She was wearing a pants suit the colour of a ripe mango. In Taali no woman, no matter what church or mosque, wore trousers. Sister Josephine had told the girls in the school that trousers on a woman showed up all sorts of cracks and crevices that didn't need to be publicized. "A man carrying a bag of gold is not going to write *gold* on it, is he, girls?" And the girls had laughed and shouted "No, Sister Josephine."

Then they unloaded the doll that looked to Gladys like a dead girl, maybe two years of age, with yellow hair and blue eyes that closed when Reverend Bilhouse laid her down on her back on a pile of fold-up chairs. The crowd edged back. Reverend Bilhouse started laughing at the villagers who were afraid of the doll and at his wife who was afraid of the villagers. Then he shouted in Abule, "It's just a pretend child."

The children were skittish for a few minutes but curiosity soon overcame fear and they moved closer trying to sneak a feel of the skin on that pretend child. Mrs. Bilhouse tried to shoo them away, hissing and flapping her hands as though she were trying to get stray chickens back into a pen.

"Look at them, David, full of guinea worm and filthy. I don't want them to touch Angeline. We should never have come north."

"They're all God's children, Pam. We knew it wasn't going to be easy. But this is the mission God gave us and He is with us."

Then he pulled the real baby from the back seat of the pick-up. Pink hat with lace and covered head to toe in pink. Nothing that bright and colourful had been seen in Taali before. Gladys had never seen a white child before. The baby looked dreamy as an angel in the catechism books, light enough to float away as she lay in her father's arms, blinking at the crowd as though she'd just fallen from heaven. Gladys looked up at the pale, faded blue of the sky. Angeline's eyes looked like the sky after a rain, clear and a blue that looked like forever.

Some village men were now joining the crowd around the car. Among them was her father standing tall and proud under the baobab. She dropped her eyes, afraid he would disapprove of her being out in public with the children and these strangers. He was looking for a husband for her, someone who would pay ten good cows for his prized daughter who could read and write.

Gladys had been allowed to attend the boarding school in Talon as long as she had only because the headmistress was a big strong sister from the south, one of those rare women who could intimidate Gladys's father. She allowed

Gladys to attend for free, waiving school and boarding fees to keep what she called her star pupil.

But this year, when she came home from Talon for Christmas holidays, her father had refused to let her return to school. "It's time for you to become a wife," he said. He had made himself invisible on the two occasions when Sister Mary had come out to Taali to talk to him about Gladys's absence from school.

He was looking at her now, almost smiling, beckoning her over to where he stood with the men. He told her to translate his words into English for the Reverend, then moved forward, shoving her ahead of him. Soon he was shaking the white man's hand, bowing and smiling to expose his teeth stained orange by kola nuts. Her father didn't smile like that with anyone she knew.

In the heat of the afternoon Gladys shivered. She kept her eyes on the ground as she struggled with the correct English words to tell Reverend Bilhouse that her father was happy to see him. Her father nodded energetically, as though he had been put on the earth to welcome just such a church man. The reverend replied in Abule, but her father wanted her to translate everything he said into English anyway, as though he were the chief and she his *linguist*.

Gladys's father followed the new family up onto the porch of the old stone house that had been empty since Father Carlos left. Gladys went back to the compound to finish her cooking, eager to tell her mother what she had seen. The older women in the compound chewed over the news that night with their *tuo*, fascinated by the presence of two white babies — one stillborn, one chubby and alive.

"We've had enough religion in our village to make the dead cover their ears and pray for peace on earth," her mother said about the new missionary. "Let us hope, Gladys, that they'll be like the full moon and that they won't keep shining their light for too long here."

Gladys lay awake a long time on her mat that night, wondering what would happen now in Taali. Churches and missionaries meant two things: schools, which she loved, and religious rivalries, which spelled big trouble. People were still mourning the dead from a fight a few years back when the imams gave orders to burn down the Catholic church that was going up beside the mosque. She had liked the priest, Father Carlos, who had cajoled parents in the village to send their children to the school. Her father was the first in the village to be baptized by Father Carlos. He had pretended he had only one wife and the priest had pretended to believe him. Now there was a young girl — younger than Gladys — whom her father was courting as number three. That was why he needed to marry off his firstborn daughter; he needed the cows to pay for his own new bride.

The fire had destroyed all the boards for the new church and two workers had died from cutlass wounds inflicted by Muslim assailants (according to the Christians), by Christian assailants (according to the Muslims). Father Carlos had been recalled to Talon where religious rivalries were kept in check by security forces.

For a while after Father Carlos left it had been peaceful in Taali. Those like her father who had accepted the sacraments went back to their old ways, consulting fetish priests about spirits and spells, omens and oracles. But then the Muslims, belonging to two different branches of Islam and two family lines competing for the chieftaincy of the village, started feuding among themselves. The two marabouts, who were on different sides in the chieftaincy dispute, got everybody stirred up and butting like billy goats about who really saw the moon first and when Ramadan started and when it stopped each year.

And now a new Christian church would enter the fray. Her mother was right. She fell asleep in the middle of a prayer, asking that they would decide not to stay.

She wondered a week later if her prayer would have been answered if she had ever finished saying it. By then, her father seemed to have become the new reverend's assistant and one of his first tasks was to find Reverend Bilhouse a reliable and responsible girl who could help out in the big stone house.

"Gladys, you are going to start to work for Reverend and Missus," her father told her one Sunday. Gladys's mother sat quietly stirring porridge, feeding the fire as he spoke. Her face remained an impassive mask and sweat dripped down her nose and cheeks. To Gladys, she looked old — older than even her grandmother had when she died the previous year.

"Get dressed and come," he said. No one in the compound said a word. Gladys got up from the stool where she had been picking lice from her small sister's hair. As she dressed in her hut she thought she heard someone weeping, but when she stopped to listen she realized the sound was coming from inside her. She had been so sure that eventually, when her father realized there was no one in Taali who would pay the high bride price, he would let her go back and finish school. Now that was impossible. Her father hadn't found her a husband; instead he had found her a job.

The only good dress she had was too small for her now. It was pink and filmy, with rows of blue and white flowers in a wide band around the hem. Her brother Paul had sent it to her from the capital three years ago when he wrote to inform the family he was planning to go on to university and wouldn't be returning to the village that year for farming. Then, it had been the most beautiful thing she had ever seen. But now? It wasn't anything like the dresses and suits Mrs. Bilhouse wore. The dress was too short; her breasts had grown since she last wore it for her grandmother's funeral. It wasn't right at all. She tugged at the elastic waistband, trying to pull it down to cover her knees. Only small girls showed their knees. Not big girls with breasts like papayas, who passed blood each month.

Pam Bilhouse looked Gladys over, smiling as though she, or Gladys, were slightly handicapped. "I'm glad you want to work for us, Gladys. I need a good girl to tend my baby correctly. I'll be teaching and assisting Reverend, so you will have plenty of work to do." She laughed, the sound of a pot breaking into shards. "But I guess you people are used to hard work. I believe you'll be happy with us."

Gladys stared at her feet. No more algebra and neat lines on paper and English poems. She didn't know what it meant — tending a baby *correctly*. She had tended Ben, and the two babies from her father's second wife, carried them on her back when their mothers were busy cooking or fetching water or firewood. When they tired her out she used to pinch their legs, hard, so they would cry to get off her back and their mothers would take them.

There was some pleasure in knowing that other girls her age would be jealous of her in that big stone house. If only her dress were longer, not missing a button so that the dark skin of her belly showed through. She nodded to everything Mrs. Bilhouse asked. She did not dare to speak inside those strange stone walls.

At first she didn't know how to do anything right. She had to learn to iron and fold clothes and clean under beds and wash windows and to sweep floors with a broom that had bright blue bristles and a long handle. She was used to handling grass brooms, bent double and sweeping hard to raise clouds of dust. That way she could tell dirt was being moved. But Mrs. Bilhouse taught her how to use the long one, taking care not to spoil the bristles. Mrs. Bilhouse was patient with her, and kind, especially if she were in a good mood and not remembering how much nicer it was in the south of the country. She said they had run a Bible centre there but that the reverend wanted to convert the north too where Islam was so prevalent. She said she was sorry she hadn't learned to speak Abule like the reverend. "My husband is so good with Africans. No matter how stubborn they are, he never loses his patience. He cares so much. You can tell by how fast he learns those languages. I just can't seem to learn them like he does." She said she was sure that under her tutelage in the school, adults and children of Taali would learn English. "After all," she said. "English is the national language, isn't it Gladys."

At the end of the first week Gladys raced home to tell her mother everything, and to show her the sleeveless, cotton dress Mrs. Bilhouse had given her for work. She told all the women in the compound about the room she had in the boys' quarters behind the house. She didn't tell them the roof had holes in it through which she stared at the stars at night, or about the rats that lived in the back of the toilet and sometimes swam in the bowl.

She made them all laugh with her story of the white, padded nappy with plastic on it that she had put in the tub with the other clothes to wash, and how Mrs. Bilhouse had laughed too when she found it and explained that this was a "disposable diaper", to be thrown away after one "doo-doo". Children had immediately taken it from the garbage pile and torn it to pieces, salvaging the plastic to wear as hats.

She didn't tell her mother how Mrs. Bilhouse yelled when she found Gladys looking through her clothes, fondling the crispy cloth. "You musn't ever do this again, Gladys," she said. "It's an invasion of my privacy." Gladys had learned a lot of new words in a week. Privacy. Bathtub. Indecent (her dress). Disposable. She tried hard to please the white woman, who meant to teach her things she had never learned in school.

She had learned so much that it was difficult to imagine that she had, even a week ago, considered herself schooled. She now knew that she was not supposed to sweep the table with the broom she used for the floor. She knew which brush was for the toilet and which was for the wash basin, and she knew all about germs and how they were spread. She now washed her hands at least a dozen times a day.

When she went home on Sunday afternoons she was amazed at how far she had progressed, how much she knew, how ignorant the villagers suddenly seemed to her. She chastised her mother for doing her private business in the bush rather than a toilet, even though her mother had never seen a toilet. Her mother didn't say that she was getting tired of Gladys's lectures, but she and the others in the compound began to laugh at the "white ways" she brought home, and Gladys noticed that rather than learn from her they were making fun of her.

She stopped going home every Sunday. Sometimes her friend Alia would come to her room and they would just talk — about Angeline, about boys and girls and what went on between them, about the pros and cons of having a man all to yourself as Mrs. Bilhouse did. Gladys was beginning to think that the Reverend and Mrs. Bilhouse weren't really together, not in a biblical way. They slept in separate rooms and she had the impression that there were no visits back and forth at night.

Church had started in earnest under the tree. About half the village now showed up because the rains had come soon after the reverend arrived and harvests were the best in years. Gladys's father had convinced the congregation that this was because God had added Taali to his list of Christian villages. Her father took his role as assistant very seriously, bossing people around, trying to get labourers to volunteer their time to build the new church that was slowly taking shape across the street from the stone house.

Then Christmas came, and so did Paul. When Paul was small, her father gave him to his rich uncle in Talon. The uncle was a Party man and contractor who would raise and school the boy. Everyone in Taali knew that Paul was smart; Gladys's father was the first to tell them that his son was a student at the university and that when he finished he would return to the village and share some of that city wealth with his family. People had stopped asking when this would happen. "We hear that your brother is going to be a student all his long life, Gladys. Maybe he's going to teach us how to make money grow on trees one day. Ha ha." The women would have to wipe tears from their eyes, they laughed so hard about her father's boasting.

They didn't say anything, though, when Paul came during semester breaks. He didn't put on airs, like others who left the village and then came back wearing their knowledge and modern ways like an Independence Day parade. Paul spent his time in Taali with the elders, obeying all the village rules, pretending that despite his sophisticated clothes he was still one of them. He told Gladys that he was studying history, particularly the history of the Abule people. Gladys was proud of him but unsure what to make of his odd manners and words.

Although her father bragged about his educated son, Paul set him roaring like a pack of lions every time he came home. This year, with the Bilhouses there, it was worse. Paul was refusing to be bullied into the labour force for building the New Dawn church and would not help with the block moulding, even when his father ordered him to do so.

"You disobey your own father?" he roared.

Paul didn't say anything, just stared up at the night sky as if he had an assignment to count the stars. He had his hands in the pockets of his town trousers. It was a Sunday evening, and Gladys was waiting for the storm in the compound to pass before sneaking out of her hut and back to the stone house.

"I ask you, you disobey your own father? We need a church and school here. You think you're too good to soil your soft, schooled hands? You will help here like everyone else. The Lord says so."

It became far too quiet in the compound, because Paul wasn't answering, not right away. Gladys crouched in a corner with the smaller children cowering behind her, fearful of the wrath of their father, their lord. Pots sat untended over flickering fires that Gladys's mother had abandoned, having fled to the safety of her hut. Gladys watched as Paul marched up to his father and looked down on him as though he were a louse he had picked from his hair. Then he started to talk, almost in a whisper. "Father, I do not intend to build any white man's church for any white man's gods. He's got such good connections with this god, then why doesn't his god build it for him? We don't need to hide away inside some dark house to talk to our gods. Our gods are all around us. You hear me, Father?" Gladys slowly exhaled.

Paul turned and went into his hut. He came out with his blue travel bag. "I'm leaving," he said, not looking at the wide-eyed family members crouched around him in the dark compound. Gladys was sure that he would never come back. She decided his spirit had really left them a long time before that, probably on the day he got in her uncle's car and headed for Talon, a scared and dusty little village boy staring solemnly out the window at his mother and sister and father, pretending to be brave, not even waving goodbye.

The school and the church were built without Paul. Mrs. Bilhouse taught children in the morning, adults in the evening. Gladys was aware of the palaver rumbling around the village at night among the people who didn't think education was good for the children, putting ideas into young people's heads, making them consider themselves better than their elders, too good for planting yams and cassava. Like Paul. Like a white man. Although Gladys noticed that the reverend sometimes worked in the fields with the farmers and didn't act as if he thought he were too good to dirty his hands.

In the end, six women started attending the evening literacy classes and thirty kids became regular pupils in the school, mostly because of the free paracetamol, chloroquine and cocoa drinks. The chief and the Imam even sent their older sons to the school, if not to the Sunday services. It looked as if peace would prevail.

Gladys was working seven days a week with a few hours free on Sunday afternoons and evenings. The money was paid to her father, who said he was saving it for the children's secondary school. The reverend had bought him a new wireless to listen to the BBC in Hausa and a new watch that beeped the same time as the BBC bells. He had also given her father a blue motorcycle with a yellow sun painted on the petrol tank, on which he went out to other villages to spread the word about the New Dawn Church. To tell them that this was their last chance for salvation. "Join up or burn," said her father, simplifying the Christian message to edify the illiterate heathens in the villages.

Gladys felt restless but could find nothing to complain about. Mrs. Bilhouse had given her some dresses that didn't fit her any more because Mrs. Bilhouse was getting as skinny as a beggar while Gladys was getting some flesh on her bones. Reverend Bilhouse kept her supplied with yams and rice donated by church members and Mrs. Bilhouse allowed her to take leftovers from their table. She had also bought some white cloth to make Gladys a uniform and bandana for her head, just like the uniforms the public health nurses wore when they came to vaccinate children.

In the mornings after Mrs. Bilhouse went to the school Gladys dressed Angeline up as prettily as the doll that sat on a white dresser in the corner. She smothered the girl's yellow curls with bows and dressed her in cotton smocks with miniature rainbows and flower gardens on them, each with socks to match. Angeline was up and walking and always laughing. One day she opened her mouth to smile at Gladys and out came the word "Mama".

"I'm not your mama, Angeline. Your mama hears you say that and you and I will share the caning."

"Mama," said Angeline, hugging Gladys's knees. They giggled together.

"She's smarter than five village kids put together," Gladys told her mother who came from time to time to the stone house to see the miracle child Gladys was raising. "She can talk English and she can build things and break things and build them again." Her mother would shake her head and smile but never had much to say on the subject of the Bilhouses.

On other days, Gladys put Angeline into the stroller that was prettier than the bougainvillea growing around the veranda of the stone house. It had a red and white umbrella to keep Angeline from getting a sunburn. They went strolling up and down the road impressing their audience although the wheels got stuck in the mud and the sand and the ride was rough.

"What god have you been seeing to put an angel like that in your hands, Gladys?" The people of the village began to call Angeline "Little Owl" in Abule, and Angeline started answering back. In Abule.

Sometimes if she wasn't in the house cleaning, cooking, washing, she took Angeline out behind the boys' quarters and sat in the sand under the mango tree. Angeline played in the sand while Gladys cooked yams for herself and pounded them into *fufu*. Gladys took her on her knee and showed her how to hold the pestle to pound the fufu, until she learned how to spread her own knees on the stool and pretend she was an African mammie pounding the fufu too. Gladys was nervous when they played this game — afraid that Mrs. Bilhouse would see her letting Angeline behave like an African.

"We're here to bring these people up to our level, not to lower ourselves to theirs," Mrs. Bilhouse said to her husband one evening while Gladys was dishing up yam chips and steak. She was responding to the reverend's suggestion that they bring traditional drummers in for the Sunday services. "Drums are heathen, David," she added. "Thank you, Gladys, that's all now." Gladys wished sometimes the reverend would argue with his wife, but he seemed to go deaf around her — all the more strange because she knew he hardly stopped laughing and talking with the villagers, and even with her, when Mrs. Bilhouse wasn't around.

Gladys had no time to go inside the new church although she admired it from the road. It was a fresh-looking, whitewashed building with arched windows and a big yellow rising sun over the door, underneath the words "New Dawn". Mrs. Bilhouse spent very little time in the house with her daughter. Whenever her mother was around Angeline seemed to cry a lot. Mrs. Bilhouse was preoccupied with her teaching and doing the church accounts and she came out to Gladys's quarters only once a week to inspect the toilet which she would lock for a week when it failed her inspection.

Mrs. Bilhouse had been complaining since the beginning about the condition of the big stone house — the leaking roof, the smelling septic tank, and the unfinished concrete floor on the veranda which she wanted redone in terrazzo. Just before the Bilhouses' second Christmas in Taali, workers came to renovate the stone house. Gladys was sitting with Angeline playing with plastic blocks when the truck arrived full of machines and tools and three men. Mrs. Bilhouse told her they were carpentry and masonry students from a training centre in Talon which was run by white men. "My husband seems to think they're very skilled, so I think we can trust them, can't we, Gladys."

It didn't look to Gladys as though Mrs. Bilhouse trusted them at all. She cancelled classes for a month to stay home and oversee the work. Gladys and Angeline were relegated to the playroom with the door shut while this was going on.

"There's so much dust, Gladys. It wouldn't be good for Angeline to breathe it. Better you keep as far away as you can."

On Sundays if she weren't needed for chores at home, Gladys would try on one after another of her new dresses, the ones that no longer fit Mrs. Bilhouse. If the Bilhouses had gone out somewhere Alia would come and tress her hair and she would paint Alia's fingernails and toenails whatever new shade Alia had found in the weekly market. Mrs. Bilhouse forbade Gladys to paint her own. She also discouraged visitors on the compound, but Alia knew how to be discreet and used a footpath that led to the boys' quarters through a maize field in the back.

One Sunday the Bilhouses left early to hold the church service in a neighbouring district. Alia came around in the morning. She was five months with child by now and she told Gladys that she was going to marry the man, a rice farmer in the next village. "I'll be second wife," said Alia. "But my rival is old and ugly so I'm not worried."

Alia's bulging belly pushed against Gladys's shoulder as she worked on her hair. "What's it like, being with your man?" Gladys asked. Alia laughed and told stories that made Gladys wipe her eyes and cluck her tongue and wish she were doing the talking, not the listening.

"What is so funny?" came a voice. They both looked up, startled by the intrusion; no one came to the stone house when the Reverend wasn't there. It was the tall labourer, the one who seemed to be the boss. Usually he was covered in cement and paint and wearing a green, yellow and red crocheted cap like a Rasta man. Now he was dressed like a man in one of Mrs. Bilhouse's magazines, in a white t-shirt and fancy blue jeans and shiny black shoes that looked like hooves. They both started laughing harder.

He seemed unaffected by their giggles as he walked over and sat down on the roots of the tree. "I'm Jonas," he said. "From Talon." He was Goroni and spoke to them in his language which most tribes in the region spoke to communicate with each other.

Alia smiled at him while winding black thread around the ends of the tiny braids on Gladys's head. "What are you wearing on your feet, Mr. Jonas?" she said in Goroni.

He glanced down, lifted a leg and swivelled his ankle, admiring his shoes. Then he took a cloth from his back trouser pocket and dusted each shoe carefully. "Shoes," he said, in English. "Don't you Abule girls speak English?"

They giggled some more and Gladys was afraid to look up at him. He smelled different from men in the village. Dangerous but nice, like acacia blossoms at dusk. And he had his hair cut square on top as though he had been sitting inside a cardboard box

"She speaks English, Mr. Jonas," said Alia, in Goroni, jabbing her finger into Gladys's back. "As for his hair, Gladys . . ." she whispered in Abule, putting a hand to her lips to stifle her exaggerated laughter.

Jonas caught their glances, patted his hair and told them the cut was called "don't mind your fucking father". Alia nodded but she didn't understand the words. Gladys glanced around to make sure no one had sneaked up and could hear such profanity. She hoped God was busy elsewhere just then and hadn't heard.

"You're Gladys, right?" he asked, in English, which he spoke like a teacher.

Gladys nodded and Alia snapped her head back into place, to continue the braiding. "What's your name?" he asked Alia in Goroni.

"Alia."

"How have you girls been keeping out here in Taali?"

Gladys didn't say anything. Alia was pulling so hard on her hair that she felt her brains might soon come out. Alia tittered and pulled harder, when it was obvious Gladys was going to play demure and dumb like a good village girl.

"Villagers," he said then, standing up and stretching. "Catch you later." Gladys wondered where he had learned to talk like that. Catch you later. Must have been something he learned at that white man's school in Talon. There were jitters in her legs and her belly.

"He has his eye on you, Gladys," said Alia when he was gone.

"You think so?" Gladys laughed. "Father will lay the cane on him, he finds him talking to me. I'm Father's prize cow. Think what Mrs. Bilhouse would say." They both doubled over with mirth but after they stopped laughing and wiped away their tears, Gladys didn't feel talkative at all. Alia hummed a high-life tune as she finished with all the tiny braids and left, just before the blue pick-up pulled up.

That night Gladys didn't cook and there were no leftovers from the Bilhouse table because they had eaten in the neighbouring village. She was agitated and not at all hungry. Even a day away from Angeline made her realize how much she needed that small girl. One day the Bilhouses would leave Taali, leaving her alone here, unmarried, childless. An old woman with no husband and no children was usually a witch and was sent out to Kukuo for de-witching at the shrine. If the birth certificate that Sister Mary had made for her was right, she was close to eighteen years of age.

She lay on her side, staring at the photograph on the box beside her bed. Reverend Bilhouse had taken the photograph the first Christmas. Angeline was asleep on Gladys's back, snuggled there inside a blue and white wrapper. Gladys was standing with her side to the camera her face turned so that she stared straight into the camera's eye. Angeline's face was also turned towards the camera, but her eyes were closed. Her own face gleamed in the light from the flash. It was very black, as Alia constantly reminded her. Alia used bleaching cream to give her face "colour".

She sat up and removed her blouse, looking down at her full breasts, her round belly and thighs thick and strong under her wrapper. She felt ripe and ready for plucking like the March mangoes growing from the fragrant blossoms on the tree outside. The generator was coughing and sputtering. But over the pounding noise it made she thought she could hear music coming from the stone house — the strange, sorrowful music the Bilhouses always played on Sundays. It reminded Gladys of a lost goat bleating for its mother.

She turned quickly when she heard the step outside her door. She was uneasy about the creatures that came out in the evenings. "Yes. Who is it? Is that you, Sam?" The watchman who slept on the front veranda rarely came behind the house. Not since the day Mrs. Bilhouse had found Sam and Gladys sitting on the ground talking in Abule and told him she would sack him from the place if it happened again. "Sam?" There was no answer but she could hear breathing other than her own. "Mrs. Bilhouse?" Fear made her voice small and plaintive. She hastily slipped on her blouse.

"It's Jonas. Gladys, open the door." He was whispering.

She started to pray: Lord in Heaven, lead us not into temptation, deliver us from the Devil.

"Gladys, open up. What do you fear?"

"I don't fear anything," she said in a frightened whisper — and stood up, pulling her wrapper around herself.

"Then open the door."

"It's not locked," she whispered.

The door swung open and Jonas moved quickly inside, shutting and leaning against it. He was still in his Sunday clothes and he looked into her eyes as though examining a bowl of fufu into which he was about to put his hand. She felt it in her stomach. Like worms.

He moved forward and she backed up until she could go no further and was against the far wall. He reached out to touch her face, as though she were a child. The same way she touched Angeline when she and the small girl were alone together. Her knees went numb as though she'd had malaria for ten days.

"You look nice, Gladys," he said, taking her gently by the shoulders and guiding her to a sitting position on the edge of her bed. "I like you."

He took off her wrapper with his eyes, then gently eased it open with his hands. She closed her eyes but she knew he was removing his jeans. He eased her back onto the bed, covered her with himself. She didn't know that pain and pleasure could be the same thing, tearing her in two.

She knew she was not supposed to like it, because she had been told over and over at school and in oblique ways by Mrs. Bilhouse that it was deadly sin with a man to whom she was not married. It was okay for Alia. Her god didn't make rules like that. But Mrs. Bilhouse and Sister Mary had a different god who was particular in such matters.

Mrs. Bilhouse was always saying to her husband that the African people had to rid themselves of their "bestial urges". The reverend always let her talk like that, as if she were the head of the household and he only a child. Gladys wondered now if she was too African, because she liked it too much and only half heard herself call Jonas's name as though she were trying to reach him from across the stream that separated Abule-land from Goroni-land. This man who was easing a hunger inside her was a stranger, not even Abule. A Goroni. Her father said the Goroni were awful people. She whimpered, suddenly afraid.

Jonas put his hand over her mouth, gently so that it rested on her lips, and whispered "Quiet, Gladys. It's okay. I will never hurt you."

Afterwards he said nothing, just lay with her for some time. Then he got up and put his jeans back on. He passed her her wrapper, and then he turned his back. "I've been watching you since I came. You're nice, Gladys. I want to marry you and bring you back to Talon."

"You have to ask my father. I don't know if he will let me go. I'm a working girl."

"There are lots of good families in Talon. You could work for them minding their children until we have our own children. I've got work too. I'm the supervisor at the vocational training centre. I have money."

"You have to ask my father."

"I'll do that. The work here is almost finished."

During the day Jonas pretended he didn't see Gladys, although he always winked and smiled at Angeline when their paths crossed in the stone house. He had taken up humming as he worked, melodies that Gladys didn't know but would remember for the rest of this life and into the next ones. He still wore his Rasta hat, the colours of the flag that they had raised every day on a tall, straight pole at the school in Talon.

Mrs. Bilhouse never gave the workers any peace. Gladys had the impression she wished they could stand outside the house and just reach in with their arms to do the work they were contracted to do on the walls, the floors and the ceilings. She was always beside them, pointing out how poorly they had done something. Gladys watched Jonas out of the corner of her eye and concocted errands to do in the kitchen so she had excuses to pass through the hallway where they were working on the ceiling.

Once he took his shirt off to paint in the bedroom and Gladys, who was putting on Angeline's shoes, held her breath, wondering if Mrs. Bilhouse could hear her heart pounding in time to the movement of the muscles in his back. "Please get dressed, Mr. Jonas. This is a Christian home and we do not like indecency," Mrs. Bilhouse said, coming into the room, her face red as a palm nut. Gladys scooped Angeline up and ran outside, trying to stop the fit of giggles that wouldn't let go of her stomach.

She no longer walked with her feet on the ground. Even when she took off her plastic slippers and walked barefoot around her room in the evenings, she could not feel her feet on the solid earth. The reverend seemed to notice her euphoria, and smiled at her over the soup she served for dinner. Mrs. Bilhouse asked him what he was smiling about, so he stopped noticing.

On Thursday evening Jonas came again to her door. After he lay with her, and the sweat had begun to drip from their foreheads down their temples and onto the sheet as their breathing slowed, she asked him what her father had said.

"He wouldn't see me. I tried sending messengers, but he refused to talk to them. I'm sorry, Gladys."

She sat up sharply, like a cobra.

"I even wrote him a letter, sent him fifty thousand conies. I wrote that you could stay here until your job is finished and then come. He didn't even take the letter. Just tore it up and threw it on the ground. The boy brought the pieces back to me. I still have them. Not the fifty thousand though."

Salt stung her eyes and she wiped away the sweaty tears.

"You could run away with me," he said.

She shook her head.

"Think about it." He gave her a piece of paper with his name, Jonas Jakpan, and his address in Talon spelled out in neat block letters. "You can contact me. I want a good wife like you. Someone who would educate my children about all the things you teach Angeline. I built a house with two rooms. Think about it."

"I can't . . . not if my father won't agree. I can't leave Angeline. Not now."

Jonas and his workers left the next day. Mrs. Bilhouse asked Gladys what was wrong but she didn't answer. Later Mrs. Bilhouse gave her a new white Bible with a zipper that closed around the book like a woman's wrapper. "It's wonderful to have the house to ourselves again, isn't it, Gladys? Those workers were awfully dirty people, I thought. They've left their smell behind them. Don't they ever wash?"

Angeline was hugging her legs as if she would never let go of her "Mama Gladys" and Gladys felt sick with two kinds of love.

After a few weeks she was able to put Jonas out of her mind during the day but kept the piece of paper with his name on it inside the zipped cover of the Bible, with which she slept for solace. Except to return his greetings she stopped speaking to her father altogether and he didn't appear to notice. He was too busy being the white man's man.

At Easter, Angeline would turn three and Mrs. Bilhouse planned a special birthday party. She went to Talon and invited some Christian families. Gladys had never seen so many white people in the village as there were on that Easter Monday. There were balloons in colours she had never seen before. The guests brought along pastel-coloured cakes with flowers and tiny golden leaves on top that made her think of heaven. Some of the people were sleeping over and every room in the house was full. Some of them were nice to Gladys. One couple, who slept on the floor in the school on mats like villagers, gave her some books as gifts.

Mrs. Bilhouse told her she was to serve the ladies tea and cake and look after the children, make sure they each got a *mineral*. The men would be taking their tea and minerals on the front veranda after they had a look at the new church.

That day Gladys felt as though she had grown a hundred new pairs of hands. She was in the kitchen setting out the dainty white bowls of sugar and the pretty blue and white Sunday teacups on the tray when she heard the white ladies talking about her as though she had been born without ears.

"Gladys? She's been with us from the beginning. I don't know how I would have survived here without her. She's a lovely girl and she's so good with Angeline. You know, I think these people get along so well with children because they're like children themselves," said Mrs. Bilhouse.

"Is she married?" Another voice.

"Oh no, her father says she doesn't want to marry. Gladys is no fool. She knows she's much better off with us than she would be living in the village with a local man. Even some of our most devout men still take many wives and abuse them."

There was some laughter; it wasn't the kind that made Gladys want to join in.

"But the girl is pregnant."

Gladys's knees went weak as though Jonas had just touched her, and she couldn't steady her hands enough to pour the milk into the pitcher. It ran off the table onto the floor.

Mrs. Bilhouse was laughing. "Pregnant? Gladys? No. They all have stomachs like that. You know she eats very well here with us. My husband seems intent on fattening her up, always giving her yams. When she first started she was all knees and shoulder blades." She was still laughing, but nervously now, as though she just remembered that the kettle had been on the fire all day.

Then they started talking quietly like spirits in the night and Gladys couldn't hear any more. She stood leaning on the counter with her elbows locked to keep her knees from buckling. She didn't hear Mrs. Bilhouse come to the kitchen. "Gladys, we are waiting for the tea," she said, colder than the freezer compartment of the refrigerator. Gladys looked up at her, smiling and trying to make her smile. Mrs. Bilhouse just stared at the roundness of her belly and Gladys knew that she knew.

That night towards midnight when everyone had gone to bed and the generator had been turned off, Mrs. Bilhouse came to the kitchen again. Gladys was on her hands and knees, washing the floor. "Are you pregnant, Gladys?" She didn't answer. Mrs. Bilhouse repeated the question, the toe of her white shoe moving onto Gladys's hand with the rag to stop it from going round and round.

"Yes Missus," Gladys said, as softly as she could.

"Who is the father?"

Not your business: thought Gladys. "I don't know, Missus," she said, finally.

"You don't know?" Her voice went high as a bird's. "You don't know? I think you do know. In fact I think you and I both know, you little whore. I suppose this has been going on the whole time, right under my nose . . ." She moved away and Gladys started wiping the black and white tiles again, going round and round with the cloth, as if she could eventually wash them away. "Get out of my house now. Get out. Curse you. Go back to the Devil where you came from."

Gladys got up and took off the white apron, performing each movement very slowly. She carried the bucket of water out back and poured it gently over the potted plants on the back steps as she had been instructed at least every day for two years. Then she started to collect up her things.

The night was far too dark, no moon at all, when she walked away from the stone house. She didn't know where she was walking. She was just as afraid of what walks on the earth during the night as everyone else in Taali, but as she walked, for the first time in her life she feared nothing at all.

Evil spirits could come and take her. No Angeline. No Jonas. Nothing. Father waiting with a cane. That was all. That was nothing.

But no spirits came to her. Maybe it was true what the reverend said, that the spirits didn't exist. Just God and the Devil. And since she was the Devil's work God was not minding her. Things went round and round in her head. Maybe she shouldn't have said anything, refused to admit it. She wanted the baby, that was for sure. It was hers, the only thing that was. But if it was the Devil's work, then better she didn't bring it forth. Then she could keep Angeline, her little girl. She thought she was walking towards Talon, that her steps would lead her back to the road. There would be a lorry tomorrow. But she had no money. Everything she had earned had gone to her father. She could sell some of her dresses and the white Bible wrapped up in the cloth bundle on her head. She would keep the photograph. Maybe the kind visitor from Talon who gave her the books and asked her questions about her schooling would take her. But what if Jonas didn't want her any more? Someone like Jonas probably had lots of women in Talon. She was just a dirty and stupid village girl. She was walking in circles.

Dawn was coming when she slipped quietly into her mother's hut. Her half-sisters had taken over her old hut. She lay down beside her mother on the floor. Her mother reached out and put her hand on her daughter's head, as though she were small again. "Sorry," she said. She knew, too. That was the way of Taali.

Gladys woke up from a dream, in which she was cooking meat in the stone house and Jonas was waiting for his meal at the table. It was her father's voice that broke the dream into slivers, daggers that pierced her stomach. He was yelling as though he had seen Satan. He dragged Gladys out of her mother's hut and into the middle of the compound. Chickens and a baby goat shrieked in indignation but scattered and disappeared like the rest of the family members when he began to beat Gladys with the stick. She covered her face with her hands to save her eyes but did not fight back and did not cry out. He hit her head, her face, and when he had pushed her onto her back with his foot, he kicked her belly. At that instant, she began to scream. It was not a human scream. Nothing like her mother's sobs when her husband beat her. Gladys's father threw down his stick and fled, covering his ears. Maybe he thought he had unleashed the Devil in her. Maybe he had.

He drove away fast on his motorcycle and for a few minutes no one moved. Gladys was silent. Then the women started to whisper, then to talk, then to yell at each other. Blood was spurting from Gladys's nose, and her mother wiped it away with the hem of her wrapper. It was as the women picked her up to carry her into her mother's hut that blood began to come from her vagina. The women brought water and washed Gladys's forehead as the foetus came out.

It was a little wrinkled thing that the Devil might have made. There was no need to cut the afterbirth on the premature baby and Gladys's mother took the whole thing, wrapped it up in some white lace Mrs. Bilhouse had sent her from old kitchen curtains, and took it in her basket to bury in the sacred grove.

Gladys fell into a deep sleep, still bleeding. Her mother sent Ben to fetch Reverend Bilhouse, to see if he had some medicine to stop the bleeding. He came a few minutes later with Mrs. Bilhouse, who carried Angeline in her arms. Mother and daughter were crying. The reverend was angry, not replying to his hysterical wife who was sobbing and shouting, "I didn't know this would happen." She tugged at her husband's arm, but he shook her off. "I didn't know. I thought the child was yours. You always cared more about these people than you cared for me. Oh my Lord in heaven, forgive me."

The Reverend Bilhouse and the women carried Gladys out to the pick-up, ignoring the hysterical white woman on her knees on the mud who was shouting about how she hated it here, how she had tried her best. Angeline was screaming and Ben picked her up and tried to calm her on the way back to the stone house. Mrs. Bilhouse staggered behind. "Not my child. Leave her. Put her down." Ben ignored her, as he would any lunatic on the roadside.

Gladys's breathing was shallow, but the bleeding was slowing. The reverend drove her to Talon where he spent an hour waiting for the doctors to come out of surgery to tend to Gladys. He had her admitted as the sun set red on the horizon in its own pool of blood.

There was no blood in stock in the hospital and the doctor gave her plasma and told the reverend that there was no cause for alarm. The girl was young and strong and she would survive, just needed a day or two to recover from the accident that caused the miscarriage. He didn't ask for details and the reverend didn't offer any; he could see the suspicions on the doctor's face, the same ones his wife wore when she told him Gladys was pregnant and that she had dismissed her.

The next day he went back to see her. Her bed was empty and the nurse didn't know where she had gone. The other women sharing beds and mats in the ward shook their heads dumbly when asked if the girl had said anything to them about her destination. "Beat a girl like that and wonder why she runs off," said a toothless old woman to her neighbours after the white man and the nurse had left. "The girl knows where she's going-o."

The next day the Reverend Bilhouse drove his wife and daughter to Talon. Since Gladys had left, Angeline had been hysterical, calling for "Mama". The reverend had interrogated his wife who had finally calmed down enough to guess who the father was. They drove to the training centre and were told that Jonas was not at work today. They might find him at home. They got directions, followed roads that weren't roads, through mazes of crumbling houses, until they reached the new brick house with the green gate. Jonas was outside, leaning against the wall with his arms crossed, as if expecting them.

"Have you seen Gladys?" the reverend asked.

Jonas looked up at the sky, then smiled at Angeline who had stopped crying. He moved his eyes from Angeline's face slowly and faced the reverend with a smile. He reached down, rubbed his hand over Angeline's curls, smiling. His smile died when he turned to look at Mrs. Bilhouse. "I suppose I have." He bent and put his ear to Angeline's ear. "Your mama will be fine now, Little Owl. God and I are looking out for her." He hummed a high-life tune as he opened the gate, went inside and closed it.

A week later the Bilhouse family packed their possessions in the blue pick-up and drove out of Taali for the last time as the first black cloud of the rainy season swept across the north and unleashed a torrent of rain that drowned out the sound of the pick-up and washed down the road in front of them like a river of blood.

Hombre

If they spoke of him at all they called him Hombre. No one seemed to know how he came by the Spanish nickname, an odd appellation in French West Africa. In town, people said that Hombre had at one time been a captain in the President's special security force and that he had trained with a handful of elite African officers in France and Canada.

They said he had received the coveted gold medal from the President for his superb work in putting down tribal strife in 1972 when some Abule and Goroni intellectuals, inspired by their tribesmen in the neighbouring country, had threatened the unity of their young African nation by trying to form a political party.

But then, even when pressed, the people of the town would say no more. Hombre was crazy — a *fou* — an outcast of no fixed village or tribe or nation. He didn't conform to any of the rules for behaviour in *nouvelle afrique*. He wasn't interested in high-life, discos, clubs, cars, ready-to-wear clothes, women or "democracy" as his President — a despotic billionaire — practised it.

It was from Gary, a fellow volunteer, that I learned more about Hombre. Gary had already been there three years and I was a relative newcomer, so he tried his best to fill me in on some of the local mysteries and characters. As Gary heard it, Hombre had just up and quit the army one day. He did so by loping out of the country's largest, most prestigious military camp, shedding his smart green uniform as he went until he was stark naked and running down the centre of the Boulevard de la Libération howling and chuckling like a hyena.

The men working on the new road to the President's village, European and African alike, shrank back into the ditches when they saw the black apparition nearly flying down their new highway.

Gary told me that he heard the story from some eyewitnesses to the captain's defection in the bar that very evening. They slurped beer and whisky and shook their heads in dismay. One of the road crew claimed to have seen a large hooded vulture swoop down in front of his grader and land on Hombre's naked shoulder. It was already common knowledge that the vulture had stolen the captain's human spirit *and* his national identity card.

The captain had fought his last battle in the President's security force, imprisoned his last counter-revolutionary and fired his last shot at a traitor in the Name of the President and National Unity and Peace and Brotherhood. He was no longer a part of the People's Democratic Revolution.

I had been there only three months and I had yet to see this lunatic they called Hombre.

I was called an *animatrice* in community development. My job was to motivate the town's women — encourage them to adopt modern living habits — to wash their children daily, not to overdo the starch in meals, to boil the water they fetched from a fetid stream on the outskirts of town, to plant woodlots rather than cutting down forest trees for firewood and to take up productive handicrafts in their spare time. Income-generating activities like knitting and crocheting, for example.

To my chagrin, I found the women were somewhat unresponsive to my mission. So I was seeking help, some advice from the government officials who had drawn up the Popular and Democratic Revolutionary Development Plan. One evening I finally managed to track down three of these men at the town's most popular bar. They invited me to join them for drinks. They were from the Ministry of Democratic and Popular Development in charge of my development project. However, one among them had just that afternoon taken delivery of a new silver BMW saloon car from Germany and they were preoccupied with the car's features. I had no opportunity to speak of the dilemma I was having with the women and the project.

So I drank beer and glanced about the roadside bar. I spied a shadowy form lurking near the pyramid of cigarette packages, a display of Marlboro and Benson products at the road edge.

That was my first glance of Hombre — two metres of sinew draped in black rags, as majestic and lean and well proportioned as a Greek column. The bits of cloth looked like oil rags but he had cleverly wound them around himself and tied them at his waist with a chord so they looked like a knee-length monk's habit. The cloth fluttered about his knees and arms in the light evening breeze. His feet were bound in matching black scraps, soled with tire rubber.

He was standing over the slouched form of the teenage cigarette vendor sporting sunglasses and a t-shirt that said "America kicks butts". The vendor stared at the ground, apparently fearful of Hombre's vulture-like presence. At last he tossed a single cigarette and a match to the ground, not offering Hombre a glance.

That tall man swooped down with astonishing grace and swiftly retrieved the ill-got booty. He brushed off the cigarette on his skirt, pulled a red plastic cigar tip from the depths of his rags, and using it as a holder, he lit the cigarette. Over the flare of the match his eyes met mine.

My stomach rolled and I hastily turned away but not before those glittery eyes had made themselves felt in my gut or before I had registered the mocking half-smile on his lips. Sinister, I thought.

In spite of myself I turned again a few seconds later to find him. He was striding away, so erect he was almost leaning backwards. He smoked his cigarette with the debonair cockiness of a yachtsman.

After that, Hombre seemed to pop up everywhere I went. My mission to enlighten the women in town took me into its heart — dank and foul quarters where the huts housed squabbling families of twenty or thirty, where there were no toilets at all, where children were born and bred like flies. I would wind my way into the valleys on my *mobylette*, humming to myself to keep my spirits up and suddenly there he would be, sitting contentedly on a rubbish heap smoking a cigarette in that red holder, scavenging discarded fruit from a sewer ditch, drinking water from the same festering source and rolling it over his tongue as if it were a rare, vintage wine and he a legitimate taster of such things. Or he would be lying on his back under a baobab tree, cradling his head in his hands, his long legs crossed while the dangling foot tapped out some secret rhythm. The audacity of that vagabond knew no bounds.

Once I passed and saw he had dozed off on the roadside; children had gathered and were prodding at him with sticks and taunting him with jeers. He stirred and sat up and they fled wailing as if they had just woken the Devil himself.

God knows, I tried to avoid his glittering eyes and that smirk he always bestowed on me when I passed on my mobylette. His face, handsome and noble as it may have been, could be nothing other than the visage of madness. It started something aflutter in my stomach as though I too had some awful bird of prey winging about inside. I was convinced he was completely crazy, even if I didn't exactly go along with the vulture story.

Then, a few weeks later, he began to appear not just during the day as I rode through town but also at night, in my dreams. He would be *right there* at the foot of my bed with his arms outstretched and his black tatters hanging like bat wings.

I would wake, crying, in a lather of sweat and get out of bed to check the locks on the doors. Despite the oppressive heat, I would close and bolt all the shutters. I began losing not just sleep but also weight. Hombre was becoming an obsession. I needed help but was afraid that the enlightened young doctors in the local clinic, fresh out of European medical schools, would scoff at my trauma. My African counterparts were obsessed with cars, not with the jetsam the *nouvelle societé* left in its wake, spirits like Hombre.

As a last resort, I decided to visit a traditional medicine man by the name of Doctor Z, whom Gary had told me about. He had healed Gary's dislocated shoulder. Perhaps he could exorcise Hombre from my soul.

On a Friday afternoon I headed out to the village where Doctor Z practised, winding my way past all the men in their billowing robes heading home from the mosque. I was leaving the crowds behind and was on my way through the coffee plantations on the fringes of town when I saw Hombre. He was sitting on a tree stump, smoking, and I would have had to drive right past him if I stayed on the path. His blazing eyes were on my face. I swerved and reflexively covered my eyes with my hands. My *mobylette* went out of control and landed on top of me, in the coffee plants.

When I opened my eyes, Hombre was standing over me just as he had in my nightmares. When I tried to scream he put his hand on my mouth. With the other he pried the motorcycle off me. He began to feel my legs. His hand smelled clean like lavender soap mixed with choice tobacco. I had no choice but to submit to my awful fate.

"*Vous avez cassé une jambe,*" he said to me in a deep and soft voice. I gasped, but not because he had told me my leg was broken. It was said that Hombre had lost the capacity for human speech and could only utter the guttural squawks of a vulture. He scooped me up tenderly in one of his long arms, uprighted the mobylette and climbed on. Holding me firmly against him, he headed the bike back down the rutted path I had just travelled.

The pain in my left leg and ribs was unbearable. I sobbed into his black rags, biting my tongue until I tasted blood to keep from screaming as the little motorcycle bounced over the ruts. Through a film of agony I saw vaguely the horrified stares of the townspeople before they fled into dark doorways. I can only imagine what a picture we must have made — Hombre with his black tails flying, grinning madly as he clutched a short, blond captive to his chest. And me, paler than white with the pain and the realization of my nightmares.

Hombre knew which twisting paths led to my house and once there, he recovered the key hidden on the doorjamb without consulting me on its whereabouts. He carried me over the threshold in his arms as though I were a child, not the twenty-five-year-old woman I was back then.

He laid me out on my mattress and then disappeared for a time. I could hear him outside whistling. Was the melody *Greensleeves?* I'm sure it was.

He returned with two wooden pickets from the fence that surrounded my compound. Then he deftly removed my jeans and fashioned the pickets into splints. I lay deathly still, breathless with fear. Mentally, I said thirty Hail Marys.

Hombre busied himself with one of my sheets, tearing it into strips, which he wound around my leg. When I whimpered he cast his dark, shining eyes on me. There was light in those eyes. It was not the light of madness.

I don't know how long he sat with me mopping my forehead with a damp cloth. With my head cradled in his lap I must have dozed off under his gentle caresses. When I woke I reached for his hand and murmured his name.

He was gone.

I blinked my eyes, trying to clear my senses in the harsh fluorescent light. The room was full of people and it was night. Mike Barnes, my field supervisor, and Doctor Doug Billings, the field medical officer, were poking at my ribs and legs. A truckload of gendarmes wearing khaki and slinging pistols were rummaging through my possessions with no respect for me or my privacy, as if I'd been murdered and they could track down the killer in my dresser and on my shelves. Everyone was shouting at once, conjecturing on Hombre's motive for attacking me, and planning the manhunt to track down the culprit, arranging for vehicles to get me to the airport in the capital for the morning flight to Paris.

I closed my eyes, aware somehow that Hombre was still close. I could smell his lavender presence, recall clearly his soothing touch. I was surrounded by crazed officials and authorities. I could not shut out reality or their loud voices.

Dr. Billings and Mike heaved me onto a stretcher and the gendarmes trooped out into the night to find Hombre.

"Easy now, Deb. Stay calm. You're going home. You'll be just fine. We'll give you something for the pain. Don't worry." That was Mike.

"No, Mike, no, I . . ." That was all I could gasp before Dr. Billings squeezed the breath out of me, then forced a needle into my arm. As I coasted into the drugged oblivion, I saw him. He was naked, skipping and whooping with joy as he headed across a field of weeds, until suddenly I lost him and could see only an eagle thrusting skywards with great flaps of its black wings.

I made the mistake of telling the doctors back home what had happened, about Hombre and they refused to allow me to return to Africa. They had a fancy term that I forget now — what they really meant was that they thought Africa had thrown me off my rocker.

That was years ago but even now, but only in the dead of night, I sometimes feel His presence and wake in a sweat even with the cold midwestern winter winds whistling through my open window. He still answers my call with a gentle hand on my arm. And I whisper His name, careful not to wake my husband snoring beside me. He's never been to Africa and he wouldn't understand.

Act of God

The wind blasted through the louvres like the cold breath of death, waking Jillian up. The red numbers on the radio alarm flashed — 3 A.M. A crack of lightning coincided with the thunder and a gust of wind that shook the house. Sheets of lightning thrashed at the sky.

Then the power went out. No more red flashing lights to tell her what time, no light to remind her what century it was.

She lay awake, suffocating in the dark, listening to the storm recede, disappointed that it had not unleashed its torrential rains on Talon. The harvest would fail if the rains didn't come soon. She had asked the women farmers with whom she worked in the villages what they would do then. "We will suffer," they said. "Sometimes when God has given us too many gifts, He has to take some back, so we will know how to suffer."

The blackness was complete. She dreaded the depth of the night here. It crowded her, brought fears and doubts. What if the people really hated her, the foreigner come to "help" them? What did those smiling market women really think of her? Did her African co-workers on the rural credit project secretly resent her being there, collecting a salary ten, fifty times higher than theirs, money her country was ostensibly giving to theirs? Was this guilt a western medicine, a placebo to replace real suffering?

She wondered what lay behind the smiles of her counterparts on the project. Had all the friendly village women welcomed her to their country with open arms only to shut her out of their lives?

The neighbourhood cocks were silent — even the sounds of the night insects were muted as though the crickets were downcast by the betrayal of the storm that came without rain. The doubts and undefined fear kept her awake until dawn shone its faint grey light through the windows.

In the kitchen she turned on the tap to fill the kettle and nothing happened. Damn it to hell. Another water cut. Water cuts threw her into confusion, disrupted the routine that permitted her to fabricate a sense of belonging here.

The power was still off and the refrigerator was already defrosting on its own, leaking water onto the kitchen floor. Power outages soured her mood the way they soured the milk in the silent refrigerator.

She searched for batteries for the radio and found only an empty package. Threw it on the floor in despair. That meant no morning news. Without those shortwave newscasts from world capitals, the isolation grew. Detached, dispassionate voices reading news helped her remember a world where she had once belonged.

She slammed the kettle into the sink. "No power. No water. Do you want me to die in this damn hole?" She was shouting now. She wanted to fill the silence, the loneliness, the vacuum in the house with her rage.

She put a hand over her mouth. What if someone was passing? A watchman perhaps, going home from his night's work? What stories would start to circulate? "White madam be lunatic-o, and proper."

If she complained at the office about the lack of power and water, people would commiserate. Bukari, her driver, would say, as he always did, that the water and sewerage corporation was making some extra money again by shutting off the pipes so that the Talon water mafia — the men who owned tanker trucks — could sell water to people and "grow fat".

He told her that people in Talon could always go out to fetch water at Independence Valley. That was the name they had given to a half-finished, two-storey warehouse on the outskirts of town. It had been started under the country's first President after independence. "But then the money was finished like always because the Big Men chop it," he told her. "Underneath that building, there's water. They wanted to store grain there, it was going to be a silo. Now it's just full of water from the rainy season. It is not good water, but the people go down there whenever the water is off. It's not nice, the stairs are steep and the girls fear the place."

Bukari was the one who recommended and then found a water tank for Jillian to keep on her compound for these emergencies. But Bukari was a rebel, someone who, at least in his mind, tackled the criminals who were the authorities. When she asked Mary, who cleaned and washed twice a week for Jillian, about the water shortages, Mary would shrug and smile and say, "It be an act of God, Madam. God no be blind. He see what awful thing people do nowadays-o. So he send the storm, but the rain do not fall."

Jillian picked up the kettle, slipped on her flip flops and went out into the grey gloom of the early morning. Dark clouds scudded past on the dawn breeze. Above them was the pale blue promise — threat — of another sunny day. She longed for a week of rain, the kind of weather that made people back home complain because it spoiled summer barbecues and days at the beach. She walked around the house to the water tank that was settled unevenly on four bricks behind the garage, mentally thanking Bukari for his foresight and ingenuity. She fiddled with the lock on the faucet, thinking that if things worked here — if the water corporation provided people with water as it was supposed to — she wouldn't have to lock the faucet on the tank to keep all the women in the neighbourhood from helping themselves. In fact, she wouldn't even need the tank.

There were so-called experts out in the villages working on wells and dams; in town, where there was a water system, it didn't work because of corruption and neglect. So why did *she* feel so guilty? She had been fighting the guilt since she came a year earlier. But the only defence she had against guilt was anger, and that didn't help.

She tossed the padlock to the ground and squatted to fill the kettle.

"Morning, morning, Madam."

Aisha, the tomato girl, was standing a few feet from her, smiling. The metal tray of tomatoes on her head dipped as she bowed. Jillian wanted to tell her to go away. Normally she rather liked the visits of the tomato girl who came most days in search of a few coins in exchange for a few tomatoes. But right now Aisha irritated her, standing there in her rags, cloaked in need.

"I don't want any tomatoes this morning," Jillian said. Aisha grinned. She understood almost no English. She lifted the plate of tomatoes from her head and began to select the best ones, firm as Madam liked, from the little tomato pyramids arranged so neatly on the tray.

"Fifty fifty," said Aisha, holding up four tomatoes.

"Okay," Jillian said finally, kicking the tap closed. "Give me two piles. For one hundred conies." She went inside, put the kettle on the stove, lit the flame, then searched the basket of odds and ends on her table for a hundred coni note. She tried to make out the face on the bill, but the brown note was caked with grime — she wondered which of the country's leaders it was.

She was studying the note as she came around the garage, looked up in surprise when she heard the sound of water running and saw Aisha squatted beside the tank.

"What do you think you're doing?" Jillian shouted.

Aisha looked up, startled. She leapt away from the water tank and upset the jug she had been holding under the tap. She and Jillian stared at the yellow plastic jug that had once held motor oil. It lay on its side and vomited the water out in glugs that sounded human.

"Watah, Madam," said the girl, timidly.

"No water," Jillian said.

"No watah," said the girl, pointing across the main road to her neighbourhood of mud and thatch huts.

Rage flared inside Jillian. It was not reasonable, but rage never was. It moved away from the small and fragile girl, snarling like a fanged beast as it turned back on itself at its source somewhere deep inside her. There was something new and dark and awful in there, in her gut, more malignant than cancer.

She picked up the padlock and snapped it shut on the faucet. The girl flattened herself on the ground, flinging one arm over her head in self defense. Jillian's rage evaporated; shame flooded in, nauseating her.

She sighed. "It's not that I don't want to give you water, Aisha," she said, trying to sound gentle. "But I can't give water to everyone. I know you need water but if I give you water, I have to give everyone water. You should all march to the sewerage corporation and break it down. As long as you can come to me, the real problem will never be solved . . ."

The girl was crawling away from her, trying to get the tray of tomatoes onto her head and to retrieve the water jug at the same time.

"No, don't do that. It's okay. I'm sorry." Jillian moved towards her, wanting to make amends, to stroke the girl's small bony shoulders that poked out through gaping holes in her pink t-shirt. But Aisha lunged out of her reach and started to run. Tomatoes rolled off the tray and the empty water jug swung from her hand as Aisha ran towards the gate.

"Come back, I'll give you some water," Jillian said, but the girl was already through the gate and across the road, too far away to hear. Jillian picked up the fallen tomatoes, cradling them against her stomach and wondered what had happened to her, when she had become so hard.

The power came on at dusk, but the water was still off when she got up the next day. She listened vaguely to the morning news from former Yugoslavia. Did she care what happened in Hertzasomething? What world *did* she still belong to?

Then she headed out for a day in the villages where she would explain, again, the credit system and how the repayment had to be made. The money, even the few dollars the women's groups were allocated, always came with rules attached.

On the way home that evening she engaged Bukari in another discussion about local corruption, asked him how the water corporation could get away with the deliberate water cuts.

"They're just wicked people," he said. "They want to chop our money, that's all."

"But why don't the people do something about it?" she asked. "I mean, demonstrate, or . . ."

He didn't allow her to finish. "The police will shoot us or arrest us. They always do."

She thought that over, wanted to reply but couldn't find anything to say. Instead she stared out the window at the crumbling mud houses, leaning on each other, one after the other, home to thousands. Stones were laid in rows on top of the sheets of tin roofing to keep them from blowing off. The rusted heaps of tractors, the rusted containers and the wrecks of cars made her angry at her own world that foisted machinery, doomed to break down, on the country and turned it into a junkyard. Discarded plastic bags, in which pedlars sold water, were caught up in the dust devil ahead. Mangy dogs loped across the road with its valleys and humps, not a road at all any more. Gangs of boys, bare but for scraps of cloth that were once shorts, chased tires they propelled with sticks. They were laughing and they waved as she passed.

She noticed that the concrete skeleton they called Independence Valley looked deserted. "There doesn't seem to be anyone fetching water there, Bukari. Does that mean the water came back on?" she asked.

"No," he said. "Three girls fell in yesterday. They were fetching water from below and there was some pushing because the stairway is very narrow and they fell in. One of them couldn't get out. So no one will go there now."

"That's terrible," she said. Jillian turned around to look again at the abandoned half-finished building in that gravel wasteland but her view was obscured by the cloud of red dust their Land Rover left in its wake.

The next morning she was up early, to watch the sun splash light and early heat across the compound. She ran from the kitchen when she heard the "Morning. Morning!" She tore outside, barefoot, to catch Aisha and make amends for her behaviour two days earlier.

It wasn't Aisha. This girl was smaller, even thinner. The plate of tomatoes looked as if it could squash her. Aisha's junior sister perhaps. "Tomato," said the girl.

"Where's Aisha?" Jillian asked. "My tomato girl?"

"Fifty fifty," said the girl.

"Aisha *bene*?" Jillian persisted, trying out one of the few Goroni words she had learned over the past year.

The girl cocked her head to one side and answered in Goroni. Jillian held up her hand. "Wait, I'm coming," she said, dashing inside to find her Goroni-English handbook.

"Now," she said, "say that again, *biala, biala*." Slowly, slowly. The girl repeated herself, slowly. Aisha . . . something. Just one word. Jillian flipped through the dictionary, looking for a word that resembled the one the girl kept repeating: *Ofieme*.

There it was. *Ofieme*. "Drowned?" she whispered.

The girl nodded and the plate of tomatoes tipped dangerously. "Fifty fifty," she said.

Masks

If I tell you what I saw, will you help me sort it out, Ali? I remember the smallest details, all of them. My recall is almost perfect. But recall has nothing to do with understanding.

You were taking me out to see funeral masks. I insisted on driving the Land Cruiser because it belonged to the Fulton Foundation which gave me the fellowship. We cruised out of the capital and headed out on the super new highway that led north up into the most remote part of the country. I commented on the good road and you said that it belonged to the Economic Recovery Program, which meant all that pavement still belonged to foreign banks.

But you had your nose stuck in a book and didn't seem too keen on chatting as we drove out of the capital. So I amused myself picturing an African student on a fat fellowship from some cultural foundation in his country heading off to the USA to do, say, a thesis on the cultural implications of the majorette's uniform. And I pictured the kind of welcome that poor sod would get in downtown Midwest America at a Fourth of July parade, with a camera and notebooks and questions about the cultural significance of the baton. Probably get tossed in the slammer and beaten up and not in that order. The poor shall inherit our garbage but not our bad manners.

I wanted to share this thought with you but didn't because you were busy reading. I was dismayed to see that it was a book by a well-known *Africa expert* and I was a little afraid you might think I was going to write something like that about my fieldwork. I wondered what you were thinking of his patronizing treatment of the people he studied, the people who entrusted him with their secrets.

After driving for awhile I began to feel a strong urge for a cup of coffee. But there was nothing in the way of cafes on the roadsides at all. Just those fabulous baobabs and crafted villages of thatched huts. A few old men with straw hats pedalling along peacefully on their bicycles. And goats and sheep that kept popping out of the nettles and scrub on the side of that ribbon of pavement like obstacles in Felix the Fire Eater — that's a computer game I was into as an undergraduate, Ali.

If I hadn't been fast on the brakes it would have been curtains for you and me. And the goats and sheep too. Not to mention that brand new Land Cruiser.

I was yawning and thinking that for the first time in my life I wouldn't complain about a roadside billboard broadcasting the proximity of a fast-food restaurant where coffee could be had "to go". But just about then you closed the book and surprised me by asking if I believed in *juju*.

"No," I said.

"Why not?" you persisted.

"Because, well, it's complicated. I think everything can be explained by the simple power of the mind. I guess I've lost faith in even that because in America they've perverted all the mystery and wonder of parapsychology and psycho-kinesis to sell their tabloids that can be read by a half-witted six-year-old. So all that's left of the supernatural is sold right beside the bubble gum and breath fresheners at supermarket check-out counters."

You didn't respond to my muddled lecture. You were sitting straight in the passenger's seat, staring at the dashboard as though it were a television screen. Or a crystal ball.

At that point you'd been working as my assistant for only a week. Before that I'd spent three weeks in the country drawing and photographing masks in the National Arts Centre. Mostly, though, I'd been trying to get a grip on the names of the twenty-one different ethnic groups in the country. It always helps to have some idea of whom you're studying before you start drawing conclusions as to the cultural *meaning* of their motifs — or masks. Right?

"Why do you ask me about juju?" I continued.

"It's important," you said. "We're going out to this village to watch a funeral ceremony and look at masks, which may seem straightforward to you. Believe me, Roger, it's not. There is a lot more going on during these ceremonies than meets the eye. The masks you will see are masks that no one has ever seen before. They are spirited up for special ceremonies. The men wearing the masks are not, in fact, men. They are the masks. Spirits. If anyone dares to suggest that they know the man underneath the grass and wood and skin it's grounds for death. Or banishment. You want to be careful, and diplomatic. Run any questions through me and I'll translate them, edit them before they reach the elders."

"Fine by me, Ali, you're my guide," I said. "I'm just a simple student of fine art from the U.S. of A."

"I always say one thing to foreigners who come to my country . . ." you continued, as though I hadn't spoken. Then, instead of saying anything more, you started making weird clucking sounds in your throat.

"Well?" I asked eventually, getting impatient.

"You're here to learn and to ask questions. Don't meddle in what you see. The people are not freaks in one of your Manhattan Island fun fairs."

"Next you're going to tell me you've been to Manhattan Island, I suppose."

You said, "Yes, Roger," with this solemn nod that made me realize you weren't joking.

"When was that?" I asked.

"When I was studying."

"You never told me you studied in the States. What did you study?"

"Masks. From here."

"No kidding." I laughed. "That kind of makes me seem redundant and superfluous, doesn't it?"

You paused. I could see you were working on a polite answer, master of good manners that you and your people are. "It makes me the perfect guide for you. I am sure that your study will be different," you said. "You will see things through a different peep-hole in your own mask."

"My mask? In the States, Ali, the only time we wear masks is on Halloween." I think I was already starting to feel nervous around you and when I'm nervous I always talk too much. "All across the States, mothers run out to Safeway just before Halloween and buy costumes and masks made in Taiwan. Last year it was Batman. This year all the little kiddies are Teenage Mutant Ninja Turtles, Donatello or Michelangelo. There's a whole promising generation of American kids who think Michelangelo is a masked and caped mutant do-gooder turtle."

Ali, you sure could be *quiet*. Impossible to know what you were thinking.

"Course," I continued, "it isn't very safe any more to let your kids go carousing and cavorting with the heathen spirits on Halloween." I wanted you to know that I didn't think there was any connection between our crass Halloween masks and the ones we were heading to see. "These days there's a good chance your own little Donatello will get a razor blade in his apple or a shot of crack in her chips."

You looked aghast. At least I thought you did, so I hastily added, "Don't take me so seriously. I'm kidding. Really. I mean it happens but not that often."

"Oh. I see," you said slowly. Enigmatic as usual.

Do you know what it's like trying to read your eyes? Or the eyes of anyone in your country if they don't want you to know what's going on inside? Forget it. On our side of the world we've spent the past few centuries writing things down and now we're cramming all that information onto silicon chips. You guys have all that — and a whole lot more besides — in your heads, tucked away out of sight behind your eyes. If you're not invited inside to share some of this, then you better stay right where you are on the doorstep, in the dark, staring at the welcome mat.

Shit, that's where you left me.

You went back to your book and I concentrated on getting us the rest of the way before I died of dehydration. I guzzled bottle after bottle of water, trying to keep up with the transpiration rate. You didn't take a single drop. Said you weren't thirsty. Are you really and truly human, Ali? You know, ninety per cent water and all that?

We arrived in the village at four that afternoon, but the heat was still potent enough to make my head swim. The dancing had already been going on for two days. You told me not to get excited yet, that these were just the regular dancers. The women wore red and white halter tops and grass skirts that revealed strong dusty brown legs. Bare feet on the soft brown earth, stamping up a dust storm. They had strips of cloth around their ankles, which were embroidered with beer caps so that one dancer could wake the dead with the rattling. Human tambourines. Those tassels they wore around their middles, which exaggerated the gyrations of their hips, stirred things up in my nether-regions. That embarrassed me. I hope you didn't notice. Seeing as you had told me not to get excited. Yet.

I started snapping pictures, while you explained that this was a harvest dance to thank the spirits and the deities for another year's supply of food.

The masks were due at dusk. So you told me.

Before that, however, the villagers plied us with *zomkom*, a delicious beverage made with water, millet and fresh ginger root. Two chairs fashioned from split palm trunks lashed together were placed before us, as was a tub of water for washing our hands. Then a parade of girls brought us bowl after bowl of local delicacies — pungent sauces full of greens and groundnut oil, stews and massive lumps of *tuo* — a porridge that looks like leavened bread dough and tastes better than my mom's Cream of Wheat.

"What's this?" I asked, withdrawing something round from my plate. It was slippery between my fingers. There were no spoons and I was trying hard to master the skill of eating with my right hand, as you were doing.

"That's an eye," you said, with your mischievous smile. Enjoyed that, didn't you.

I let it fall with a plop back into the stew. The girls who were hovering nearby watching us — me — with unabashed curiosity, filled the compound with their laughter. You said something to them in their own language and they laughed harder.

"It's not a human eye, it's from a sheep. You can't refuse such a delicacy. There are testicles in there too, but they're all chopped up. Good for your virility." You wiped your mouth with the back of your hand and smiled.

"Ali, I'll be sick if I eat this."

"You won't be sick. Don't be squeamish. By early morning you'll be glad you ate it. It's going to be a long night."

I watched you chewing on a rubbery tidbit you had fished from your stew. "I hear something," you said.

I heard nothing.

"Yes, a car. I hear a car," you said.

Moments later, not one but two Nissan Patrols pulled up in front of the chief's palace, a hut indistinguishable from the other huts in the village except for its size and the bits of old metal bowls and pots that were embedded in the wattle and daub.

Seven white people emerged from the fat vehicles like slugs coming out of cocoons. "Oh my God," I said. "Who the hell are they and what the hell are they doing here?" I know I was being unfair but they were the last people in the world I expected or wanted to see right then.

You rose and said, "I won't be a minute, Roger, I must greet them." You put your bowl on the ground. I took that opportunity to drop the eyeball into your stew.

There were two women, two men and three teenagers. The Nissans were parked rakishly next to a crumbling mud hut. Their doors were still wide open so they looked like a magazine advertisement for the Paris–Dakar Rally. Drivers in the front seats had already taken advantage of the recliner buttons on their seats and were settling in for a well-deserved rest.

"They're from Talon," you told me when you returned. "Mr. Arnold, the fat one in the purple shirt, is with the water project in Talon, and that's his wife in the green batik and those are his kids. The others are just visiting him — his relatives, he said. The man who brought them is Imoussa, Mr. Arnold's cook. He's from here. Looks like you're going to share the funeral with some of your countrymen." You grinned at me, then picked up your bowl and plunged your hand into the stew. You didn't say anything about the eyeball.

At that point, half of the fun had gone out of my adventure. I didn't want to share my *unique* African experience with a bunch of bloody *tourists*. To be fair, I'll begrudgingly admit that the Arnolds turned out to be decent people — at least they weren't loud and obnoxious and they didn't brag about voting for Reagan or anything like that.

What got me was that you and I had to wait to meet the chief until the Arnolds were ready . And first they had to be served zomkom and plates of tuo and I had to watch a re-enactment of my own introduction to stewed eyeballs. The teenagers were too polite to shout "yuck" but they rolled their eyes at each other. The two women looked scared shitless and didn't touch anything, just kept wiping their faces and hands with handkerchiefs.

You told me not to be impatient. The masks would not appear until all the visitors had been taken to meet the chief.

"How long have you been in the country?" Arnold asked me, as we headed in to the chief's palace. "Oh, almost a month."

"Mmm. What was it you're studying?"

I had no intention of getting into a half-baked discussion of my research with a nuts-and-bolts man like that. I didn't ask him who he was but he volunteered the information anyway. He was an engineer, he told me, and he and his wife had been in Talon for three years.

"And what was it you said you were studying?" he persisted.

"Masks," I said, eventually.

"Masks," he said. "That sounds interesting. That's what we came to see. Imoussa was telling me all about the funeral and the masks and he's been promising us for a year he'd get us to an authentic ceremony. I've got four battery packs charged up and ready to go, and a couple of spotlights. Filming is a hobby of mine."

"I prefer stills," I said, a bit too fast. "Of course, that's my line of work. I'm actually a painter myself but I'm here to study the art of the masks, you know, motifs and their meanings."

Arnold glanced back at me briefly before ducking to enter the palace. You sidled up beside me inside the dark hut which was lit by a single kerosene lamp hanging in the middle of the hut. "I'll do the talking," you whispered. "You don't address the chief, just his *linguist.*"

You had me stumped there, for a minute. I mean, to me, a linguist was an academic who studied languages, and their development and cultural implications. But you saw how confused I was and pointed to that wizened old man who was squatting in front of the chief, to whom strangers were supposed to address their words for the chief.

The chief was a tiny shrunken old man sitting on the cracked concrete floor of the hut with his back against the mud wall. His feet were tucked up inside a heavy hand-woven cotton robe.

You slipped forward and spoke with the linguist in Goroni. "The chief welcomes you to his village," you announced, finally.

Imoussa bowed deeply and you presented my gifts — the bottle of schnapps and the kola nuts — to the chief by laying them at his feet. I caught a glimpse of the chief's eyes then. They were all white, even the pupils.

"Jesus, the chief is blind," I whispered to Arnold.

"Yeah. River blindness. Onchocerciasis. When the parasite reaches the eyes it turns them white and causes permanent blindness." It shouldn't have bothered me that he knew that but it did. Meanwhile, you were busy telling us what the chief said.

"The chief hopes you will find the funeral interesting. He says it is two years since there has been a white man in his village and he says that he has been waiting patiently during that time. Because the last white man who came here promised to dig a well for the village. His people are forced to take their water from the river which is a good long walk from here. He thanks you for your gifts."

Arnold piped up then. "Please tell the chief that a team of drillers is being trained now in Talon and that we hope to be out here within a month."

I could have kicked him. I was miffed that the villagers would agree to show *just anyone* their highly prized secret masks in exchange for a couple of wells.

It was complicated and slow–going, all that translation. First you spoke to the linguist, who then translated for the chief, who began to nod his head slowly and reply, and then the whole process had to be repeated.

"The chief is most grateful for this good news," you said at last. "He says the children in the village have been very ill with guinea worm and diarrhoea, and he hopes that when a new well is dug this will improve. He informs you that the masks will soon arrive."

You and Imoussa herded us back out into the moonlight and scared up two benches for us to sit on. At first I found myself sitting beside three blond-haired teenagers in Reeboks and neon t-shirts. I moved away fast. I put my arm around your shoulders and put some distance between us and the Arnold clan, making sure for probably the umpteenth time that you knew what I wanted to see.

"You've got to make sure you tell me everything as it happens. I'll be doing the photography, but maybe you could just talk into this tape machine while I'm doing that so I don't miss anything," said I, as though addressing a simpleton. Then I showed you how to work the tape recorder.

"Fine, Roger," you said.

I'm cringing now. Does that help at all?

The dancers and drummers were working up a frenzy before us. Imoussa and Arnold had disappeared, probably gone to set up their tents. I decided to put them out of my mind. I wanted to get some of the drumming on tape and you and I moved through the dancers, snapping and taping. I was getting as worked up as the dancers. They were performing a courtship dance, in which the girls went down on their hands and knees, and pumped their hips while a man straddled them. Their backs were arched and they wiggled their grass skirts and jangled their leggings. It was fantastic. For the first time in my life I felt a little sorry not to have a video recorder.

Then Arnold was back, setting up two high-powered, battery-run spotlights that illuminated the entire area, casting the assembled villagers into relief. They were standing about ten deep in a tight circle around the dancers who created their own aura with dust. I was worried about the effects of the dust on my recorder and camera not to mention on my nose. I suffer from asthma, probably because I grew up in a polluted steel town. I tied a blue and white handkerchief over my mouth, PLO style.

I had to prostrate myself, belly on the ground, to get a shot of a woman dancer whose face was frozen into hypnotic ecstasy as she danced past me. Her back end was going like a honey-bee's that has just discovered a tree full of apple blossoms. The intensity of the drumming had increased about a hundredfold. I scrambled to my feet. The crowd on the far side had parted, to allow massive bulky forms to come shuffling through into the limelight. At first glance, they looked like dancing bears. But I realized that they were in fact the masks — grass-covered forms swaying slowly to the beat of one enormous drum. The other dancers moved back into the crowd while ten of those *forms* took their place in the centre.

You were right. Those forms had nothing to do with men. They were mounds of grass rising out of the earth, wearing heads of eagles, vultures, cobras. All sharp angles, jagged lines, bright reds and blacks. They were beautiful and hideous. Alluring and repugnant. Like fat snakes on the slither, one could not take one's eyes off them for fear they would strike. Strike at what? I was hypnotized. I imagined trying to write my dissertation without abusing superlatives. It must be wonderful, I thought, to be released from this ludicrous urge to try to capture the essence of life and spirituality with puny words. It must be wonderful to allow things to happen, to allow images to register without trying to analyses them. But the Fulton Foundation would never go for that.

I kept up my vigil, moving cautiously around the edge of their circle dance, capturing the images — the geometric wizardry of the masks — in two-dimensional photographs. You followed me in a crouch, whispering explanations into the microphone.

Masks that no one had ever seen before — covering faces that no one would ever see. "Wild," I mouthed, again and again.

Occasionally Mr. Arnold and I crossed paths. He had his nose up the objective of his video camera and I had my eye glued to my own camera. Each of us continued on our way as though the other didn't exist. I didn't notice when the rest of the Arnold clan headed off to sleep. The moon had set by the time I suggested to you that we too flake out for the night. I remember how great it felt to lie down. But that's all I remember because I was out like the proverbial lights that — besides Arnold's — didn't exist in that village.

I don't know what woke me. There was no hint of dawn on the horizon. The drums were still beating but with less urgency now. It was a slow steady beat, something primordial and futuristic at the same time. I rolled over. The camp-bed was narrow and it was too hot to even think about using my sleeping bag. Mr. Arnold's spotlights had been extinguished but there was a flickering glow over the village. I assumed that the villagers had lit a fire and perhaps were already preparing the next day's feast.

My ankles, where skin was exposed between trousers and desert boots, were a burning mass of bites. I wished I had brought a mosquito net or the dining style tents that the Arnolds had. I scratched like crazy, wondering how you could be so still, wondering why you weren't bothered by the mosquitoes. I wished I was anywhere but in that village with no fan to keep me cool and no nets to keep away the mosquitoes. Finally I gave up trying to sleep and sat up, thinking some of my precious drinking water would at least cool the bites. I was hoping my movements and restlessness would wake you so you could commiserate with me in my misery.

I reached for my flashlight and shone it about. That's when I saw that your bed, a few feet from mine, was empty. I got up, drawn towards the strange glow over the village. I moved slowly and stealthily, ensuring I didn't get ahead of that reassuring beam of my flashlight. I tripped on the tent pegs of one of the Arnolds' tents. Someone inside was snoring loudly.

The smell of smoke was strong but there was no fire I could see. An orange glow flickered over the whole village like a neon sign advertising an after-hours casino. It was an ethereal kind of light, no source visible.

Just before I entered the ring of huts that encircled the open area in front of the chief's palace, I stopped and turned off the flashlight. I dropped to my knees, peering around the corner of a hut.

There were faces everywhere, thousands and thousands of faces *made only of light*. They filled the sky, looking down on the hundreds of figures dancing in front of the chief's palace. The masks — what *you told me* were the masks — were gone. And there, on the periphery of it all, you were.

Your face was alight, luminescent as though the fire were inside you. I could see every bead of sweat, every line. But your face was not any one face. It was like rubber, first alight with euphoria, then wracked by grief, then sombre and stern, like the bust of a great (but long-since deceased) visionary. Indeed, as I watched, all of the dancers underwent the same transformations, while their bodies obeyed the beats of the drum as though chained to it. You had no bones — you were hallucinations, reaching skyward with your arms, beckoning all those faces. You flowed. Your feet *did not touch the ground.*

I woke in my camp-bed with my mind on coffee. Plain old everyday coffee, for God's sake. I glanced over and there you were, sleeping peacefully on your camp-bed. The sun, barely over the tops of the scrubby Sahel trees was already sucking sweat out of my aching and tired body. You lay on your back and I examined your face that was illuminated by the rich morning light. You were just Ali again. Behind me the Arnolds were already up and moving around. They were brewing coffee on a camp-stove. I decided that by the light of day and given what I had seen, it wasn't so bad having someone so mundane and on-the-surface there after all. I wandered over towards their campsite in search of coffee. Drums were beating in the village. The day's ceremonies had already begun, or else the night's had not ended.

Mr. Arnold was telling me a little about what had impressed him the night before and, with a cup of his instant coffee loaded with canned milk and sugar firmly in my hand, I was feeling disposed to listen to him. He said that he was a collector of masks — especially old ones he acquired through Imoussa. He indicated that he hoped to get one of the new ones we had seen last night. Imoussa was bargaining on a price for this priceless *objet d'art*.

We were interrupted — by you. "Good morning, everyone. I hope you all slept well." You looked fresh and seemed bright and cheery. *On the surface.* I could almost convince myself that I had dreamed the dance of the rubber masks.

We left after receiving a wealth of gifts from the villagers who abandoned their drummers to come out and see us off. The chief gave me a goat and two white cocks; the village women handed me about two hundred guinea-fowl eggs.

Mr. Arnold got his mask, the eagle face, for free.

We allowed the two Nissans to get well ahead of us, because our vehicle, while luxurious and new, had no air-conditioning and we had to drive with the windows open drinking in the dust that the Arnolds' off-road Nissans left in their wake.

You started reading that book again, so I slipped the cassette you had made during the dance of the masks into the tape deck in the car. I listened for about a half hour to your descriptions of each wooden mask — what the motifs symbolized — spirits of trees, crops, fire, water, soil. The python, sacred to the people of the village, was pervasive. "The swirling and twisting of the figure wearing this mask is symbolic in itself. For this is the python, the totem of the founder of the Goroni people, the creator of the chief, the progenitor of the chief's lineage."

I reached over and ejected the cassette, tossing it onto the dashboard in frustration. You looked at me quizzically, working a chewing stick over your teeth like a lathe.

"Ali, those guys in the grass and the wooden face masks with the horns. Those weren't really the secret masks at all, were they?"

"What do you mean?" Innocence was painted on your face as thick as the ochre on the wooden masks the evening before.

"I mean, you've got other masks, more secret. Ones you really won't show to any outsiders, right? Those wooden ones are the ones you put on when curious strangers come but they're not really the secret ones are they?"

You removed the chewing stick, looked sideways at me and smiled. "Roger, this is your dissertation. I'm your guide, but I'm not going to write your dissertation and do your analysis for you too." You laughed, banging me a little too hard on the shoulder. I removed a hand from the steering wheel to receive one of those finger-snapping handshakes that you always used to indicate that some kind of understanding has been reached and that there is no need to delve any deeper. *That to delve any deeper would be incorrect.*

I've written my dissertation and handed it in. It's cut and dried. It's bullshit. There was no room in that academic treatise for anything that even came close to what happened. They would accuse me of writing fiction. Of being the victim of hallucinations or spirit possession. Spirit possession is the nice term they use for this in academia and it's okay as long as it's your subjects who are experiencing it while you, the analytical and dispassionate student of human life and art, remain dispassionate and write it all down like it's a recipe for brownies. But I saw it too and that's just not allowed in this so-called era of rationality and Fulton Fellowships. So what do I do now? Forget or try to understand?

That's why I'm writing to you, Ali. I still don't understand it. Were you telling me I never could? That you've been a step ahead of us all the time?

Second-hand dream

Wambolt let the *Herald Tribune* droop to get a better view of the petite woman who had just come into the cafe. His wife had once been shaped like that, but twenty years of marriage and four children had saddled her with forty excess pounds and stretch marks right up to her mouth. And she was back home in St. Albert. Light years away.

The girl was available, he guessed, or she wouldn't be in the Normandy Cafe. She didn't look new to the trade but there was still something vulnerable there, an innocence that caught in his throat. Her taut blue jeans were short enough to reveal slim brown calves and ankles that wobbled as she stepped out in oversized, shabby red pumps. Like a chaste little girl parading about in whore clothing — second-hand, from top to bottom.

Wambolt butted his cigarette and returned his eyes to the newspaper reluctantly. Three gruelling months in the sandswept north, pouring concrete and bulldozing villages and trees out of the way for the new hydro dam, had left him with plenty of money and a concupiscence wanting to be spent.

Four hours in the city and he had a good start. Five cold ones under his belt. The *Herald Tribune* had provided the latest NHL results — his Oilers were out in front. Soon, though, he would have to do something about a girl for the night, or the week. He could always get up and move now to the Safari Fever Club, but it was still too early for action there . . . he worked his eyes over the girl's face and body again.

She was leaning against the bar, chatting with the bald-headed barman who owned the Normandy and the Safari Fever Club next door — and ran a number of the girls who frequented both places. Wambolt laid the newspaper on the table and leaned back in his chair, balancing it on its spindly legs as he rested his indecision for a couple of seconds. The girl was laughing as she turned casually to scan the cafe. Her eyes rested on his for a second before she lowered her head and stared at the floor.

Dodie had been on the Boulevard for three years, on the job since noon. She'd made her round of the cafes frequented by whites and by wealthy Africans — mostly contractors or men from the ministries.

Business was miserable. That afternoon she had been in and out of the Normandy four times, smoking cigarettes and sipping Fanta. She was out of cigarettes and down to her last thousand conies. Barely enough to get her into the Safari Fever Club later. But business didn't start there until after midnight. She was feeling tired. In the village she would already be cooking the evening meal, getting drowsy as night fell. But this was the city.

Nights weren't for sleeping in the city. Tomorrow morning, when she returned to the odoriferous quarters just around the corner, her uncle would again demand money and her aunt would plead for a few conies to buy rice. Dodie's two-year-old twins, John and Paul, seemed to be shrinking and both had a skin rash. There were simply too many children for her aunt to feed. Latest count was fifteen. The extended family had grown because last year's rains and crops had failed. More family members had migrated to the city looking for work and charity. There was no work and the charity in her auntie's house was stretched thinner than a ribcage.

Dodie had to get out, as Clementine had done. Lucky Clementine. Clever Clementine. Clementine and Dodie had come from the village to the city together. They'd worked the Boulevard for one year when Clementine met Wolfgang — a German volunteer who worked in community development or something like that. At first he was just one of Clementine's regulars. Then he asked her to move in with him. Eventually he married her and took her back to Germany when his contract finished. Dodie's jeans were a gift from Clementine when she came for a visit last year. Clementine was sophisticated now— a stranger Dodie dreamed of becoming.

She moved slowly away from the bar and towards the door. She held her head high as though a pot of water were perched up there. That was what she had escaped by fleeing the village. A future with heavy loads on her head and babies on her back. No future at all. She reminded herself of this every time homesickness struck and she began to ache. For the village. For its *human* comforts.

She squinted into the traffic on the boulevard. Yellow headlights and bright spotlights still dazzled her. In Europe and America all the streets would be as magnificent as the Boulevard of Liberation. A husband like Wolfgang and she would be able to live like the white women who came to the Normandy each afternoon — breathless in frilly cotton dresses, wearing glimmering watches and gold chains draped around pale, scrawny necks. The women looked too thin, as if they never had enough to eat. Their skin looked dried and cured like the hide of a skinned goat. But their children were plump like rosy, scrubbed piglets. They had white socks and shining hair, and their whining and crying earned them outrageously expensive dishes of ice cream bathed in cherries and shaded by exquisite miniature umbrellas.

She'd seen videos from America. People there were rich and always busy with love affairs and fine jewels and lots of parties. There were no uncles and aunts haggling for a few conies, no open sewers running through the compounds, no dirt or disease or poor people. If she could make her way to France or Germany or America, her mother would forgive her for leaving the village. And in return, Dodie would send her family the world — radios and televisions and videos and hair dryers and blenders and perfumes and shoes and baby toys and bedsheets in shades of heaven.

On her last visit, Clementine told her, "White men are civilized, Dodie. But Germans are the most civilized, even more than the French and the British. Wolfgang says Americans are foolish, like children. As for me, I much prefer Germany to all the other places. Germans are so clean and they know how to get things done. You should see their *autobahns*. Everyone has a Mercedes or a BMW."

Dodie had sat silently, listening while she pictured herself in one of those cars. She didn't tell Clementine that she wasn't up to caring whether a man was German or American, or to admitting that she didn't have a steady man yet. She wasn't about to dismiss any chances. Perhaps that was why she didn't dismiss the big, sloppy white man hiding behind the newspaper. Men in videos were never sloppy. This man didn't look rich at all. He smoked local cigarettes, drank local beer and wore no gold. White men were strange, as if they wanted to hide their wealth. John and Paul's father hadn't looked rich either. And he had had untold wealth stashed away in his locked closet and briefcase. But he didn't stay in the country long enough to share it with her.

The large man drinking beer in the corner of the Normandy vaguely resembled Wolfgang, unkempt and thick in the middle. The battered, dusty jeep parked at the curb probably belonged to him. It had plates from Talon, so she figured he worked up north somewhere. She brushed a hand over the corn rows on her head and tossed the long, plaited pony tail of synthetic hair over her shoulder. She stood in the doorway, her back to him and waited, but not for long.

He touched her elbow. "Hey beautiful, want to drink something?"

She turned and smiled, following him to his table, where she dropped into a chair opposite him. He lit a cigarette and offered her the package. She withdrew one and waited for him to light it. She smoked silently, maintaining a bored expression as he progressed through the standard preliminaries. She thought it odd that whites, who tended to be so senseless about basic things in life, always asked her questions as though *she* were the simple one.

Wambolt ordered a double whisky for himself and asked her if she would like a beer.

"I'd like a Heineken," she said.

She didn't need to ask him about himself because he seemed eager to talk. He said he was Canadian, that he worked in the north and that he had five days of leave in the city. He asked her which part of the country she was from. She told him one of her grandfathers was white and that she'd lived in France for a year at her uncle's villa. "Near Paris," she said.

"Never been to Paris except at the airport," he replied. "I don't generally like the Frogs. Faggots most of them, with their perfume and little purses." He laughed. She didn't know what faggot meant but decided not to ask.

Two hours — four whiskies for Wambolt — later she was showering as he told her to. She didn't tell him she had washed just before coming to the Normandy. The tiled hotel bathroom was clean and it smelled nice. She wished John and Paul could see a place like this, just once.

Twenty minutes after that, Wambolt was spent and snoring beside her, trapping her under a heavy arm. She wanted to get up and turn on the television, but she felt it wise not to wake him. In spite of Clementine's belief in the gentle white man, Dodie knew that as the white lie it was. Wambolt had been rough with her, manhandling her onto her stomach to take her like a ram in the village. Except rams didn't wear condoms.

She lay very still and imagined that this air-conditioned room belonged to her. This was a big house in a distant city, where she lived with Wambolt and John and Paul. But Wambolt, in this dream, was gentle and loving and he wore a suit and tie all the time.

She told herself that everything was going to be okay. Even if he decided once was enough and dismissed her in the morning he would pay her enough to see her through tomorrow.

In the morning, after breakfast in bed, Wambolt took her again but more gently this time. At eleven he told her to get up because he wanted to go to the beach. On the way through the lobby, he stopped in the hotel boutique to buy her a tiny green bikini that looked like something she would put on under her clothes during her days.

She lay down in the waves beside Wambolt, trying to keep her body hidden in the white froth of the breakers. It was okay to be nearly naked in a hotel room, but on the beach it was awful. Wambolt said he wanted to teach her how to swim. He was talking to her as though she was a little girl, so she tried to behave like one — giggling and wrestling with him in the water like the small white children who were there with their parents. He still hadn't paid her and she worried that her aunt had no food for John and Paul.

Over dinner in the hotel room she spoke very little. She laughed when he told stories about the stupidity of the African labourers who worked for him. She didn't hound him for money but she calculated how much he owed her for the weekend and wondered when he would finally pay her and send her home.

On Sunday morning, he suggested she go home, fetch some of her things and move into his room. He gave her a thousand conies for the taxi fare. She walked home to save the fare, and passed eight hundred of the conies on to her auntie. She kissed her boys goodbye. "I don't know when I'll be back," she whispered. "But I'll send you nice presents, so don't worry."

Wambolt drank a lot and when he was drunk he stopped paying attention to his wallet. In the next few days Dodie was able to take out a few thousand conies while he slept. She considered it a small advance on what he owed her. She bought shoes and socks for her boys, a sack of rice for the family and paid for a new coiffure for herself, a headful of tiny polyester braids that reached her shoulders. She didn't go back home but sent the gifts to her family with a young boy who often performed errands for her in return for tips on where men carried money on their persons.

Wambolt seemed happy with her. He bought her Benson cigarettes and gold earrings that matched the golden package that the cigarettes came in. He chose a pair of gold and silver sandals and a shimmering white evening dress from the hotel boutique which she wore to the Safari Fever Club. He said she outshone all the other girls.

During a slow dance that night in the Safari Fever Club he sang the words to the song into her ear: "I will always love you."

"I love you, too," she whispered back.

Then four of his colleagues from the north came in and joined their table. They all wanted to dance with her too, and Wambolt kept pulling money out of his wallet to pay for more champagne. She tried not to think about John and Paul and how she could have used that money. Instead she drank a lot of the champagne and laughed as much as she could because Wambolt and his friends were laughing. When the club closed, Wambolt put her over his shoulder and carried her to the car. She felt terribly dizzy and was afraid she would vomit all the champagne she had drunk.

One of his friends was carrying a girl named Vanity and when they got in the car, the friend suggested they go to a local photography shop called Foto Love. The green and red fluorescent lights sobered Dodie a little. The two couples took turns on the crimson velveteen bedspread, while the photographer moved around making suggestions about the positions they should assume while the flashes made her head feel like it had exploded. They had to wait a long time for the man to develop them, and Dodie fell asleep with her head on Wambolt's lap while they sat on the couch in Foto Love.

The next night Wambolt told her he had to leave for the north again, that he'd be there for three months. He would not be returning to the city until it was time for his annual home leave in July.

"God, I'd love to take you to Canada, Dodie. My wife bitches and my kids whine. I never get any peace."

She crinkled her brow and clucked in sympathy. He caressed her face as she fell asleep beside him.

He was unable to sleep. Lying on the bed with his arms behind his head, he eyed her. He doubted he would ever find a Canadian woman as obedient, compliant and grateful for small nothings as Dodie. And certainly not one with her physique. He'd had plenty of women over the past decade working in Africa. That was one of the fringe benefits that came with the tax-free money. But he'd never had one quite as devoted or sophisticated as Dodie. She was young, sweeter and brighter than the others. And she never demanded money for her family, as most girls did after a few hours.

Dawn was showing when he kissed her mouth and woke her up. "How would you like to come with me to the north for a couple of months?" he asked.

"Oh, that would be nice, Wambolt," she said, as he edged her head and her mouth down where he wanted them. At times like this she concentrated on the trees by the stream where she had fetched water as a child. By imagining the smells and sounds in that grove as she and her sisters bathed after filling the water pots, she could stomach anything.

Abule-land, where he worked in the north, was a remote and heathen place as far as Dodie knew. She feared the Able people who lived there. They were barbaric warriors and it was said that they often raided other tribes, stealing girls. But Wambolt had said he was in a special camp with "no spearchuckers allowed". And he said the camp had electricity and running water. That was a big part of her dream.

To her own surprise, she liked it in the north. Except for the cooks and the houseboys, who all came from the south, no Africans were permitted inside the tall wire fence that separated the camp from the surrounding villages.

She strode through the local market, heard the Abule women calling her the white man's girl. It turned out that the Abule people weren't so bad after all. She joked with the market women, teasing them for picking lice out of each other's hair like baboons and wrapping themselves up in soiled cloths like beggars. She had a chauffeured vehicle at her disposal and a weekly allowance to do the shopping. Each week she saved a few thousand conies to send back to the city and her sons.

Much of the time, Wambolt seemed not to notice that she was there. He worked late on accounts and spent a lot of his evenings in the camp canteen with other white men, drinking and watching videos. She was always ready for him when he came home with needs only she could satisfy.

Sometimes, in the privacy of their bedroom, she asked him questions about his country and he would talk to her as if she were his wife of several years.

"Canada's really a great place. In the summertime we have barbecues in the backyard or head up to the lake and the cottage. I've got a motorboat there, and we all get sunburned. Come down on me again, would you Dodie bird . . ." He held her head in place until she swallowed it all.

Dodie tried to imagine what it was like, this lake as big as an ocean. A land of huge houses, as though everyone was a president or a minister. Lots to eat and drink and boats with motors and no one had to work. She pictured John and Paul as handsome grown men, in suits, carrying the keys to their shiny cars in one hand, briefcases in the other.

"Is it awfully cold there?"

"Naw. Well, sometimes, but not in the summer. No, in the summer there's no place like Canada. Blue skies and green grass." He rubbed her head roughly. "You want to come along?"

The weeks flew by, much more quickly than they ever had on the Boulevard. She revelled in leisure and luxury, even put on a few pounds. She chose new dresses and cosmetics from a European mail-order catalogue and sent away her order form without telling Wambolt. She ignored the warning that delivery could take up to six months, hoping she'd still be here. Her favourite items, the ones she most looked forward to getting, were the matching Mickey and Minnie His 'n Hers night shirts. As she flipped through the catalogue's pages she thought she had derived as much pleasure from life as it could possibly offer.

She now bathed three times a day and used up a bar of soap in two days. She made sure his clothes were clean and well pressed so he no longer looked so sloppy in his jeans and t-shirts. He seemed finally to have stopped worrying about catching something from her because he had stopped using condoms when they came north.

She cooked evening meals for him, always something African, a piece of steak or chicken with groundnut sauce. On Saturday nights she served drinks when the men in the camp gathered in her living room to play cards. They seemed to hate her country and other places they had worked in Africa. Always laughing about it. But they were nice to her so she guessed they didn't hate *all* Africans.

On Friday morning, two weeks before Wambolt was supposed to leave for Canada, she went to work in the kitchen, deciding to throw all her weight behind fate. She pounded the *fufu* herself with a heavy wooden mortar. Over a charcoal fire in the back she prepared the hot sauce that Wambolt loved. She grilled each piece of antelope separately. All the ingredients of the splendid feast, save the champagne and the wine, were African, none more so than the herbs Dodie lovingly sprinkled into the sauce. They were powerful herbs that her tribeswomen used to mellow out their men, to keep their husbands from beating them and to stimulate their gentler manhood. Men were really like children, her mother had told her years ago. They needed a woman's hand to guide them, to power them. But secretly. Men must never know how women controlled their lives and fate.

When the meal was laid out like a chief's banquet on the table and protected against flies with a sheet, she turned her attention to her body. She washed and anointed herself with cocoa butter before putting on her white lace dress. She thought about opening the perfume that Wambolt had bought for her at the hotel. But in the end she decided to leave it unopened just in case something didn't go according to plan and a time came when she needed something to sell.

Wambolt, already happy after a few rounds with the boys in the canteen, was titillated by her extravagant preparations. After dinner he belched loudly and pulled her onto his knee before she could clear the table. He kissed her, making her face burn with the beard he was growing. Then he took her to bed. "I want to take you with me. Pack you in my bags," he said. "Wouldn't that set the bitch to barking?"

She lay awake most of the night. He was taking her to Canada. She would have to send word to her family.

Wambolt woke her up, saying that he had to make a brief trip to the capital to check on some business.

After he left, she hopped a bush taxi and travelled south to her village. At first her father and his wives were angry. But Dodie's mother was quick to see the advantages of the match for her daughter whom no respectable local man would now consider taking as a wife. Eventually she managed to convince Dodie's father that the financial benefits accruing would compensate for having a foreigner in the family. Dodie promised to send plenty of gifts.

Wambolt and Dodie spent the final weekend in the capital in the same suite in which they had consummated their relationship three months earlier. Wambolt was distracted, hardly taking notice of her. He had business appointments with local contractors and visitors from the World Bank who were partially financing the dam. Dodie was left alone with her own problems.

Dodie, just back from a day of mourning and funeral arrangements, was sitting on the bed watching Wambolt dress. She hated to leave now because John and Paul had fallen sick with influenza which was reaching epidemic proportions in the crowded quarter of town behind the Boulevard. Two cousins in the family house had already died. Still, it was now or never, if she was going to get out.

"Well, tonight's the night, Dodie."

"Do you have the tickets?" she asked.

"Course I do. How else would I be able to leave?"

She hesitated. She had vowed never to nag Wambolt. Or not to trust him. He had told her she could trust him. "You're my number one girl," he had said. But still . . .

"I mean *my* ticket," she whispered.

"Your ticket? For what?" He breathed in, struggling to get his belly into the grey flannel pants. "Dodie, run down to the lounge and get me a beer, will you. I've got some calls to make before I go."

"But Wambolt, isn't it that I need a ticket to go on an airplane?"

"An airplane? Why? Where are you going?"

"To Canada, with you . . ." She kept her head down.

"Dodie what kind of shit are you pulling? You're not going anywhere. You're going to wait right here for me. I'll be back in September. Christ, do you really think I could take you with me?"

"You said you were going to pack me in your suitcase." She stood and moved to him, running her hand over his belly, smiling up at him so hard that her lips hurt.

He pushed her gently away and turned to the mirror. His reflection smiled down at her as he smoothed his thinning blond hair. "Dodie, good God. You scared me there for a minute. I thought you were serious. St. Albert's no place for a girl like you. Here . . ." He pulled his wallet from his back pocket. "Here's fifty thousand conies to keep you off the streets until I get back. Now be a good girl and go get me that beer." He gave her rear end a pat and shoved her towards the door.

When she was gone, he checked again that he had all his papers and closed his briefcase. He glanced in the mirror again, making his reflection chuckle at Dodie's prank. He was going to miss her, no doubt about that. On the other hand, he was not unhappy to spend a month with his wife who was a good mother and not a bad woman either. Bossy and demanding but with good intentions. A little on the heavy side but he couldn't really complain about that any more, not with this belly of his that had grown so it hung over his belt buckle. Yeah, she had a tendency to bug him about his drinking or the time he spent away from his family. But she knew who buttered her bread and paid for the ranch-style home in St. Albert, and on recent visits home she had been almost charming most of the time. He hoped Dodie would be back soon with that beer.

She stuffed the bills into her bra and stumbled numbly down the carpeted hall, away from dreams of boats with motors and toys and shoes and ice cream. Fifty thousand conies. They spent that in one night at the Safari Fever Club. It would barely be enough to enrol John and Paul for one term in nursery school. She already owed the doctor ten thousand for the flu medicine. She strode past the door to the television lounge where *Dallas* covered the giant screen with visions of the American Dream. She knew now it was all a mirage, no more accessible now than those memories of a beautiful glade of tall trees where she had once fetched water as a child. She went through the sliding glass doors that kept the warm air and the locals out of the hotel. She ignored the hisses of the liveried doormen and hailed a taxi.

It took the man at Foto Love almost an hour to get around to finding the negatives and another two hours to print them up. He charged her twenty thousand. She dashed him five thousand conies to accompany her to the Commissariat, where he had friends who did business with him. Her last twenty-five thousand conies and another hour were spent convincing the two police inspectors to take action.

He couldn't figure out what had happened to her. She'd been gone four hours and he had to leave for the airport at eleven. He sat in the bar, his suitcase beside him, drinking beer and waiting for her to come back. He had checked out of his room angry at Dodie for running off like that. Let her sleep in her own home for a change. Obviously, he had spoiled her. She would have to get her things back from the hotel management.

He guessed there had been more trouble at the family home. Christ, there was always someone sick or dying in her family. At five to eleven, he went out into the hot and sticky night air and hailed one of the waiting taxis. As he was getting in, two plain-clothesmen approached him and demanded his papers and then announced that he was under arrest for defiling a teenager. They showed him photographs. He gave them fifty thousand for the photographs and they thanked him, wishing him a safe journey as he pulled away in the taxi.

Shortly after midnight, Dodie left the Commissariat. She walked to the hotel, but the room had already been cleaned and the hotel management said Mr. Wambolt had taken all her possessions and left nothing in the room. She walked home barefoot — the evening sandals were useless in the slime of the back paths leading to the family house. She calculated her net worth. She had two thousand conies that she always kept tucked away in her brassiere.

It took Dodie some time to get back on the Boulevard after that for she discovered she was pregnant a week after Wambolt left. Paul died of malaria shortly before her son, Christian, was born. Three months later she was back in the Normandy, sporting a pair of shiny black high heels and a pair of black tights to match — all good quality merchandise from the second-hand market. She thought she saw Wambolt once, arm in arm with another rented woman at the Safari Fever Club, but he didn't seem to notice her. She didn't go closer because she had nothing to say — nothing that would interest him.

Live birth

Barbara's first impression of the Langadi Health Centre is that it does not belong there. It is too new, too white, too pristine for the surroundings.

She switches off the engine of the Suzuki and stares at the building, blazing white in the gloomy, hot haze of the harmattan. A red dust devil scoops up dried leaves and bits of paper and races across the wasteland surrounding the new health centre. She blinks and it is gone.

The health centre has been financed by the International Federation for Mother and Child. The IFMC is an organization she had never heard of before she spied the advertisement in the *Sunday Times* right above the crossword puzzle. *International Agency Requires Public Health Nurse, obstetrics and administrative skills necessary. Two-year post in pleasant rural West African setting.*

Pleasant rural West African setting? Looks like a Hollywood depiction of the world after the nuclear holocaust. Baked red earth with twisted trees tortured by drought. She minds the heat terribly. But at least the physical discomfort helps her forget how many other things hurt inside her. And have been hurting ever since she walked out the door of the house she and Jim built together. Jim is there now, probably asleep with his lover.

And she's here in this desolate post. Had there been any other applicants for the job? What converging lines of chance, of probability — improbability — put her in Langadi on this day, at this moment, in this lifetime? This is her first time in Africa; her first time off her own continent. If Jim had stayed with her, she would probably never have strayed from home.

She yanks the key angrily from the ignition. The thought of Jim does that to her. Since the divorce she has refused to see him and they have corresponded only by letter. She still can't believe he left her. These are things that happen to other people, not to Jim and her, childhood sweethearts, professional people, thirteen years of marriage. He has stolen her prescribed future, the comforts of growing old together. Laughing at grey hairs and wrinkled foreheads.

She pulls on the emergency brake although there is no need for it on this flat bit of dusty road which seems to stretch forever, going nowhere at all and certainly not up or down. But she is not in a hurry so she takes her time to perform each step correctly. She wants to get off to a good start. She musn't hurry. The battered old truck she followed north, into Talon, had the words "No Hurry in Life" scrawled across the wooden bumper in red and yellow letters.

The country representative of the IFMC must never have learned that bit of folk wisdom. When Barbara met her in the capital the woman had wasted no time at all. She even talked fast, rushing through the preliminaries, handing her the keys to the jeep, telling her to spend the first night in Talon so she could check in at the Regional Department of Health. Then she sent Barbara on her way seven hundred kilometres north — armed with the statistics on child mortality, stillbirths and deaths of mothers during childbirth that rolled off her tongue like numbers in a tragic game of bingo.

She left Barbara with the impression that her job was to rewrite the statistics overnight. Barbara wishes that woman were here now to impart some of her frenetic willpower. The hotel in Talon had no water or electricity but lots of cockroaches. A drunk Canadian with the unlikely name of Wambolt had tried to pick her up at the Point Ten bar when she sat down there to drink something cold. And the Regional Department of Health in Talon was closed. Nor there was any sign of the nurses she was supposed to pick up there.

Now she's arrived at her destination and she feels overwhelmed by what lies ahead, worried because she doesn't know what *does* lie ahead. Isn't there supposed to be someone here to meet her, greet her? The village seems deserted.

She wants a shower, a drink and some food. First though, she has to find her quarters. She steps out of the jeep, lugging her suitcase from the passenger's seat. The country representative said the quarters were behind the clinic.

She didn't say how small they were. A tiny square hut with a green door and a window with green shutters. It's as freshly whitewashed as the health clinic. She drops her suitcase and returns to the Suzuki to fetch the rest of her belongings and the medical supplies.

She was wrong about the village being deserted. About fifty children have surrounded the jeep. They are using their fingers to write A, B and C in the dust covering the blue paint. Some speak an English she can almost understand. All of them are fighting over her luggage, wanting to carry it to the hut where she is to spend one hundred and four weeks of her life.

She tries to still their squabbles, to keep track of the boxes they are carrying. When her few possessions are inside the house she is drenched in sweat. She hands out a few coins, tries to shoo them away. When it is obvious they're not going anywhere, she closes the door on them and turns around to survey her new home. There is no water, no furniture and no kitchen.

She sits down on her suitcase in the middle of the room that is her house and bursts into tears. She feels so badly about crying that she cries harder. She has lost the reflex to turn off the tears. She hears Jim's voice: "Get a grip on yourself, Barbara, it's not the end of the world. We can still be the friends we've always been." She keeps bawling like a baby that's being weaned by its mother.

Hurt. Humiliated. Homesick. Jim and his lover are probably waking now and going at it, however it is that two men go at it. She wonders for the hundredth time if she would feel better if he had left her for another woman, rather than that long-haired man with thighs like twin oaks and those Clark Kent glasses. She thought gay men were supposed to be effeminate. Would it have happened differently if Jim hadn't got mumps on their honeymoon and could have fathered a child, or two? If only . . .

She is shocked into subdued sniffles by a knock on the door. "Hello. Is anybody home? Hello?"

"Yes. Yes. Um, just a moment please, I'm coming . . ."

She stands hastily, straightening blouse and skirt and wiping at her eyes with a fist that comes away wet and brown, the colour of the roads she has travelled. She opens the door, but only a crack.

"Oh, excuse me, Madam. Sorry to disturb you. My name is Salifu. I'm the teacher in Langadi, and I wished to welcome you and to see whether there might not be something I could do to be of assistance to you." He has eased his way inside and stands before her, blinking like a stand-up comedian. He is short, well, a bit shorter than she, which doesn't necessarily mean he is short. She is six foot one, an even six foot if she thrusts out one hip and slouches. She feels disoriented. How come she has the impression that *she* is looking up to *him*?

She can feel the flush and a faint annoyance that he has managed to enter without waiting for her to open the door and invite him in. She rubs at her eyes some more. "This dust." She hopes he didn't hear her crying.

"Oh my goodness," says Salifu, glancing about the small room. "They've neglected to furnish your quarters. That was left to the villages of Langadi and Kakadi as their contribution to the health centre. But I guess they didn't agree on who should do what, so no one did anything." He speaks with a very faint impediment, a slight slur that runs his words together. It is a gentle sound, soft like a ball of fur. She examines his face — trying to pinpoint a physical infirmity that could account for the slur. His face is normal, even nice. There's a hint of a smile hidden away in the luxurious growth of a full beard.

She blushes again when she sees he has caught and deflected her inquisitive stare which she fears borders on the suspicious.

"Sorry, Mr. Salifu. How rude of me. I haven't even returned your greeting. My name is Barbara. Barbara Walsh. Please call me Barbara. I hope someone informed you that a new nurse was coming to open the clinic."

"Pleased to meet you, Barbara. We have been waiting for you. I wish to welcome you on behalf of the communities of Langadi and Kakadi. Please, you must be hungry and thirsty. Did you come all the way from the capital this morning?"

"Yes. Yes. Yes to everything." She tries to laugh, sounds as if she has asthma. She feels silly with relief that she is not alone. "You can see I have nothing to cook on, nothing to eat on, nor to sleep or sit on for that matter. Or to wash in. There is no water anywhere. In fact, you've come at the right time."

"I am happy to be able to help, Barbara. We so desperately need health workers in this area. You wait small. I'll be back in a while with everything you need." He's too earnest and formal, she thinks. He must be mocking her.

In less than an hour, Salifu has rallied a dozen village children who come bearing broken furniture, a three-legged chair and a table to match. He also brings a man he calls a fitter, who adds the missing legs and a lot of nails to make the chair and table functional. Then he disappears again.

By late afternoon, there's even a kapok mattress covered with maize sacks sewn together like a quilt. When the children have finished bringing these second-hand amenities, they gather at her door to stare at her and giggle. But then Salifu is back again to chase them away. This time he has brought a housemaid and cook — Mary — who comes bearing charcoal pots and cooking implements, which she immediately sets up behind the house. Salifu hands Mary a yam and a guinea-fowl and she begins to cook.

As they stack the boxes and medical supplies on shelves in the clinic Salifu tells Barbara a little about the village — that market day is on Saturday and where she can buy meat and eggs, cold minerals to drink. She pictures icy bottles of healthy drinks from the bowels of the earth and says she's looking forward to some mineral water. He explains that "minerals" is a generic term for soft drinks like Fanta and Sprite and Coke. He says she can get clean drinking water from the village borehole but it's gone very salty in the past few years. She can use it for clinic needs. He recommends that she buy river water from the boys who fetch it in drums each day, boil any she intends to drink.

Barbara wants to share her dinner with Salifu and Mary. Mary declines and goes home, promising to come in the morning. Salifu accepts. Barbara is aware of the quiet murmur of voices in the village. There are no vehicles and there is no electricity.

The complex logistics of running a clinic without power and running water strike her suddenly like running headlong into a wall. She feels like a neophyte despite her degree and all those years of experience in public health that led her — misled her — into believing she knew a lot.

They move to the front step of her house and watch the sun going down while the smell of their dinner, guinea-fowl in groundnut oil, serenades the pink evening. She offers to pay him for the food. He refuses, saying it is his welcoming gift to her, his obligation as her host in Langadi. She starts to feel much better listening to Salifu's voice if not his words. She has the impression he thinks she can't manage on her own. This makes her feel she can. He lights a kerosene lamp that reduces the world to a small and cosy place just big enough for two on her front step.

At eight the next morning, scrubbed and feeling brisk and efficient in her white uniform, her hair pulled into a professional knot on the back of her head, she opens the front doors to the Langadi Health Centre. There is so much to be done. Most of what they need is still in shipping cartons and the staff must be briefed on the operating rules of this brand new clinic. She wonders when they will show up.

Word has spread quickly. There are dozens of women and babies and children lined up quietly, expectantly, at the door.

From that minute there can be no looking back — no time to look ahead either. There are supposed to be two nurses and four nursing assistants here but none comes. This means that instead of just supervising and training of staff, as so carefully outlined in the official project documents, Barbara *is* the staff. Salifu comes to her aid again. He has somehow managed to recruit two trained birth assistants from the village to work for next to nothing. They are willing and helpful but neither has any formal education beyond primary school.

They run out of syringes and surgical gloves at the end of the first month and she has to spend her evenings sterilizing the used ones. She goes to Talon again to ask for the promised nurses and the supplies but can find no one who seems to know anything about these arrangements. She calls the country representative in the capital but she has travelled to Geneva and won't be back for a month. No one else in the head office in the capital seems able to offer any advice. She gives up and drives back to Langadi.

Salifu often comes to help but his visits are not pre-arranged or regular. For days he is not around; then he's there each evening for a week, making himself indispensable. An extra pair of hands and a friend with whom to share her dismay at the health needs of the women and children. He says he is trying to negotiate with the Langadi and Kakadi chiefs in the area, asking that they mobilize villagers to construct small huts around the clinic where patients from each community can wait for treatment or recover afterwards.

But he says the chiefs are unwilling to do this unless the clinic will accept adult male patients too. She says this is impossible without staff and supplies.

"This mother-and-child federation seems to have forgotten that men get sick too," he says, with barely suppressed anger, something she has not seen in him before.

"Yes, Salifu," she says. "You're probably right but there's nothing we can do about it. Anyway, it's better than no clinic at all, isn't it?"

"Not necessarily," he replies, heading out of the clinic and slamming the door. If she weren't so tired she would follow him, ask him to talk to her and explain what he means. Instead, for the first time since she's come, she goes to bed and cannot sleep. Ghosts of Jim and his lover tiptoe in during the night, when her defences are down, and they move into her bed, crowding the worries about Salifu and the clinic out of the room. So she gives up on sleep and returns to the clinic with her lantern where she keeps busy organizing medical records and writing a report to the federation about the poor planning that went into this clinic. She writes until she can open the doors and welcome the yellow dawn. And Salifu.

He has brought his sister, Zenab, who will hand out numbers each day to keep the queues orderly. This should help keep peace among the patients. Sometimes women have to wait for three days before she can see them and the clinic is starting to look like a refugee camp with people camped out on mats around it. And the statistics are still grim — for every ten live births there are three stillbirths.

As the weeks pass she is glad she has no time to dwell on her own pain, although she still remembers each night as she lies down to sleep that another day has passed without a letter from Jim; he had promised he would always be her best friend even if he was no longer her husband. She's aware that there is still a small abscess of pain somewhere behind her eyes that could pop and spread its poison through her body any time. But she's much too busy trying to heal real wounds to allow one inside her to fester and seep.

One Saturday, Salifu comes with the fitter and the materials to construct a simple shower in the hut out back so that she can stand under a flow of water instead of squatting and pouring calabash after calabash of water over her body. As she watches him she is reminded of Jim and his enthusiasm when they were building their house. Then she realizes that she is glad it's Salifu and not Jim she's watching and is startled by this feeling that seems to combine hard-earned tiredness with happiness. It's as unfamiliar as her new surroundings and has endeared itself the same way — without warning or effort.

Six months into the life of the health centre things are not exactly quietening down but they are smoothing out. She doesn't bother keeping records for the federation any more, despite the rule the country director insisted Barbara follow so they could monitor the "impact of the project".

She has no time to write the monthly report and keep statistics because she's too busy lancing abscesses, counselling women on the recipe for rehydration formula, giving antibiotics to calm infections caused by guinea worms in legs and feet, delivering and weighing babies. Salifu has arranged with someone in the Talon health department to have a nurse come out on the weekends to share the workload. Brenda is very quiet, has a reassuring smile that she uses on Barbara and on patients to show them she has things under control.

Sometimes, if Barbara has a spare minute — this being only very late at night or very early in the morning — she wonders how the people coped before the centre was there. Not just Langadi and Kakadi but all of the thirty or so villages that are sending their sick, maimed, pregnant and malnourished to the centre. By the *thousands*. She learns she can manage quite well on a few hours of sleep a night and sometimes on none, that if the need is there she can work thirty-six hours without a rest. It is so wonderful to feel useful. Needed. Not that patients at home hadn't had needs too. But she had been pushed into public health administration and that meant pushing paper, not nursing away pain.

Still, there are days when the whole enterprise strikes her as hopeless. Even with the birth assistants, they lose three infants in just one month. Mothers bring their infants at the last minute after prayers and traditional medicine have proved ineffective.

With school on mid-term break Salifu starts to come every day on his bicycle to help out. He is all smiles and full of greetings in the four local languages he speaks. He pulls the most urgent cases out of the long queue of patients, produces still more wooden benches and mats out of nowhere, keeps records and an inventory of medicines in stock. She has more time to tend to malnourished babies and sores.

The Tuesday morning that she stays in bed, suffering from her first bout of malaria, a five-month-old baby dies after it goes into convulsions brought on by fever. The birth assistants flee, rather than cool the little overheated body.

"They think that when a child has convulsions, it is possessed by spirits," Salifu tells her that night. He has brought her some bitter liquid, which he calls tea, to treat the malaria. "They always run away. That's how it is. Please, you drink your tea."

"I can't, Salifu. Just the smell makes me want to vomit. I've taken chloroquine." She is not comfortable lying in bed while Salifu watches her. He often gives her the impression her white skin is translucent, that he is looking right into her, at her knotted-up insides. Sometimes she thinks he's causing the knots in her belly to form. She wishes he would leave, not hover around as though he's the nurse and she's the invalid. As soon as he goes she will fling the plastic tub of medicinal tea out the back door.

"This is better than chloroquine. How can you expect all your medicines to work here? Is there malaria in your country?"

She shakes her head.

"Then why would you think you know all the cures? This tea is made of local barks and leaves that we have always used to treat malaria. Trust me. Our doctors do know some things. Many things." He grins. "Particularly about ailments of the soul that lay you open for other, more physical ailments." Although he is looking at the far wall as he says this, she can feel his eyes on that little nub of pain deep inside her, much deeper than the malaria headache.

She doesn't want to talk to him about this. She doesn't want to talk to him at all right now. Sweat trickles down her forehead. "Salifu, please," she says.

He leaps to his feet. "I must leave you to sleep. You drink the tea and tomorrow you will feel better, in two days time you will be up and around, bringing forth babies again. Drink the tea, Barbara. It will help."

She does not dump out the tea but sips it all night, gagging but keeping it down. Salifu is right. She is back in the clinic on the third day. While she lay in bed, she planned a series of lectures for the assistants on the causes of convulsions and how to deal with them. But when she's back on her feet, she realizes there is no time for lectures. No time to think.

That day two women give birth unattended on Barbara's bed, because the birth slabs are occupied. They can get two women on the awful concrete slabs at one time, they discover, but even that emergency space-economizing measure cannot eliminate the problems. Anyway, she is beginning to wonder who came up with the idea that concrete birth slabs were an improvement on traditional birth methods in the relative comforts of mud huts.

She speaks to Salifu about the women's strength and pain thresholds. "They don't cry out, Salifu. Not one woman. Not even the teenage girls. They're strong." Salifu nods. "Some of them would be put under anaesthetic in my country, or at least given an epidural. Breech births and tearing are not enough to make them even whimper." Salifu nods again. He stifles a yawn. She's not telling him anything new, she can see. And anyway, it is late. They have been taking inventory together and the night has settled over the clinic like a soundproof blanket. Some nights even the insects are quiet.

"It makes me feel, well, unworthy somehow." She leans against the wall, realizing he has been watching her re-arranging things that are already arranged. There is a smile on his face. Is he amused by what she says or by what she does?

"It shouldn't," he says.

His hand closes over her elbow as he ushers her out of the clinic. "You have your own strengths and weaknesses. We have ours."

Brenda and Barbara usually close their Saturday in the Concorde Bar. This is the only bar in Langadi. By almost any standard, it's a dismal place overrun by flies and rats. But Barbara is slowly and inexplicably beginning to love the Concorde. The dirt no longer bothers her. It's just part of Langadi, and there's not much to be done about sand and dust that sweep down from the world's biggest desert and cover half a continent for six months of the year. And if the Concorde's owner has been able to get kerosene for the refrigerator, the beer and minerals are almost cool. The porch in front allows her a panoramic view of the village of Langadi, with its brown, mud-walled huts interspersed by a few tall kapok trees, a few shops with tin roofs and that white health clinic. Beyond that there are gnarled acacia trees and dust. This is how large her world has become.

"It is not easy in my country," says Brenda one Saturday, after they've exchanged tales of their lost husbands. "My husband decided he wanted another wife. That is illegal in our church, so he made up a story about my unfaithfulness and divorced me. The real trouble is that I can't bear children."

"He divorced you for that?"

Brenda laughs and Barbara admires her perfect teeth, the dimples on her chin, the sheen of sweat on her face that seems to glow in the yellow light of the hurricane lamp. "Barbara, you're something."

Brenda is drinking Fanta, but Barbara's had a bottle of beer and she feels lightheaded, giddy, happy. She's tempted to tell Brenda about Jim's sterility and how he divorced her for a man — see if that makes Brenda laugh. Decides against it. The beer has made her less discreet than usual, but not indiscreet enough to touch on the untouchable. "Brenda, why don't you find a new husband?" she asks.

"It's not easy-o! The men here, they're not serious. Especially if the wife can't give them children. How many children do I deliver every day and I can't bring forth one of my own? God works in strange ways."

"But what about someone like Salifu? He strikes me as a good man. A serious man."

Brenda laughs again, then looks skyward where two vultures are circling. Market day always draws vultures. Barbara wonders where they come from.

Talon? How do they know it's Saturday, that there will be meat and carrion in the market in Langadi?

When Brenda speaks, her voice is subdued. "He's taken, Barbara."

"Salifu? Taken? By whom?"

Brenda glances at Barbara quickly. "You mean you don't know?"

Barbara shakes her head, hoping Brenda will say more. But Brenda doesn't and she doesn't want to ask again. It embarrasses her that she doesn't know even that much about him. Annoys her that Salifu himself has never divulged a single thing to her about his personal life. Then again, she hasn't breathed a word to anyone but Brenda about her own, about Jim. Not even to her own mother, who thinks that they are just living apart, temporarily.

The next night after they have closed the clinic, Salifu comes out back to sit on her doorstep and drink tepid red hibiscus tea. She asks him questions, amazed that she has never done so before. Amazed, too, that he answers. She learns that he was born in Langadi, the son of an Abule mother and a Goroni father. His father was the chief of Langadi. But he is dead now.

"My father was a forward-looking man," Salifu says. "He sent me to a boarding school in Talon when I was seven. Then I went on to train as a teacher when I completed my A-levels."

"Are you married, Salifu?" she asks quietly, almost in a whisper, hoping to diminish the crass, loud sound of her curiosity.

He waits a long time before answering. And when he finally does he is staring into his teacup, murmuring as though he's reading his reply in the tea leaves there.

"I was married. My former wife came from the south. I met her when I was at teachers' college. Then we moved north to Talon. I was teaching there. But she hated it. She called it the 'bush'. Said the people were 'backward'. Imagine how she felt about Langadi. She came here only twice the entire time we were married. Last year, just before my father passed on, she moved back to the capital and took my three children with her. I still send her money for their schooling but I hear she is going to marry a rich contractor. I have not seen my children since she left."

"My husband left me, too, Salifu. But we didn't have any children for me or him to take."

"Sorry," he says. She wonders why he asks for no details. Is he not interested? Or is he too polite to pry? She's glad, either way. She knows that Jim can't hurt her any more but the humiliation can, and still does.

"Why did you leave Talon? Come back to Langadi?" she asks.

"I promised it to my father. The school had no teacher. Before my father died he begged me to return, to share my education with my brothers and sisters of the village. My father's rule was peaceful. A time of small prosperity and big hope in this area. He was a great statesman in a small state."

"State?" she says.

"Yes, the Goroni state. It includes everything between here and Talon. The Abule state starts on the other side of the river."

"I see."

"My mother was an Abule woman. She was my father's second wife. I think he married her to make peace between the Abule and the Goroni in this area. That was just around independence. Things were better then. That couldn't happen today; a chief marrying a woman from another tribe. We've moved backwards."

"What do you mean, peace?"

He glances at her, then away. "It goes back a long way, Barbara." She likes how he says her name — softly so it comes out almost like Baba.

"Tell me, Salifu, I'm interested. Really."

"The Goroni and the Abule are traditional enemies. The Abule live to the west of here; Kakadi is their capital, the seat of their chief. Long ago there were wars. After independence, my father and the chief in Kakadi kept the peace. They lobbied for development. The new chiefs are younger men and they lobby for power and land. If they have to they'll go to war for either."

"War? Between Langadi and Kakadi? Are you serious?."

He pauses and she feels she has said something wrong. "Sorry, I didn't mean to offend you, Salifu. I guess I have trouble understanding what they would accomplish by fighting."

"It is the same for me. But both the chiefs are young men, short on enlightenment and wisdom. They have visions of power, which neither has the right to possess. I am afraid these men will cause serious trouble."

"What kind of trouble?" She swallows the last of her tea. The picture of chiefs strutting about in tiny villages of wattle and daub expounding on power and glory makes her want to laugh. But at that moment, with Salifu's round eyes on her, she does not feel at all like laughing.

"You will see, Barbara. The new chiefs are full of treachery," he says. Then he smiles enigmatically. "You are tired. I am tired. I must go."

She wants to ask him to stay a little longer, to tell her more, but cannot bring herself to do so, not when he has that distant look on his face.

That night she lies on her mattress scratching at mosquito bites on her ankles. She is thinking about his face — the soft contours around his nose and his eyes, the tribal scars running up and down his cheeks. "We wear our addresses on our faces," he said once when she asked him about the scars. Her hands lie on her stomach but they are imagining the feel of his thin shoulders in those threadbare shirts in flamboyant colours which echo the vivacity of the savanna trees in full blossom during the drab faded days of the hot dry season. She hears the muted sound of his voice in the African night. Those polished vowels and slippery consonants. How has all of this crept up on her so silently? She does not sleep at all.

She goes to the clinic just after dawn. She feels a jubilation which emerges in snatches of happy popular tunes as she prepares swabs, syringes and birth instruments.

At seven thirty she opens the doors. The jubilation dies quickly. Where are the women and children? The assistants? Mary? It's Saturday, but there's no sign of Brenda either. There is no one here.

No one.

She walks outside into the sunshine, sneezing. Confused. What has happened? Here's the church and here's the steeple — open the doors, see none of the people, do you know the reason why? She recites this rhyme aloud. There is no one to hear her talking to herself. "Do you know the reason why?" she repeats, almost shouting.

"Barbara, sshh."

She whirls around, flushing. Brenda is coming around from the back in her green uniform. "Look at that," she whispers into Barbara's ear, pointing to the clinic.

Barbara looks.

At first she thinks Brenda must be drawing her attention to the grime on the walls. It has been so long since she has stood outside the clinic that she has not noticed how brown and dirty it has become in just ten months. Then she notices the red lettering over the door. Langadi Health Centre. The word Langadi has been painted out and just above it, in shaky red letters, still gleaming wet, someone has painted "Kakadi".

"Oh for heaven's sake," she says. "Is *that* why no one is here?"

"Yes, Barbara."

"That's ridiculous."

"No, it's not. It's disaster."

The morning heat bears down on her. The village is deathly quiet and no one comes to the health centre. It is as if someone has decided that it is contaminated with some deadly and highly contagious disease. Quarantined on the flat, empty plot of land. Cows munch contentedly on the few remaining blades of grass that have been missed by other livestock. There are no people to shoo them off today.

Barbara wonders if she should go to Talon and telephone the office in the capital. Brenda says she should. She decides to wait for a second opinion, the one she depends on, the one she needs, Salifu's.

By mid-morning, she is in a rage. "Brenda, how can they be so damn stupid? What difference does it make what the clinic is called? It's for everyone!"

"No, it's not. It's for women and children, mostly. And they don't count much here. Please don't use profane language. Especially not now."

"You know what I'm going to do? I'll paint the bloody name myself. Langadi-Kakadi Health Centre. As if a name matters." She storms out the doors, across the road, past the market — all deserted — to the fitter's shop that sometimes has a couple of cans of paint and a brush or two for sale. The doors are closed and there is a padlock keeping them that way. She tries to recall if she's ever seen anything padlocked in Langadi.

She heads off at a jog for Salifu's. She has only been there once, for a meal with his sister, Zenab, and several nieces and nephews. It is well outside the village and the sun on her head has made her feel faint long before she arrives. Zenab meets her at the door, says Salifu has gone to Kakadi. She says they had heard drums of war coming from Kakadi and Salifu has rushed there to try to negotiate something with his mother's family. Her English is poor. Barbara is doubtful that she has understood correctly. But the words "Go home, Barbara," are clear, like a cock's crow.

She is too angry to go home. She jogs back to town, glad she's lean these days and that the worst of the sun's heat is gone. She marches smartly to the Concorde Bar, hammers on the closed door and demands a bottle of beer.

A voice behind the door. "Madam Barbara, we are closed. We are all leaving Langadi. You must too."

"I don't care. Just give me a beer, and I'll take it with me."

"The beer is warm. Please go home."

"I don't care. Give me a beer."

"Please, Madam Barbara," he says as he opens the door and looks around before moving onto the small porch. "There be danger. I give you beer but I do tell you they come now and we be in danger. Brenda did go on a lorry to Talon. She say you must go. I go now. I foot it to my village."

She stares him down, as surprised as he is at her sudden stubbornness and rudeness. He brings her a beer, collects money and disappears back inside, closes the door. She is alone. She might be the last person on the face of the earth after doomsday.

She pulls a chair to the front of the veranda and sits down to drink the warm beer. She puts her feet up on the wobbly fence. It is not at all seemly, a nurse in a filthy white uniform with her feet in white shoes that are now dusted the colour of the baked earth, propped up like a rancher in a western saloon. But there is no one watching her except a cow and three goats, all of which look ready for the slaughterhouse. She clucks her tongue and the cow averts its eyes and ambles off. She has the impression it is shaking its head but decides that is just her mind misbehaving in the heat and the unnatural silence. The goats climb a small mountain of garbage and forage on yam peelings.

She shuts her eyes, swilling the tepid beer. She is sure that things will return to normal in the morning. She concentrates on making it happen. She would love to have another warm bottle of beer, and another, and another. She would like to get terribly drunk and let her thoughts swim away to a deserted beach with palm trees. Away from whatever danger there is here. Why does she feel no fear?

She pictures herself hammering on the door again, demanding more beer. But she's not drunk enough. She's only a little tipsy from the beer, which is indeed very warm. It has gone straight to her brain, bypassing her stomach, which is growling with hunger. She hasn't had anything to eat since last night.

Dusk descends on the town on a faint breeze and then the night settles in with stillness.

She looks at her watch but it's too dark to see the time. She stands up quickly, too quickly and feels dizzy. The indignant anger that sent her running three miles to Salifu's and back has been replaced with a feeling of loss that mounts as she nears the clinic and her home. Brenda is gone and the clinic is locked. She realizes suddenly how dull life would be if she didn't have the clinic to run and Salifu and Brenda for company. Strange — she has no other friends here. She sees hundreds of people every day, greets dozens, exchanges pleasantries with many, and yet only two are people she thinks she *knows*. Perhaps she is wrong. Perhaps she doesn't know them at all.

It is much too early to sleep and she is not tired after the first idle day in ten months. She thinks about things she should do, eat for example, but doesn't even know what food Mary has out there in the shed that serves as a kitchen and pantry. Anything Mary does have would require a lot of cooking. Anyway, she's no longer hungry.

She finds herself thinking about Salifu, then looks for something to keep her mind off him. But there is nothing. Jim and his lover and her house — even her mother — no longer exist except as elusive fragments of a shattered life that is no longer hers.

At nine o'clock she is listening to short-wave news and trying to write a letter to her mother. She can't think of anything to write and the BBC news is depressing; more outbreaks of fighting all over the world, in places she has never heard of. It takes some time before she becomes consciously aware of the roaring sound. At nine fifteen Salifu bursts through her door. Her initial thought is that he has received her telepathic messages and has come to scoop her up in his arms and tell her he knows how she is feeling because he feels it too, about her. She actually moves two steps forward.

"Barbara, you must leave. Everyone in the village has fled. They are coming."

"Who's coming? What are you talking about, Salifu?"

"The Abule are coming. Please, get your valuables. You can drive this night to Talon."

"Salifu, I've . . ." She stares at him, noticing how dirty, dishevelled and tired he looks. The first shot rings out, a popping sound and a whine, very close. It is followed by terrifying howls that only human beings can make. Howls women back home make in the final stages of labour; howls she has never heard here.

She runs straight into Salifu's arms, practically bowling him over. He grips her shoulders with surprising strength, pushing her away from him and looking up slightly into her eyes. "Barbara, now you must try to understand. They have started to fight. It began over ownership of the health centre but it has grown into a full-fledged ethnic clash. Thirteen are dead in Kakadi. The Langadi chief led his warriors there today and burned down their granaries. We have sent word to the military barracks in Talon but I don't know when they will arrive to stop it. The Abule have come and they want to destroy the clinic. You must go. Quickly. Now."

The roaring is louder now. Salifu is speaking directly into her ear. It is difficult to believe that the shouts and screams reaching her are human voices. A mob is not quite human, she thinks.

"I fear it is already too late," says Salifu. He keeps his arms on her shoulders, then pulls her to himself. This is when he should kiss her. She doesn't even know if men and women kiss here.

"Will you come with me, Salifu?" she is whispering. His hair and his beard tickle her face.

"No, I cannot." He has his hands lower now, around her waist. "But now I fear you cannot go either. They are already here."

More shots. There are screams. The smell of smoke is suddenly overwhelming. Salifu takes her hand and pulls her to the door. He opens it silently, pulls her down to a crouch behind him and they move that way behind the milkweed bush beside her front porch. Grass torches blaze and shadowy figures writhe in the eerie, flickering light. It is hard to separate the sounds from the sights and smells.

The orange glow of fires in the village lights the sky like a premature dawn. "The clinic will burn just as the village is burning," he says quietly, gripping her elbow. "It should never have been built here. I told them that when they built it. I told them they had to find a neutral site, between the villages. At the river, where Abule-land and Goroni-land overlap. They wouldn't listen."

"But Salifu, the health centre was here to save lives. How can they do this?" She breaks loose from his grip. She can hear the breaking of wood. "They're breaking down the doors. We have to stop them."

"You cannot stop them, Barbara," he says, his voice buried in the hot sounds of battle. "If you go there they will kill you, not because they want to but because you are in their way. You must hide in your house. They dare not touch that. If you interfere now, both sides will try to implicate you." He places a firm hand on her shoulder, turns her around, pushes her back inside. He slips the deadbolt across the door and closes the wooden shutters. He stands with his head bowed for a moment before he comes to her.

"They won't disturb us here. We will stay low." He extinguishes the flame in the lantern and she cannot see his face. She can only feel his hand as he pulls her with him, as he leads her to the mattress on her floor. She lies alone in the darkness, listening to the sounds of the crazed mob outside. She is terrified now. Shaking with the fear that she didn't know enough to feel all day. Salifu sits on the floor, close enough that she can smell him. He tries to calm her, tell her that the Abule do not hate her, will do nothing to her if she stays inside and out of their way. She starts to cry, the way she cried that day she arrived and he walked in on her — uncontrollable sobs.

"Stop," he says. "Please Barbara." His words do nothing. It is his hand on her forehead, the light sweep of his fingers over her cheeks and chin and then lower, on her shoulders, that makes her stop and roll over to meet him as he lies down next to her.

She is not sure when the sounds of the angry mob fade into silence. When they awake at dawn and open the door, they see the smoke from spent fires. There are birds singing, but the human population of Langadi is gone. The village has been gutted by fire. Salifu tunes in the national news. The first item on the news is that the First Lady, the President's wife, made a speech decrying teenage pregnancy. Then the news reader says that the army has been called to Langadi to stop an ethnic clash that has been sparked by a feud over ownership of the health centre.

In Langadi, there is still no sign of the army.

Salifu goes out back to boil water for tea and porridge. He tells Barbara to pack her things, that she must leave right after breakfast.

They are just finishing their porridge when five army trucks full of men in fatigues roar to a stop down the road, drowning the clinic in clouds of red dust. A few minutes later the country representative pulls up behind a blue police van. She wastes no time on pleasantries and appears not to see the ruin of the health centre. She says Barbara has been recalled to the capital where she will have a month to report on what happened. They will send her to a new posting then, probably in the south.

She is to follow with the police escort and the country representative. The military are moving through the village to check for casualties and have taken up positions on the outskirts of town. Salifu is taken for questioning, and Barbara refuses to leave before he returns. The country representative loses patience, says she has an important meeting in the capital early the next morning and drives away following the police van. Barbara agrees to meet her next day at the IFMC headquarters.

He comes just as she finishes her packing. He sits quietly on the old wooden chair with the broken plastic strings. He says that the army has imposed a curfew and that there will be an inquiry. Each side has hidden their dead and injured and is claiming victory over the other.

She stuffs the rest of her clothing into the suitcase, then sits on it to fasten the oyster locks. She looks up at Salifu, appealing to him to say something about her, and him. But he seems so dispassionate about the big tragedy all around them, how can she expect him to show passion for something so small and selfish as feelings they might have for each other?

She sighs and closes her eyes, readying herself for the departure. A few minutes later she hears the click of the deadbolt on the door and his footsteps as he comes to her. She holds back the tears until, on the other side of the ecstasy he has induced, they start to seep out onto her sweat-soaked face.

"Can't you come with me, Salifu?" she asks, finally. The words sound superfluous. She wipes her eyes. "The dust," she says, trying to smile.

He shakes his head. "I would like to but you know I cannot."

She counts off seconds, thinking that she deserves years not seconds of the happiness she feels with Salifu. He touches her face, turns it to his, holds it there between his hands.

"I can't go with you," he says. "I promised my father I would stay and teach my people. And now . . ."

"I understand, Salifu. It's okay." She tries to wrestle free. He holds her in place, inspecting her face. Then he rolls off her, onto his back.

"When peace is made, maybe in the next century, or the century after that, everything will have to be rebuilt. The school. The houses. Everything." His eyes seem to be shining. At first she thinks it's because he's already making plans for salvaging the peace and dreaming of Langadi with schools and health centres, of the bright future he is going to shape. She props herself on her elbows so she's looking down into his face. He closes his eyes and she sees the tears seeping out from under his lids.

"Salifu. You can't do anything here now. Please, think about coming with me. You can teach anywhere. We can save money and when the time is right, when there's peace, you can come back. You're not breaking your promise to your father." She touches his face, and he opens his eyes.

"Do you believe that?"

She nods.

"Why do you ask me to come with you, Barbara?"

"Isn't it obvious?"

"I don't know. I don't know white women."

"You know this one. Better than anyone else."

"I would like to come with you. Not because I want to leave here. Because you cannot stay here and . . . I would like you to be my wife."

She will file those words away, pull them out in years to come, when Salifu is no more than a happy memory. Examine them. Replay them. Hear them again and again. Right now, though, she can't because she's afraid if she does, they will disappear, or be taken away from her like everything else she's ever had that was good. "I thought you were already taken, Salifu. That's why I didn't..."

"Who told you I was taken?"

"Brenda."

"She's clever, Brenda. Then she knew before either you or I."

Barbara cannot breathe, let alone speak. Happiness can be suffocating too.

"We must go," he whispers. "But we will come back. One day we will come back."

Returning

The city felt terribly different. Had it changed so much in three years? Or had she forgotten the squalor, the poverty, and the heat and the despondency she could feel when Africa was all around her. Karen wondered if the three years in Canada had reduced her tolerance, broken down her defences just like her body's immunity against malaria and the heat.

The heat. She brushed the wet hair back off her forehead and adjusted the sunglasses on her nose. She felt people were staring at her as she trudged along the road. She would have liked to inform all of them — those aloof and smug expatriates in their air-conditioned cars and the hawkers who hooted to her to come and buy — that she had lived here for five years. She had returned for a job interview.

For that, she was supposed to present a seminar on a subject of her choice and field questions from the research staff afterwards. The institute concentrated on the causes and effects of desertification and she had prepared a seminar on bush fires in the Sahel. She had worked as a freelance journalist in this city. She had thought herself quite an expert on the country, as arrogant as that would have sounded had she said it aloud. She never had but she had thought it many times.

It wasn't the thought of tomorrow's interview or seminar that was causing her stomach pains, making her breath come as gasps as she walked along the Avenue of Liberty. She had already decided the job wasn't for her. She had applied on a whim. The job advertisement, *Writer/Editor, International Institute for Studies into Desertification*, came from *The Economist*. That alone had impressed Karen, smacked to her of success, of making it.

She had never made it and suspected she never would. She could never support her husband and daughter with her irregular and meagre income as a freelance writer but at the same time she didn't want a job where someone told her what to write.

So Paul, a management consultant, pulled in the money. He paid for the house; she paid for a bathroom mirror. He paid for the floor tiles; she paid for the broom to sweep them. She had never been on the inside of a career path, never had a permanent job that offered her designated office space and the comfort of a monthly salary. Paul told her it would be good for her to be on the inside for awhile. For appearances' sake she had applied for this job.

Six months later she was on the shortlist and back here in this city in a landlocked country on the edge of the Sahara going to an interview for a job she didn't want.

She had been excited about returning. She had thought she would enjoy a few days in this city where she had been so fulfilled. She would spend hours in the market buying the souvenirs that she had neglected to buy when she lived here. She would walk in and surprise old friends, visit her old house and housestaff.

What old friends?

The sellers on the road were driving her mad — they would tear her to shreds in the market. All she wanted to do was get to the post office and call home. Make sure Paul and Sarah were okay. Make sure they were missing her as much as she missed them.

It was a long walk from the hotel to the centre of town. Somehow she'd forgotten how hard it was to get around the capital without a car or a moped. She'd mistakenly thought the institute would provide her with a vehicle and driver throughout her stay.

Two boys moved into step with her, one on each side. She grasped her moneybelt protectively. She wondered if thieves had perfected ways of removing moneybelts the way they had perfected tricks to get handbags off shoulders and money out of pockets. A man in the airplane had told her the city had become a "den of thieves". It had always had a lot of thieves, though in her five years here she'd never run up against them. She had always thought that even thieves knew she *belonged*.

"You want to buy, Madam?" The boy on her right held up a small bicycle made of wire. It was ingenious. He made the pedal go round with his hand and the back wheel spun.

Sarah would like it. "How much?" she asked.

"Two thousand."

She rolled her eyes and grinned knowingly at the boy. "I'm not a tourist," she said. "I lived here you know. Be serious. How much is your real price?" She had even perfected the jerky accent that marked the street English spoken here.

"Ah, you're from here," said the boy on her left. "We could tell, Madam. You like our city."

She smiled, revelling in their flattery even as she told herself not to be taken in by it. "Okay, okay, just tell me how much," she said, avoiding their eyes and looking straight ahead. On both sides of the road were almost solid rows of kiosks made of corrugated tin or cardboard, manned by hundreds of people who sat there all day, every day. Desperate to sell. Watching for likely buyers, someone with money. Tourists and foreigners, mostly. The road itself was clogged with vehicles bearing development agency logos, windows up, engines and air-conditioners roaring. Development at work.

Paul had driven one of those Land Cruisers and shuffled papers and plans for development projects here. She had never questioned it then. Where had her cynicism sprung from now?

Mopeds surged around her, speeding among the vehicles and up and down the dusty makeshift marketplace on the shoulders of the road. There was little room or safety for pedestrians. She was aware of how conspicuous she was on the roadside. The vendors pleaded with her to come and buy and when that failed, insulted her because she didn't stop to admire their wares and exchange greetings. On foot, she realized, she was a nobody. She hadn't done much walking when they lived here. Now she suddenly felt reduced to the level of a peasant woman. Not even a bicycle to ride on.

The boys were too close to her. She knew — had heard at least — how fast the thieves were when they decided to make their move. One would push you and the other would make the grab for money or necklaces. She glanced behind her. They often came up from behind, too. They worked in groups.

"Okay, for you, Madam, because you're from here, the price is only one thousand." The boy forced the bicycle into her hand and brushed his palms together, as though the deal were sealed.

She pushed it back into his hand, conscious that her moneybelt was momentarily unprotected. She looked into his eyes. He was no longer smiling and his eyes were hooded by heavy lids. Shifty, she thought.

"Madam, don't be like that. It's fine work, you see how the wheel goes around. Nice for Nasarah."

For the merest fraction of a second, she grinned. So he did remember her and her daughter born in this city. But then she knew she was wrong, her own little joke had tripped her up. "Nasarah" meant "white person" here. She had named her daughter Sarah, thinking that if you said it fast enough it sounded like "Nasarah". White Person. She had thought herself very clever.

"Go away," she said to the boys. "Maybe tomorrow I'll buy, but not now." They didn't leave. The boy on the right grabbed her right arm. She wrenched free, angry now.

"Stop it," she said. "I'm old enough to be your mother. You're a small boy. Don't you respect your elders?"

They laughed and exchanged some words in their own language, keeping stride with her. She was sure they were mocking her.

She stopped suddenly, feigning interest in goods laid out on the wooden cart parked on the roadside in front of her. It was heaped with second-hand clothes and shoes which came from Europe and North America by the container-load and were sold to clothe the whole continent in cast-offs. She fingered a pair of children's sneakers, lime green and bearing the all too familiar images of Ninja turtles. The frippery — the faded t-shirts and polyester slacks — was unappealing. Three young men moved in around her. They picked up shapeless shorts and blouses for her inspection, urged her to buy. The second-hand clothing was called "Dead White Man" here; the people couldn't believe that anyone living would give away clothing with so many years of wear left in it.

She flapped her hands and smiled at them. "No, I'm just looking."

She glanced at her watch. It was almost noon here, early morning at home. Paul and Sarah would be eating breakfast. She pictured them in the gleaming wooden kitchen, buttering thick pieces of whole-wheat toast in the cosy darkness of the winter morning. Paul would probably be listening to the news, half listening to Sarah telling him stories she had made up or dreamed — wherever it was her fantastic tales of monsters and wild animals came from. She wanted to get them before they left the house — Paul for his office and Sarah for kindergarten. She wouldn't tell Paul how nervous she felt here. He wouldn't understand. Did she? She had felt she belonged here. But it all had to do with their house, their friends, their refuge from the sellers, beggars, thieves.

"I felt so much a part of that miserable city," she used to tell friends after she and Paul returned to Canada. Here they had socialized with ambassadors, Prominent People in Development, the international press corps. She'd even interviewed the President on several occasions — that young army captain with good ideas, better intentions and very poor security. Shortly after they left, he had been killed in a coup.

The institute driver who picked her up at the airport this morning had droned on about the staggering rate of unemployment in the city, the poverty, the difficulty of making ends meet since the coup. He said he knew of women who had killed their youngest children to make sure that there would be enough food to keep the rest of the family alive. She didn't necessarily believe it but it was typical of the kind of thing she would use to beef up articles.

The only local people who had written to Paul and her were Emil, their former night watchman, and Alyssa, their former babysitter. She had thought she had made more of a mark on people here, had more friends than that. The expatriate friends had moved to other posts in other countries — the others had obviously not really been friends at all. Or maybe she should have written to them.

She felt utterly alone as she walked down that crowded road in the midday sun. She considered taking a small detour to see how her house looked now. She wondered if the mango trees she had planted were producing fruit yet. She wondered if the cane furniture was still on the shaded patio in front. She had not liked the British man who came to replace Paul and who took over the house. She'd only seen him twice and he had shown little interest in hearing how much she and Paul liked their "African home". He dismissed her stories with a wave of his pipe, saying he preferred East Africa. He probably wouldn't remember her. She couldn't even come up with his name.

She decided it would be unwise to visit the house that was no longer hers. She certainly didn't want to run into Emil, the night watchman. The last letter they had received from him spoke of a long and incurable illness. He said he'd lost so much weight that he doubted they would recognize him any more. There had been a finality about that letter. "I want to thank you and Madam for all you have done for me. I will remember you on the day I die." Not "until the day I die" but "on the day I die".

Naturally she and Paul had assumed the worst. AIDS. She wrote back, a short chatty note full of platitudes and vain hopes that Emil was getting better. Paul enclosed a cheque for one hundred dollars.

That was months ago. By now, she supposed he would be dead or very close to it. She didn't want to see him if he was nothing but bones and sores.

She glanced around, wary of anyone who seemed to be moving too close to her. It had been a mistake to wear the gold earrings and pendant — they were like advertisements to thieves. But they were from here and she had put them on hoping they would somehow show that she was part of the place.

Part of the place?

Ahead, vultures circled high over the hospital. It was a sprawling complex of grimy buildings and filthy labs, where most people went as only a last resort, usually to die. Sarah had been born there. Karen had gone against the advice of her friends and her husband and stayed here to deliver her child. Her blood had soaked the birthing bed and the floor of the delivery room. She had been lucky — any more and she would have needed a blood transfusion. The blood was not tested for HIV back then. That birth — her blood spilled and the pain she had endured — had made her feel she had earned herself a place in this country.

The ache of missing her daughter hit like a wave, taking away her breath, submerging her in longing to be at home. Sarah's wide brown eyes haunted her; she pictured her looking up at her from a plate of dinner. "Mommy, do you know something?" How often did she fail to listen, to answer her daughter's questions, to invite her to continue her tales? She stumbled, and a solicitous young man grabbed at her. "Madam, are you okay?"

She jerked free, reaching instinctively for her moneybelt. He backed away, melting into the sea of people in front of the hospital gate.

She looked behind her, hoping again to find a taxi. None. The city she had known had turned mean, she decided. She could die here, on the spot, and no one would care. People would gather out of curiosity. "Oh look at the dead white woman." Someone would probably deftly remove the gold earrings, the fertility pendant and the moneybelt before the authorities came to remove her body. Then everyone would walk away and forget her. She leapt out of the way of a speeding motorcycle.

She kept walking, looking neither left nor right. She knew she must appear like one of those tourists she and Paul had occasionally spoken so disparagingly of — bargain tourists here for cheap adventure and tacky trinkets.

I'm not a tourist, she told herself. I belong. I know this city.

Everything seemed to have changed, yet nothing had changed. The armless boy under the traffic light, who used his feet to hold the bowl and catch coins tossed from passing vehicles, was still there. Three years since she had thought about him and there he was. All that time she'd been away he'd been sitting here, catching coins.

From Canada, it had been hard to imagine that the city was still there. Like a tree falling in the woods without ears to hear it — did this city exist when she wasn't here to see, smell and hear it? Did she exist to these people only as a source of money? Couldn't they see she understood their problems and cared? She had always thought of herself as a caring person.

Her only ties here now were a night watchman with AIDS and a babysitter who wrote once every year. Was that all she had to show for five years of her life? She fingered the gold earrings as she waited for the light to turn green at the United Nations Roundabout. The familiar United Nations monument stood in the centre. It was a skeletal globe of metal, on which the blue continents seemed to float. It was revolving slowly. She watched as North America came into view. She had never noticed before that they had left the Atlantic provinces off the map. Her province and her home didn't even exist.

"Hey Mademoiselle, are you lost? Or crazy?" She started as the moped whizzed past her and the passenger on the back grinned back at her, vaguely curious, the way she would often smile at the naked lunatics who roamed the city roads. She'd forgotten where she was, forgotten the traffic light.

She ran quickly across the road as the light switched from green to red. A white Peugeot headed directly for her and she sprinted to avoid being hit. The man behind the wheel didn't swerve or brake. If she hadn't run, he would have flattened her. Was she now invisible?

In front of the post office she kept both hands on her moneybelt and quickened her pace. The area had always been infested with thieves. And beggars. There was the beggar woman with the twin girls. She was in her usual place, on the red sandy ground directly in front of the block housing post office boxes. When you went to check for mail each day you had to step around her to enter.

The woman showed her toothless grin to Karen, her palm out for alms. Surely this woman must recognize her. Karen had given her a coin almost every day for five years. The twins had come into the world at the same time as Sarah. This beggar woman and Karen had shared pregnancies, touched each other's swollen bellies and laughed together.

Karen smiled now. "How are you, Madam? And the twins?"

The woman rolled her eyes skyward and rubbed her belly with one hand. Her t-shirt was torn and her wrapper poorly wound around her waist. Her brown stomach was baggy. The other hand remained outstretched, waiting for charity, something to be put in it that she could put in her belly. Good God, she was pregnant again. Karen looked at the twin girls, their tiny thin arms and their round bellies, too round to be healthy. They sat, one on each side of their mother, dumb. They had not grown at all. Sarah, also four, was twice, no three times their size. Their faces were wizened, eyes lifeless, their bodies were those of malnourished toddlers. She bent down to smile at them. They looked back at her, unsmiling and silent. She'd seen more life and curiosity in the eyes of roaming sheep. She reached out for their hands, but they remained motionless. She stood up too fast and put her hands to her eyes while the blackout passed.

The woman was still gesticulating, pointing now to her mouth. Not a hint of recognition.

"Don't you remember me?" Karen asked. "My daughter, Sarah? Same age as your twins?"

"Nasarah," said the woman. Her toothless grin looked like the opening to a dark hole that had no end. The white enamel bowl beside her was empty.

"I used to live here," Karen persisted. "You don't remember me?" She was desperate for some sign of recognition from the beggar woman, a sign that she remembered all those coins, those shared touches. She knew it was foolish but she couldn't seem to stop herself.

"My husband with the beard," she said. "Surely you remember him." She drew a pointed beard in the air under her chin.

The woman held up the bowl, unblinking.

Karen reached for her moneybelt, remembering she had no small change. "Later," she said to the woman. "I'll come back."

The woman's grin faded. She coughed and spat a bloody gob that landed near Karen's feet. Karen walked quickly away. She had made a fool of herself in front of the beggar woman and all those around who had watched and listened. She had demanded recognition and gratitude; for what? If the woman had remembered her, or even pretended to, Karen would, she knew, have given her the five thousand coni note in her belt. Instead she had walked off and given her nothing.

She glanced at her watch, trying to keep the present and the past at bay. She would have to hurry if she was going to catch Paul in the house.

"Madam. Madam."

She paused, with one foot already on the steps leading to the telephone office. "Madam. It's true. It's you. You're here!" A man in a tidy white shirt and pressed slacks, Sunday attire, was running towards her, with a beaming smile. She turned to meet him. At last, someone who recognized her.

"Yes, I'm back," she said, examining his smiling face, urging herself to connect it to someone she knew, had known. He looked like so many young men in the city — very lean, neat, tidy, pleasant, friendly. His arms hung stiffly by his sides. There was something innocent and almost submissive in that stance, something studied and practised, an offer of respect. An admission of subordination.

"You don't remember me?" he asked. Confusion and disappointment clouded his smile.

"The face is familiar, yes," she said. "But I can't quite place . . ."

"Madam, where you sleep."

Her mind leapt, clutched at possibilities. Her house. Could this have been one of Emil's friends? Someone she should know and recognize? She'd heard many white people say they had trouble telling Africans apart. She had scoffed at them.

"Watchman," said the man, guiding her gently.

She faltered. Emil had written that they would not recognize him any more. "Emil?" she said, suddenly relieved. "Is that you?"

His smile flowed back into place. "Yes, yes. It's me."

She reached for his hand and shook it heartily. "You've grown so very thin," she said. "I would never have recognized you." She felt embarrassed then. How could she not have recognized someone she had known so well, seen every day for five years? He seemed unable to contain his pleasure. He slapped his thighs with his hands and grinned.

"How is your, ah, sickness?" she asked.

"It's okay."

"You really are thin. But you look fine. What about the sickness?"

"I take medicine," he answered.

"And the work? You're still there? Your new master is still breaking your feet?" She chuckled, quoting excerpts of his letters back to him. He had complained bitterly in letters that his new "master" — the man who had taken over the house, furniture and housestaff — was a mean and nasty man, with a mean and nastier wife from Tanzania who, like her husband, hated West Africa.

"Yes, yes. I'm still there."

"So, how is it? The new madam is still lazy as ever?"

"Yes, yes." He joined in Karen's laughter.

"It's wonderful to see you. Paul and I were so afraid, well you know, when you wrote that letter that you weren't well . . ." Her sentence wrapped itself around her tongue, which felt dry and swollen. They had sent the money to him and written him off. Assumed the worst. Jumped to conclusions. The guilt again.

"I'm travelling on my moped," he said.

"That's nice." She wondered if he would offer her a ride. Perhaps she could get him to drop her off at Alyssa's later.

"You see, it's broken down," he continued, pointing vaguely across the street. Under each tree, self-taught roadside mechanics had set up their "fitter" shops and were busy disassembling and re-assembling mopeds.

"Oh, sorry. What's wrong with it?"

He paused. "The motor. I just want to have it repaired."

He grinned sheepishly and dipped his head a little. "I have no money with me."

"Emil," she said, mocking a madam's consternation with a houseboy who makes the same mistake twice. He shrugged.

"Okay, how much?" She opened the zip on her moneybelt, remembering that she still had no small change, only a bundle of five thousand coni notes. She glanced up to see what she might buy from one of the kiosks for a few conies, to get the small change to help him out. She withdrew a five thousand coni note.

"Nine thousand," he said.

"What? What kind of repairs are they doing? Are they going to put in a new motor, or what?" She laughed. She had thought of giving him a few hundred.

"Yes," he said.

"Okay. But I need some change first."

"Oh, ten thousand will do," he said. She paused, then dipped into her moneybelt and handed him two notes. He thanked her as he raced off, perilously dodging traffic. He disappeared behind the gas station across the street.

As she turned to go into the post office, she thought what a small town this capital really was — half a million people and she always ran into someone she knew. Then she pondered at the changes in Emil. How weight loss could completely transform someone's entire face, make cheekbones seem more prominent and cheeks disappear. But what of the tribal marks? Emil should have had three rows of the long curved scars running down each side of his face, which had fascinated her every time she looked at him, which had always reminded her of something a lion's claws had made.

She raced into the air-conditioned telephone office. She decided she had not really looked well at his face, otherwise she would have noticed the tribal marks. It was embarrassing not to have recognized him right away.

Inside the telephone office, another voice and face from the past. "Madam Karen!"

"Alyssa!"

"Madam. It's true. It's you. You're here!"

"I was just on my way to visit you," Karen said. "I have a gift for you from Sarah." It wasn't true — she had neglected to bring any gifts; had thought more about what she would buy in the city than what she should give. She would have to buy Alyssa something.

"Madam, it's wonderful you are here. How's Sarah?" Alyssa asked.

"Oh, she's growing tall. Who's this?" Alyssa was holding the hand of a little girl, blond and blue-eyed.

Alyssa bent and scooped the girl up into her arms. "This is Ilse," she said, kissing the girl on the nose, while Ilse giggled. Karen felt betrayed. Alyssa had never written that she had a new job, with a new family. Alyssa belonged to Sarah.

"I just saw Emil," Karen said. "He's been sick."

"Emil? Oh, he's fine now. He thought he had AIDS but he was afraid to have a test. Then he finally went. He said you sent him some money. He didn't have AIDS at all. He had four different kinds of worms. He's big and strong again now. He has a new job too. He's a driver for Ilse's father."

"He didn't tell me that," Karen said.

Alyssa shook her head and laughed. "Emil," is all she said.

"But how long are you staying, Madam Karen? You will come and visit us, tomorrow? I am waiting for my new madam to come and pick us now, so I'm not at home."

She thought quickly, glancing again at the small girl in Alyssa's arms. "Well, Alyssa. I would love to, but I'm going to be very busy. I'm here for some, ah, work. And I fly out, ah, tomorrow."

"So soon?" Alyssa looked sincerely disappointed.

"I must rush," Karen said, "I have to use the telephone. Wonderful to see you, Alyssa. Ilse." She tweaked the little girl's cheek, and forced a smile. Then she walked past them to the telephone wicket and said she wanted to call Canada.

Her hand shook as she dialled the familiar number and listened to it ringing — on the wall over her desk, on the table beside her bed, on the bench in Paul's workshop. Three telephones ringing and still no answer. She sat down on the stool, summoning her resolve, numbing herself, so she could go back out there.

On the roadside she stood, breathing moped fumes and praying for a taxi to pass. Heat waves made the road, and its mostly white vehicles, swim before her eyes. She eyed pedestrians coming her way, watching for potential thieves. A young man wearing a long-sleeved white shirt, grey flannel trousers and a tie met her eyes. He held a plastic pocket camera in his left hand. He broke into a smile and a run.

"Madam!" He stood before her. "You are here. It's true."

This was a face she was sure she had never seen before. Still, she didn't want to be rude. "I don't know you," she said.

She was still watching for a taxi. He blocked her view.

"I'm waiting for a taxi," she said, stepping back.

He moved closer. "Madam, don't you recognize me?"

"No," she said, truly puzzled. "I don't."

"Neighbours," he said. "Where you slept."

"I don't think so," she said. "What's your name?"

He paused. "Peter."

"Oh, Peter," she said, still not making any connection. "You're very chic today. Where are you going? What are you going to photograph?"

He held up the skeleton of a camera, looking embarrassed. "I need batteries," he said. "You see, Madam, I'm travelling on my moped but it's broken down."

She didn't say anything.

"Just there," he said, pointing towards the fitters. "You see I don't have any money. If you could just give me three hundred and fifty conies, I could fix it." She stared at him. "I mean, since we know each other."

She started to walk away.

He followed. "Madam, you haven't understood. Since we're old friends, I thought you could . . ."

"Oh, Peter," she said. "I understand very well." She adjusted her sunglasses and moved quickly away. She felt angry and betrayed. But under that was a layer of humiliation that was burning up five years of her life as though they were as inconsequential and flimsy as toilet tissue. How could she have been so deceived — by herself? She spoke to no one, met no one's eyes as she walked. She would return to the comforts of the air-conditioned hotel, and stay there, where she could pretend at least that she was not in Africa, until she could leave this city and continent — forever.

Love by dictation

When she was twenty-seven her husband took her to Africa. He had landed a posting in the embassy in an obscure West African country, and he took up his new role with a vengeance.

Margo had *time*, not just during the days but also on weekends when Geoff was travelling and in the evenings when he attended business dinners. She didn't know what to do with all that time, not here where she had no job or housework. The housestaff left her with nothing to do. If she came home from a little shopping, they would take everything out of her hands before she could get out of the car. Apparently a white woman wasn't supposed to carry her own handbag into the house. She wasn't even supposed to do the shopping.

"Sorry, Margo," Geoff said after they'd been there three months and she finally found a word for her condition — boredom. "Maybe you should join a club. You'll get used to it and make new friends and then you'll never want to go home."

She tried to make friends other diplomatic spouses but felt she was too dull and gloomy for them. She didn't play tennis which was how many expatriates here seemed to cement friendships. She didn't have children so she was excluded from social events at the international school and kids' birthday parties. There were parties for the adults from time to time but she hadn't mastered the art of conversation with worldly strangers who dropped the names of third world countries they had lived in as though they were as commonplace as brands of toothpaste.

"Now what's wrong, Margo?" Geoff asked her on the way home one evening. "You complain that you have nothing to do and when we go out, you want to go home at nine thirty."

"I'm not good at small talk, Geoff. I don't know what to say."

He put his arm around her. "No one expects you to talk or say anything. Most people there really just want to talk themselves. All you have to do is listen and smile. Maybe you're still trying too hard to please everyone." He gave her a peck on the cheek. "Your only problem is that you're still a sweet and innocent small-town girl."

After a few months she noticed that he stopped calling her sweet.

"Stop complaining and enjoy your leisure. You've got a beautiful house staffed from top to bottom with maids, cooks, gardeners and drivers. Why don't you do some volunteer work? The International Women's Association is putting on a fashion show to raise funds for the orphanage. Why don't you help on that?"

"They asked me to be a model *in* their fashion show. Geoff, you know I'm not cut out for that. Just because I've changed continents doesn't mean I have to pretend to be something I'm not. I just don't belong here."

"But this is our career, Margo. You're going to have to try to adapt, or else, well . . ." He cleared his throat as if the hamburger and not his thoughts were choking him.

"Or else, Geoff?" She put her knife down carefully beside the plate, blade facing in as it should. "Or else what?" The fork was still in her left hand. She realized suddenly how ridiculous she felt in the pretentious dining room — two of them at a table that would seat twenty, while she hid her bruised pride as she rode along on Geoff's coat-tails. She and Geoff had even taken to eating hamburgers with a knife and fork, without noticing, commenting, or laughing about their new airs.

"You're impossible, Margo. I can't say anything right. I might as well say nothing. I'll leave you alone to enjoy your misanthropy this afternoon. I'm going back to work. At least the problems there are real." He stood up, slamming the table with his palms as he did, making the silver embassy cutlery leap and rattle.

"Geoff, please don't walk out now," she said. "Please. Let's try and talk. . ." she said, as the swinging door snapped shut, leaving her alone in the air-conditioned buzz of the dining room. This fighting was new. Friends back home always said what she had smugly thought, that she and Geoff had "an ideal relationship". Male friends said how lucky Geoff was; female friends told her how lucky she was. They had a bisexual friend who said both of them were lucky.

She pushed away her plate, got up and moved aimlessly through the house, a spacious and airy two-storey villa with a balcony wrapped around each floor like a hug. The house was like an elaborate gown that she could admire on someone else, but which she could not step into without feeling like a fraud. Geoff grew up in a house like this. She didn't. She grew up in a pulp-mill town in a small bungalow, one bathroom, two bedrooms, one kid, a devoted and loving mother, a distant but decent father who worked as an accountant in the mill. With her mother dead and her father lost to Alzheimer's Geoff had become her whole family.

In the bedroom she threw herself on the bed. She lay on her back, staring through the glass doors at the leafy rubber tree that shaded the upstairs balcony as resolutions began to form.

She chose a sensible shirt dress with blue and white stripes and slipped on navy pumps. Then she packed her C.V. and a letter of recommendation from the Home for Challenged Children in Ottawa into one of Geoff's tidy briefcases and set out in the miniature Peugeot with Mohammed at the wheel. He was silent and officious in his embassy uniform.

She went first to the Ministry of Education but was sent on to the Ministry of Health. There the plump young secretary to the Director of Mental Health dialled for her boss while Margo waited, fascinated by the secretary's bright green fingernails. The woman had something equally shiny, but violet, on her eyelids which drooped as she conferred over the telephone with the director. She hung up, told Margo to sit while she typed a letter of introduction to another man in another office; the green prongs on her fingertips seemed to claw at the keys of the typewriter.

"You take this to the Minister of Social Welfare," she said, with a generous smile. "He is in charge of all children's homes."

The minister greeted her with a bountiful smile and a familiarity that suggested he already knew her.

"Madam, we are desperately short of people with your knowledge, qualifications and goodwill. Indeed, the question is not whether you will be permitted to do volunteer work but where we could best put your many talents to best use. You would be infinitely useful in the hospital, equally valuable in the mental hospital and of course essential in our orphanage. Please give me a day or two to consider this in greater depth and to discuss it with the Director of Mental Health. I will ring you as soon as we have decided how best to take advantage of your generous offer. How is your husband, by the way? He is such a competent man. However he has yet to beat me at tennis." He laughed loudly and she joined in.

Two days later the minister called to inform her personally that she could start as soon as she wished, running the school at the orphanage. He said she should call him at any time if there was something she needed, materials or advice. Anything at all, he said.

That was followed by six months of hard work as she tried to sort out her role at the orphanage. The attendants were accommodating but they didn't always appreciate her methods of teaching the children. She forbade what they called "caning". This was a struggle. There were sixty-one children in the Alimata Children's Home, ranging from six months to sixteen years. About a third of them had some sort of emotional or mental handicap. She guessed that a lot of the signs of mental retardation could have been traced to malnutrition in the early months of their lives, or even intrauterine lives, but didn't dwell on what might have been. She had resolved that if this were going to work she would have to make the best of everything that came her way, without trying to decide how it came to be.

She divided the children up into groups according to age and achievement levels, not separating those with handicaps from those without. They all had one large handicap; they were living in dismal conditions, with only three housemothers. Many of them had never been shown how to hold a pencil or a pair of scissors. The housemothers were too few, too poorly paid and too poorly supplied with essentials.

A few phone calls to the Minister of Social Welfare with pleas for materials for the school resulted in a lot of promises but nothing the kids could put their hands on — pencils and scissors for example.

She attended a meeting of the International Women's Association and solicited funds (the profits from their fashion show) for school materials. On Geoff's recommendation she also approached the Inner Wheel of the Rotary Club for money for a blackboard and tables and chairs for the classroom. This donation was noticed by the press, and a picture of her standing beside the blackboard with some of the children appeared on the front page of the daily newspaper, beside the mandatory daily photograph of the President.

She and Geoff now had lots to talk about over dinner; she could contribute something to the conversations rather than just listen to his analysis of life at the top. He didn't know much about life at the bottom.

The children at the home smothered her with their affection and needs. Her despondency had vanished. Now it was she who wanted a little more time to herself. Geoff seemed proud of her, but even that annoyed her because his pride seemed patronizing and exaggerated. He was slightly too amorous and affectionate — more than he had been back home where it all seemed more spontaneous. His studiously husbandly behaviour pleased her one minute, irritated her the next. Still, at least they would make it out of the country *together* at the end of the posting. Perhaps by then Geoff would have deflated a little, shrunk down to his normal size. Noticed that the VIP status the Africans accorded him was titular, a perk of the post, mere protocol and not a reflection of anything *very important*.

That was before *the* visit to the orphanage. She was leading the preschoolers in a rousing rendition of the *Farmer in the Dell*. "The farmer takes a wife. The farmer takes a wife. Hi-ho-the-derry-ooo..."

The children stopped singing first. Not noticing immediately that something in the room had changed, she stood in front of her silent pupils, bellowing "the derry-ooo" like a lovelorn cow. She stopped abruptly when she realized the children were staring past her. She turned to admonish the intruders who were whispering behind her back.

She had never seen the President in person before, but she recognized him instantly from the photograph that, by presidential decree, hung in a prominent place in every single public building in the country. He was not tall, not at all the majestic figure portrayed by the state press or television. He was wearing a simple military outfit that gave no indication of his rank which was captain.

Larger and much more imposing than the President were the two bodyguards who stood just behind him on either side like eagles perched on his shoulders.

"Good morning, children. Good morning, Mrs. Ogilvie. Please do not let us disturb you."

"Good morning, your excellency, Mr. President. You've surprised us. Caught me completely off guard, in fact." She laughed, and her nervousness rippled through the children in half-suppressed giggles. "Children, say good morning to your Head of State."

"Good morning, Mr. President. How are you? We are fine. Thank you." Childish little voices in a chorus of rehearsed greetings. So innocent. They did not really comprehend just who this man was. Then again, neither did she.

Geoff spoke disparagingly of him. "He's a dictator, a man with a pretentious socialist dogma and friends in all the wrong places. He has a vast fortune in Swiss banks," he said every time he found a new audience for his analysis of politics here. "He talks tough socialism and then lets the multinationals play hopscotch all over his country. His fortune is in the billions and he's claiming the country can't repay its debts because it's one of the least developed. He's also got a human rights record written in blood."

She stared at the President. This man?

"Please, continue with what you are doing, Mrs. Ogilvie. I am not in a hurry. It gives me enormous pleasure to see someone taking such an interest in our less fortunate children." He nodded and one of his bodyguards, fully armed, pulled forward one of the tiny chairs of the children. The Head of State sat down on this miniature seat and folded his arms, like the judge in a miniature talent show.

She turned her back on him, faced the children. "Okay children," she said, clapping her hands. "Let's sing 'row row row your boat.' This row starts, then this row, then this row, each row is going to row, row, row, to make the round. Ready?"

The soles of her feet had begun to sweat and she felt unsteady inside her shoes. Her trembling and lack of concentration were contagious; the children made a sorry mess of the round they knew so well.

She turned around, her face hot. "Mr. President, with all due respect, I am afraid that you make us all a little too nervous to continue."

"Of course, I understand. It's one of the sad truths of this job of mine that everyone is nervous of me." His teeth were perfect, pure white and lined up like two lines of sailors on parade.

"I'm so glad you understand, Sir." She wondered what to do with her hands; her knees were banging together. When he stood up, she was looking directly into his eyes. He should have been taller.

The housemothers were in an uproar. They and all the children gathered at the windows to watch as the President and his men got into an innocuous Peugeot sedan and pulled out into traffic, just like any other minor executive's vehicle in the mid-morning traffic. She noticed that no one seemed to notice that the Peugeot carried their President, also that as his car passed the boy without legs perched on the littered corner at the street lights, the President tossed some coins out the window.

There was no chance of holding any more classes that morning. The staff babbled excitedly away in their own languages, as they always did when they were excited about something — a child who had run away during the night or someone winning the weekly lottery. Except for the occasional "anyway" and "by all means" that they threw into their conversations, she could not understand a word of the three languages they spoke and had to wait until someone translated for her. Today they didn't translate anything. At eleven she told them she was going home for the day.

She was crashing after that nerve-induced overdose of adrenalin and deferred the cook's efforts to get her to the table. Instead she decided to go to the pool at the embassy for a swim, to cool off. She liked the calming monotony of counting lengths. She swam a hundred that day, a pleasing number from her days as a schoolgirl when "100" indicated the perfection of an assignment and consequently, as she saw it, of herself. Those were the days of youthful hope that eventually gave way to the sedate compromise of this, her adult life.

Then she dressed, drank a cup of coffee with three embassy wives at a poolside table and drove home relaxed. Her mood spawned quiet humming.

Assena handed her a message as she walked in the door. "Please be ready at four. A car will come to collect you."

"Who's this from?"

"Madam, I don't know. It was a man's voice. He said you would know who it was." Assena looked at Margo's feet; her maid's disapproval was only implied. For a woman to accept an invitation from a man who was not her husband was social suicide here. If she were from here. She was not, she reminded herself. She was an outsider, someone who didn't belong. She was not subject to their rules, she thought, knowing that this wasn't true.

"But I don't know who it is. Assena, you must ask people to leave their names."

"Madam, he refused. He said it was important. That I must be sure you received the message. He repeated it twice, and said I should write down exactly what he said, like dictation. What could I do, Madam?"

"Nothing, I suppose. Anyway, if and when a car comes, you tell whomever is driving it that I am not available."

Assena's knocking woke her up. She rarely slept during the day. Unlike people who said they especially enjoy that aspect of tropical life, the siesta, she found that it made her dozy and ill-tempered. She tended to have bizarre dreams if she slept in the afternoons and awoke not knowing who or where she was. Sometimes she woke up afraid. The fear was not defined, just a general anxiety. This may have had something to do with the new prophylaxis meant to control new strains of malaria.

She didn't wake up afraid that day; she just felt very hazy, unable to recall even what day it was. Assena's knocking was rapid and her voice querulous.

"Madam. Please. Wake up."

She could not seem to shake off the drowsiness.

"Madam, please. Oh, Madam. Please. Madam can you hear me?"

"Yes, what is it Assena?" She looked at the digital clock on her bedside table. 4:25.

She sat up. "Come in."

Assena's eyes were wide and everything about her seemed to be in motion. "Madam, please. Oh dear. The man who has come to collect you is the President's driver. He says the President wants to see you. Oh, Madam. What has happened? We must call Master at once, and tell him. They must have made a mistake. You must speak to your husband . . ."

"No, I don't think we'll call Geoffrey, Assena. Did this man give you any idea of why the President wants to see me? And please stop fluttering. You're making me nervous. I am not afraid of the President."

Assena's eyes turned to slits and she bit her lip. "No, Madam. But the man is wicked. My brother, you see, he has a friend who . . . no no, it is not good."

"Thank you, Assena," she said, dismissing the woman and her fear. "Tell him I'm coming." She stood up, stretching. "But please make sure you do not tell anyone else where I have gone."

Assena nodded, but did not look up. She had worked a long time for foreigners and had indicated to Margo that she thought they possessed little sense of reason. She told Margo what were to her terrible tales of whites she had worked for who visited ungodly things like witches villages and *juju* men, for fun!

"Do you believe in juju, Assena?" she had asked once.

"In our church we believe that it is a sin to do juju or to mix yourself in it," Assena had replied.

Margo speculated that to Assena, and perhaps to many in the country, the President would appear as the ultimate juju man, controlling all the new white magic at work in the country — security forces, television, money. There were all those whispered stories of brothers and friends and distant relatives who had disappeared, but Amnesty International had not been able to pin anything on the President. There were names but no evidence or bodies. "It's all pure speculation and heinous allegations by those with their own hidden political agenda," said the Minister of the Interior in a rare interview with the BBC. The President did not allow himself to be interviewed by anyone, on any subject.

Sometimes Margo thought fear underlay everything in this country. But at that moment — 4:29 P.M. according to her bedside clock — she felt immune to dark worries. She did not hurry; she told herself she was curious more than nervous. She bathed, sprayed her wrists with a new Gucci fragrance that Geoff had bought on his way back from Paris, put on a simple but expensive skirt and blouse (another gift from Geoff) and a pair of open sandals she had bought herself at a craft market in Toronto years earlier.

She combed her hair but applied no make-up which, since the burial of her mother, she associated with bodies in funeral homes. Then, with a regal poise she didn't feel, she walked downstairs. The driver was standing in the hall and he led her to a silver-grey Citroen parked directly in front of the door. He opened a rear door, waited until she had lifted her sandalled foot inside and was settled before closing it. He jogged around the front of the car to the driver's seat.

The presidential palace was a magnificent affair on a cliff with an ocean behind it — walls, gardens and security men in front. She had often admired it from a distance, thought it a splendid piece of architecture as long as one didn't reflect on the context or on the source of the money used to sculpt it. As Geoff did.

The car whizzed past the guards, the turrets, the gates. Uniformed and heavily armed men on duty saluted. She kept her eyes straight ahead, refusing to relent to a childish urge to wave back to them, like royalty, keeping her wrist and upper lip stiff. She was surprised by her own control and calm at the same time as she wondered at her frivolity and abandon in accepting this invitation. She told herself she had really had no choice. In this country, the President was like God. To disobey Him would invoke punishment.

They circled a botanical garden, and stopped in front of a pair of immense carved wooden doors, each of which would have permitted clear passage to an elephant, trunk raised. The driver once again moved smoothly to her door, opened it, bowed slightly and ushered her up the marble steps.

A fraction of a second before she would have run into the doors, they were opened by two men in fatigues.

A third man inside the enormous hall asked her to follow him through more doors, down more marble hallways, past more closed doors, into a relatively small sitting room with white leather chairs and white carpeting, smooth as velvet. Through floor-to-ceiling windows she could see the sun plunging into the dusk-grey ocean, extinguishing light in the hazy sky.

The walls were lined with books, superb specimens of African sculpture and some terrifying masks, each illuminated by its own spotlight. The President was seated in the middle of a sofa long enough to accommodate an extended African family.

"Good afternoon, Mrs. Ogilvie. I am so pleased that you could spare me a little time for this most welcome visit."

"Thank you, Mr. President. It is my pleasure, I assure you. An honour so great that . . ."

"Please sit down." He indicated an armchair adjacent to the sofa. She sat down and crossed her legs, keeping her eyes down. His silence prompted her finally to look up. He was staring at her but his face was devoid of expression. A master of the unspoken. Then he smiled, so spontaneously that she laughed.

Afterwards she would wish she could remember what all was said. Perhaps, she thought, he really was the master of juju that he was reputed to be. She knew at least that he covered a lot of ground — the difficulties of being a head of state in one of the world's poorest countries. The ignominy of meeting other leaders of the industrialized nations with one's hand outstretched. The constant pressure from political opponents, the dilemma of law and order versus civil freedoms that he said could turn overnight into anarchy. The tribal conflicts and the debt burdens. She did more listening than talking; she had nothing to add. She felt she knew nothing.

Then he asked her questions about herself and her home. He wanted to know how her parents were. He said it was terrible that she had lost her mother but assured her that she would one day bear children in which her mother's spirit would return to the earth. He wanted to know if her father had already chosen a new wife. She told him her father was very old and living in a home for the aged where he was cared for and fed and received the nursing he required. He thought this very sad; it would not happen in his country.

She laughed and he asked her why. "Your sympathy for my father. Do you mean because there is no home here to care for someone who can't look after themselves when they're old and sick, or do you mean it's a bad thing to be in a home like that? Or because you think it's the family that should care for him? I'm sorry, it just struck me that there might be people here who would be happy to have such a home to stay in. I meant no offence. Please forgive me."

He did not reply but there was sorrow on his face. As though her reply had saddened him. Or maybe he was thinking of the plight of the people in his country. Sitting so close to this warm and charming man, she found it impossible to believe the stories she had heard about his ruthlessness, his despotism.

Then he asked her to tell him more about her work in the orphanage, why it was that she would devote so much time to helping handicapped children when there were so many highly intelligent children in the country who needed teaching. This led them to the usual and tired comparisons between the developed and developing world and the relative value on human life and talent. But nothing that came from his mouth sounded tired.

Sometimes he lapsed into silence and she waited for him to dismiss her. She thought she could hear the roar of the waves hitting the base of the cliff. Manned by a few hundred presidential guards and God only knew how many servants, she found it inconceivable that the palace could be so quiet. It occurred to her that perhaps this was what power could buy: silence and privacy, both virtually unknown by the people here. Maybe he was tired of the silence and the privacy. Perhaps she was too.

After one of these interminable pauses, during which he never took his eyes off her — as though she were a novel he intended to finish before putting it back on the shelf — she finally said what she had been thinking since the note arrived.

"Mr. President, I don't understand why a man of your stature would call on someone like me this way. In any event, I have greatly enjoyed it. But I do think it is time I went. I'm sure you're a very busy man." She wondered where his wife and children were — Geoff said he had three daughters.

"Margo — I hope you don't mind if I use your first name, but you see I feel like I've known you all my life or perhaps in another life. I invited you here because, from the first time I saw you in the newspaper, I was enthraled. I am a married man, as you must of course be aware, but my wife and I have been estranged for many years. She keeps residence in London. I need women like you. My isolation at the top is painful. And almost total."

She did not ponder his use of the plural "women", nor did she think the explanation sounded trite or contrived. He moved in on her with more questions. Did she not want children? She did. Did she intend to dedicate her life to good works among the underprivileged of the third world? She didn't know. Would she consider staying on in Africa? She'd never thought about it. He did not ask about her husband.

She didn't recall his invitation for her to move to the sofa beside him, perhaps he had done it with his eyes but she did move. Geoff had told her stories about how wives were manhandled in this country. His surprising gentleness made what was happening seem all the more unlikely, like a borrowed bit of text from the wrong story. The word "manhandle" had nothing to do with the caresses he bestowed upon her. His whispered words sounded like incantations. She wondered if scientists had been looking at all the wrong things — hormones, electric pulses causing impulses, all those things they used to try to explain human behaviour, the prelude to love. The tyranny of love. The allure of its power. Maybe, she thought, it was all magic, sorcery, juju and spirits. It seemed natural and correct that he did not undress her or defile her need for him with the actual act.

It was midnight when she left. "You were right, Margo, I am a busy man. We will not have many opportunities. But we will have more secret meetings. They must stay secret of course. Your embassy and your government would not approve. Nor, may I add, would your husband." It was the first time he mentioned Geoff.

She was driven to her gate in a small white car, the kind of fast sporty car that wealthy men often provide for their mistresses. Feminine and classy, but a bit too racy, nonetheless.

"Where the hell were you?" Geoff was pacing the living room. Still in his tennis shorts, the long muscles in his legs were trembling. "Do you know what time it is? How long I've been waiting for you?"

"I'm sorry, Geoff, I . . ."

"You're sorry! Jesus Christ Margo." He threw the three words together, making them sound like a single name. "We were supposed to meet a delegation from Ottawa at the Novotel. I called up at the last minute to say you were sick and we couldn't make it." He looked her over carefully, breathing fast. She backed away a step, wondering how she looked to him. When had she ever felt so wonderful? She thought it was the first time Geoff had looked at her, really seen her, his wife, a woman, since they had left Canada. She knew then why his affection had felt false and ritualized. It had been. Just another of his duties in his new post. Now he was at least sincere in his anger. His diplomatic mask had fallen away to reveal a possessive man-child.

"Well, where the hell have you been?"

"I was trying to tell you. I was working. We had a party for the kids at the orphanage, and . . . well . . . the President showed up by surprise to give gifts to the kids."

"The President? Right."

"Yes, he came. He does that occasionally. Just shows up at schools to make sure teachers are doing their jobs and are in the classes and not drunk, or he'll drop in unexpectedly at the hospital to see whether the Water and Sewerage Company has kept the water supply maintained." She was exhilarated, foolish.

"How do you know? I suppose he told you and you believed it." His sarcasm couldn't touch her.

"Yes. As a matter of fact he did. After the children went to bed we all sat around and talked for a while. That's why I'm so late."

"Why didn't you take the car? Assena told me you left here in some strange car."

"They, um, the minister sent it for me."

"I was playing tennis with the minister. He didn't say anything to me about the party or a car."

"Maybe he doesn't tell you everything. Maybe he thinks some things are confidential. Maybe he didn't even know. He's not that important."

She kicked off her sandals, and walked past him to the stairs. "I'm sorry Geoff. But I'm going to bed. I'm beat."

She was already coasting into sleep when he crawled into bed and started to manhandle her in a way he had never done before. She allowed him to penetrate her physically, but told herself that he could not possibly touch that part of her which the President had just conjured up and captured for himself.

Christmas came and went. She was working long hours with the children to prepare the small show to which they invited several foreign dignitaries, who came, and the President, who didn't even send his regrets. But the show went over well. The children were talented actors with little of the shyness and inhibition in front of an audience that plagued some of the children's school plays at home.

By the end of December she told herself she felt relieved that there had been no word from the President, and by mid-January she admitted to herself that what she felt was not relief at all.

After Geoff's initial anger that night he became much more interested in her work, in her. As though he too had succumbed to the illusion that the magic touch of the President had created — that he was a well-meaning and misunderstood man, not an oppressive dictator at all. Geoff added her meeting with the Head of State to his repertoire of amusing anecdotes exchanged over drinks at expatriate parties. He and his colleagues pestered her with questions, trying to get information out of her— did the President mention anything about relations with the West and her country, what was her impression of him, what did he talk about? She said he had only expressed interest in educating small children and that she had the impression he was a sincere and caring man. Geoff stopped being so harsh in his criticism of him. When he told the story of how the President had surprised the staff at the orphanage, bearing gifts for the children, he began to embellish the tale with details with which she had never provided him. Details she could never provide him.

Word came again in February. Once again she received a dictated message that Assena gave her when she came home from the orphanage in the afternoon.

This time the note told her to inform the household that she was making a trip north to conduct a workshop on caring for handicapped children in an orphanage in Talon, the regional capital. She would be gone two nights. The car would come at eight in the morning.

As they drove out of the city, the driver told her their destination was a presidential residence in the mountains that divided the country in half like an enlarged backbone. A former colonial governor's castle on the very peak of these geographic vertebrae had been renovated to serve as a country home for the President. She had heard Geoff talk about this place that was shrouded in myth and off limits to anyone without presidential invitation. Geoff had said that in the past year two disgraced and ousted African leaders had spent time in this palace, before they moved on to European exiles.

It was a spectacular place, much more like a castle on the Rhine than anything one might expect in that African country. At that altitude, more than a thousand metres, it was cool. Wisps of cloud draped her in a comforting and comfortable blanket of damp and cool air. The residence was surrounded by rugged peaks covered with virgin forest.

He was waiting for her. They spent the first two hours walking along neat footpaths in the surrounding hills. Monkeys, sacred in the area because they were believed to be incarnations of ancestors, were everywhere in the lush growth overhead. She liked the thickness of the leaves on the rubber trees, the dark damp soil underfoot.

They dined in the middle of the afternoon, just as a rainstorm swept across the land like the final curtain. Over lunch, Nile perch from the river and steamed rice with a light pepper soup, he told her a little about the gods of the mountain on which they sat. He said that it was believed that the surrounding forests were inhabited by dwarflike creatures that could cause great mischief or good deeds, depending on how they were handled. The wine and his smile made her feel warm, although the rain had made the air coming through the opened windows almost cold.

Then he dismissed her, saying he must spend a few hours in his office, keeping up on the day's business and communicating by radio with various advisors back in the city. There were no telephone lines here.

He said they would meet again at eight thirty for an evening meal. "We have the whole night and then much of tomorrow before us."

At eight, a man in fatigues came to her spacious suite. She had just come in from the gardens where she had been soaking up the scents of the garden, which were exaggerated by the cool evening air and the dampness. She had planned to bathe and dress for dinner. She tried not to think ahead to the evening. It was difficult not to concoct scenarios.

The man did not knock and he caught her in her underwear. She clutched the dress in front of her, angry at the intrusion. He had bulging eyes like a chameleon's, which could rotate freely to spot anything edible or dangerous. He told her the President had given instructions that she be rushed back to the city as fast as possible.

"But that is impossible. He can't mean it." All the suspicions she had never felt came flooding in to taunt her now. She really was his morsel of forbidden flesh, his instant vanilla pudding, sampled, available, no longer interesting or tempting. He was already satiated.

"Madam, it is urgent. The President has been called away on some very important business. He insisted that for your own safety you be returned to your residence without delay. He specified that." Another dictated message. She threw the dress over her head, her clothes back into the overnight bag, and followed the soldier down the stairs, out the door, and into the car. They sped back to the city along the smooth road that led to and from the capital from that hilltop fortress. It was over four hundred kilometres — the best road in the country — and they covered it at speeds of up to two hundred kilometres an hour.

Once again, she walked through the door of her house at midnight. It wasn't until she was inside that she heard the shooting. It was distant and muffled, but it was unmistakeable. Rat-a-tat-tat. The man in the hat. I smell a rat. Oh, what is dat? Her mind churned out nursery rhymes.

Geoff was at the embassy, but Assena told her he had been calling Canadians in Talon all day trying to contact her. A coup d'etat was in progress, she said. Rumours in the city said the President had been killed.

"Madam, you were with him, were you not? Has he been killed?"

"I don't know, Assena. Please, I have to talk to my husband." She rang the embassy.

"What's happened, Geoff?" Her hand was shaking badly and she could hardly hold the receiver.

"A coup. Stay low, below window level. I'll be home as soon as I can."

The coup, the overthrow of a man who had been alone in power for twenty years, was bloody. News reports carried by the international short-wave stations said the President had gone into hiding somewhere in the north. The reports said a neighbouring country had been harbouring and training a rebel force of the northern Abule tribe. The Abule were intent on eliminating the President and his government which had not a single Abule minister. The local radio was off the air, except for occasional dispatches from military officers claiming control of the country.

Two days later the President's supporters, members of his own tribe from the western region, reached the capital and the streets became battlefields. The rebel Abule forces had joined up with other larger groups such as the Goroni and were already claiming they had control, even as they struggled to achieve it.

Embassies were to evacuate all non-essential staff and dependents. That was her. Non-essential and dependent. Geoff was one of three essential staff.

There was little she needed to pack. She called the orphanage and said she would be back as soon as things calmed down in the country. The housemother sobbed on the phone.

Assena knocked on the open door, softly. "Madam, may I please come in?"

Margo nodded, watched her approach.

"Madam, a man has brought you this envelope."

Assena looked as though she wanted to say something else, and Margo was sure she did not want to hear it. "Thank you, Assena. Please keep an eye out for the car. It should be here very soon. I am sorry to leave you like this. But I think this house should be safe. And my husband will be here until things settle down." Her reassuring smile failed.

Her hands trembled as she unfolded the stationery, embossed with a gold emblem, the seal of the President. He wrote, "I am sorry. Do not forget me. May we meet again one day in another place where we will continue from this magical beginning."

The airport had been closed by the rebels who, in spite of the fighting and continued slaughter in the capital, had declared their coup a success. But the rebel leader, eager to forge good ties with the outside world, was permitting expatriates to leave on charter flights coming in from London. Geoff accompanied her to the airport in the embassy van that was packed with excited and nervous spouses and children. There was no chance to talk privately with her husband. The streets were deserted by their rightful owners, pedlars and pedestrians selling and buying to stay alive. She was deathly afraid of the commandos on the corners. There was no way to tell which side they were on, which side anyone was on.

The fighting continued and Geoff stayed on, while the government waited for the American and British governments to decide whether embassies should be closed. There had initially been hope that supporters of the deposed and missing President would eventually give in and accept the new leadership. Instead the country was breaking itself up into still more factions, along ethnic lines. Phone lines were cut and she received notes from Geoff that came through Foreign Affairs. He always assured her that he was safe, that he thought he would be home soon because anarchy was breaking out in the country.

She went back to work in the children's centre she had left almost exactly one year earlier. She found solace in the cool fluorescent lights of the school, the brightly coloured posters on the walls, alphabet rhymes and benevolent masks, the plump and lively children who knew nothing of the world outside.

In the evenings, she sat in a rocker by the bay window that overlooked the frozen canal, and returned to a dream world of remembered passion and nightmares of men in fatigues.

Geoff sent more messages. It was still not clear if the President had been killed or if he had managed to flee the country. She believed he was alive and that he would ultimately contact her. She wanted to believe that she could help him get exile here. She made his need for her greater than her longing for him. She actually ached for him.

Three months to the day after the coup, an envelope from Geoff arrived in a courier bag from Ottawa. It was a Reuters news release. It was gruesome, about a mass grave unearthed beside the mountaintop palace. Thousands of skeletons. Torture chambers underneath the vast white castle. She didn't finish it. She felt as though someone had slugged her in the gut. Underneath, Geoff had scribbled. "As we suspected. He was even worse than we thought."

What could she do with her secret and her shame? The delayed humiliation and the fear that engulfed her each time the telephone rang? Her imagination ran wild, its hooves thundering through her head creating headaches that kept her home from work. "May we meet again. . ."

Each time the telephone rang, she was sure that it would be him. He would have traced her. Wouldn't a dictator like that have security forces all over the world? He might want her to hide him. He would want to come to her bed, lay his body on hers, run his bloodied hands up and down her thighs. "Like silk cotton," he had whispered. "Do you know what silk cotton feels like?" "No," she said. "Like your skin," he said. He had moved her hand gently under her skirt, urging her to feel the insides of her thighs.

The first April showers arrived, thawing the last of the ice on the canal, melting the dreary layers of March snow. The telephone rang. She picked it up. Even then the power he wielded over her was too great to ignore. She decided, though, that once she heard his voice she would hang up. She would call the police. The RCMP. The army. What would she say — that a deranged despot from Africa was chasing her and wanting her to hide him in her own house? He's my lover but it seems he's a mass murderer. But you see, I didn't know that, and I'm frightened.

She held the receiver tentatively, as though it were a loaded weapon. She was unable to speak.

"Hello? Hello? Margo? Are you there? Margo!"

"Oh Geoff. Thank God it's you." Somewhere, up there where the satellites orbited, her words were echoing. She waited until the echo stopped. "Where are you?"

"In London. I'm coming in tonight on Air Canada. The fighting escalated when they found him. He was shot down in his helicopter, trying to flee the country. We've closed up the embassy until things settle down."

"Who, Geoff? What do you mean?"

"The President is dead. The country is in a full state of war. It's been hell, Margo. Pure hell."

"Oh my God, Geoff, I'm sorry."

As she hung up she wondered what she was most sorry for — the people caught in the bloodbath, the skeletal remains of living and feeling human beings under the castle where she had stood and breathed the life of the forest and thought about earth spirits, the scenarios in her head that had played her into his embrace, or just the sudden death of her innocence? She felt as though she had just awakened from a long siesta in which she had been asleep on her feet, woken up from a dream to confront an actual nightmare.

She went outside into the wet, sweet air of the spring evening. It was like another damp day she had known — a very long time ago in a very distant place. But underneath the rich dark soil here there were no human bones, no grinning skulls. She bent over and began to pluck at daffodils, making a bright bouquet with which she would meet Geoff at the airport. She worked very slowly — she had another nine hours to practice the smile she would need to show her husband, a smile the President had taught her, wide enough to conceal a chamber of torture.

Let them live

He was headed her way. He had spotted the empty chair beside her. With a lot of grinning and mime, and more huffing and puffing, he arranged himself and his bags beside her. Ingrid tried to hide behind her paperback, hoping he would read her body language and keep quiet. He didn't.

"Excuse me, miss, do you speak English?"

She pretended she didn't notice that he was talking to her. She had taken a great liking for Morse, the aging hero of the book, who was on the trail of a serial killer. Morse was just about to explain to his deputy why he had suspected Lindsey all along.

He leaned closer and repeated his question in her ear. His breath smelled like peppermint.

"Sorry, were you speaking to me?" she said.

"Yes, and you just answered my question. I've been looking for someone that speaks English since I got off the plane here a week ago. They've got so many locals working at the embassy that it's hard to find a red-blooded American to talk to."

She turned the page.

"You come here often?" he asked.

She glanced at him out of the corner of her eye. He had an oversized, florid face and a flabby neck that disappeared into lumps and bulges in the khaki safari suit. She was constantly amazed at the number of people who came to Africa outfitted in khaki safari suits with the word "safari" on one or two of the two dozen pockets. She wondered where they found them.

"I live here," she said eventually, uncrossing her legs and re-arranging her batik skirt around her shins. She looked around the boarding lounge. Boarding lounge was a flattering description for the large hall hung with faded tourism posters that were hung with cobwebs, all shrouded by a decade of dust. When the air-conditioners went out of commission a few years ago — probably a few days after the international airport was built — someone had started methodically breaking windows to allow a flow of air. Which was fine except when one of the giant airliners turned its ass on the terminal and revved its engines prior to take-off, filling the lounge with black fumes. At least the kerosene fumes put a damper on biting mosquitoes for a couple of minutes. Right now they were having a real go at her ankles.

"You live *here*?" He shook his head. "Oh, I bet you're Peace Corps."

She shook her head and glanced at her watch. There were rumours circulating the boarding lounge that there had been a bomb scare in Abidjan and the plane had not yet taken off from there. That meant they could be waiting another two hours. Or six. Or twenty-four. The count could be days if they cancelled the flight, as happened about once a month. She ignored rumours of bomb scares. They were a handy excuse for flight delays, the rule rather than the exception in West Africa.

All she wanted to do was crawl back between the covers of the book, get through the flight and the funeral awaiting her at the other end. Her mother's death was a relief; it had been far too long coming. Her father had insisted on the life-support system that kept her breathing, even after the stroke destroyed all her mental faculties. Left a brilliant woman with tubes everywhere and a brain as fruitful as a potato. That was the last time she had been home. It had been dreadful. Her father kept begging her to stay, month after month, believing that his sheer need for his wife would eventually reactivate her brain. He had wept when his daughter left him there alone and flew back to Africa. She had never seen her father weep before that, when she told him he was being selfish keeping alive a body, humiliating the woman who once was, robbing her of the dignity she had so cherished in life.

Ingrid had already done her grieving when she sat beside the living remains of her mother in that New York hospital. Now that her mother had finally stopped breathing, her father had called her home to help him through *his* grief. She didn't want to think about it.

She turned the page to see if the pathologist would accept Morse's invitation for dinner.

"So what is a young woman like yourself doing in a place like this?"

"My husband is from here," she murmured, disappointed that the pathologist said she couldn't make it, that she wanted to take a raincheck.

"That so? Your husband? From here?" He shook his head again, as though a fly had lodged itself in his brain.

"So how long have you been living here, Miss, er Mrs . . . sorry, I didn't catch your name."

"Sawadogo," she said, not looking up this time.

"Now that's a tongue twister. Sawa . . sago . . . what?"

"Sa wa do go."

"Well, I guess that's a native name. Glad to see that you're not one of those women who refuses to take her husband's name." He lapsed into silence for a minute, digging in his jacket pockets for something. She sneaked a glance at him. It was not a safari suit after all. It was a leisure suit. The kind favoured by insurance salesmen and evangelists.

"Well I'm pleased to make your acquaintance, Mrs. Sadogo. My name's John, John Hacklestone." He held out his hand and grabbed hers in a sweaty and enthusiastic shake.

"Second vice-president of the Let Them Live movement. You've heard of us?"

She glanced at him. "No, I haven't." She sounded ruder than she really wanted to be to some poor, misplaced American from yet another well-intentioned charitable organization bumbling about in this out-of-the-way part of the world. "No, I'm sorry. I've never heard of your group, Mr. Hacklestone," she added.

He rummaged in a pocket, frowning.

"Ahh. Here it is! For a minute I thought the porters had picked me clean. Ever seen money like this?" He pulled out a wad of soiled and ragged coni notes.

"Look at that. Makes you want to put on rubber gloves just to pay for a coke. Haw. Haw. Sure is hot here, and I never thought there was a place hotter than Alpharetta in August, but looks like I found it. Mrs. Sagodo, can I buy you a Coke?"

"No thank you, I have some water in my basket." She nodded to indicate the woven basket beside her feet.

"Be right back, Mrs. Sa . . . would you mind if I asked you your first name? I'm afraid these native names just don't stick in my brain."

"It's Ingrid," she said, smiling, thinking he would be gone a while, that it would take him some time to get a drink. The green-coated waiters behind the bar were busy serving beer and whisky to young European men with long moustaches and dirty jeans, all of whom they seemed to know, half of whom she had decided were arms dealers or gold smugglers. Grateful for the break, she opened the paperback again. But it was difficult to concentrate. Hacklestone was shouting about the poor service and making so much noise that no one, not even the waiters, could ignore him. He returned triumphantly, coke in hand, and dropped into the orange plastic chair with a thud that rocked the whole row.

"Ah. You see, everywhere you go in the world, Coca Cola. And the young folks back home complain about America. What other country in the world could come up with something like Coke? You American?"

She paused a second. "No," she lied.

"You could've fooled me. Sure sound like one. Well, then, you must be Canadian?"

"Yes," she lied again, wishing she was the pathologist and Morse was inviting her to dinner. Or that she was back at home with Kwashie, editing one of his reports on medicinal plants. She wished she was anywhere but there in a hot airport waiting for a plane to go home and bury her mother. Kwashie had offered to come but they had agreed that would just make it worse. Her mother was the one who had first interested her in Africa, encouraged her to travel, and taken the result — an African son-in-law— to her heart. Her father had never liked what he called this unusual choice: "not that I have anything against blacks". But without her mother there to keep him civil she was afraid that Kwashie's presence at the funeral would only make the whole thing worse.

"Always wanted to go to Canada. Take the wife and kids up to Niagara Falls. We're opening a branch office up there in the fall, so maybe I'll finally get the chance. Sure would like to see the place."

"Yes, it's very nice," she said. She scratched at a bite on her right foot. She hoped he wouldn't ask her where she was from in Canada. The only places she knew anything about were Toronto and Montreal, because Kwashie had studied at universities there and told her his own saga of being a stranger in a faraway land.

Around them, people were standing and collecting their luggage, heading towards the doors. A few minutes later and they were deafened by the whine of jet engines as the French airliner touched down in a cloud of smoke as its tires hit the black tarmac that was hot enough to roast a side of beef.

A muffled woman's voice came over the tired public address system. She spoke in French, announcing the arrival of Flight 635 from Abidjan, destination

Paris. Asking passengers to please proceed immediately to the final security check at the departure gate.

"What's she saying?" Hacklestone shouted. Ingrid translated for him as she struggled with her basket and portable computer.

"Here, let me give you a hand with that, Ingrid." He levied himself to his feet, towering over everyone in the departure lounge. Before she could stop him he had seized her computer and slung it over his shoulder. Hacklestone led the way, pushing towards the front of the queue at the glass door. She followed, unwilling to lose sight of her computer. Sweat was dripping down his back and great dark patches were forming under his arms and on his back. The sweat stains were shaped like the African continent on a grey polyester map of the world.

Two solemn young soldiers rifled through handbags and ushered the pressing passengers through the sliding door. She retrieved her computer from Hacklestone, thinking if she moved fast enough she could find a single seat and finish her book in peace on the plane. She cleared security and moved towards the door.

"Hey, wait a minute. What are you doing?"

"*C'est interdit, Monsieur,*" said the young soldier checking handbags. She pushed for the door.

"Hey, Ingrid, wait. What are they saying? Hey, gimme that. It's mine. Ingrid, help."

She hesitated, her computer bag and basket already through the door. Logic told her to keep going. Something else, his guilessness she supposed, made her turn around and question the two soldiers about the nature of the problem. Hacklestone was busy packing papers and files back into his briefcase.

One of the security men showed her a small package of pink paper he held in his palm. In French he explained that the American man was in possession of four nuggets of raw gold. It was illegal to take unworked gold out of the country, he said.

She explained gently that he didn't know the rules but they said that even in America, ignorance was no excuse for breaking the law. They said they would have to apprehend him. She looked up into Hacklestone's big pink face and explained to him what they had said.

"But that's ridiculous!" he stammered. "I bought these legit from a young man at my hotel." She not-so-patiently repeated that his arrest was imminent.

"They're for my kids. Souvenirs!" he boomed at the guards, holding out his meaty hand for the return of the goods.

Passengers behind them were getting noisy, cursing the stupid "Nasarah", or white man, in a dozen languages.

Hacklestone kept ranting. "I've never in my life heard of anything . . ."

"Quiet, Hacklestone," she muttered. "Okay, friends," she said quietly, pulling them a little to one side and very quietly suggesting they simply confiscate the gold and give it to their boss for legal disposal. She wondered why she was helping Hacklestone, even as she was doing so. Not because he was a fellow American, she decided, but because helping people out was the African way. She was doing what Kwashie would have done.

The security men exchanged glances, aware of the impatience of the passengers behind them and then relented, putting the small pink package into a bag for confiscated goods. They pushed Hacklestone forward, telling Ingrid that they would entrust the criminal to her. They wished her luck and the shorter one winked.

"I'll take this up with someone in authority. You can't treat . . ."

"Hacklestone, they *are* the authorities," she hissed, moving through the doors as fast as possible.

The plane was nearly empty, making her wonder if there really had been a bomb scare. July flights to France were always overbooked because of the mass exodus of expatriates heading for summer. Not this jumbo. She counted twenty-seven passengers already on board, and no more than fifty had been in the departure lounge. That would mean they could all stretch out and sleep. She was beginning to look forward to the flight, thirteen kilometres above the earth, neither here nor there. Between worlds. Alone.

She settled herself at a window seat, her computer on the seat next to her. She smiled up pleasantly at Hacklestone, whom she had already decided to forget. He seemed to fill up the aisle, grinning and muttering "Excuse me" to all the passengers he bumped with his briefcase and carry-on bag.

"Lucky the plane is so empty," he said. "We can sit together. I owe you one, that's for sure." He sat down heavily in the aisle seat. "It's great to be going home, isn't it?"

During take-off he rattled on about his gratitude to her and about how much the gold had cost. He ordered champagne, then more. She opened the book and tried to read.

"You got any kids, Ingrid?"

She shook her head.

"Life isn't much without kids but then you've got all that ahead of you. Let me guess. You're twenty-something."

"Yes," she lied, snapping the book shut again in exasperation.

"My daughter's twenty-eight. She's already on her third kid. Takes after her mother! And happy as a clam, let me tell you. She's secretary of our Alpharetta branch. She's out there on the streets with the best of us, picketing the abortion clinics and writing to congressmen. Got the kids with her in the carriage. She's a militant mom, my little Sally. Not so little any more, in her eighth month." He laughed.

"I don't mean to pry, Mr. Hacklestone, but just what were you doing in Africa?"

"You're not prying at all, no, I've got nothing to hide, Ingrid. As second vice-president of Let Them Live I got appointed to do some checking up on the family planning programs that the people of the United States have been paying for over here. You know the kind of people they send out here. None too Christian. They sometimes try to slip one past us. So my organization makes spot checks once in a while. And you know what I'm carrying here in my briefcase?" He patted the case lovingly, turned it around so she could see that it was covered with neon green stickers: *Don't Abort. Support Life — God Loves Babies! Don't You? Stop the Holocaust Now. Jail the Baby-Killers!*

He leaned towards her and whispered. "I have evidence, Ingrid. Evidence that in Upper Volta the U.S. is funding a government family life program that supports abortion. What kind of family life program kills babies? I met a Father O'Brien, you know him? He took me to a girl of sixteen who had just had an abortion in the family life clinic paid for right down to the last brick by the United States government."

"It's no longer Upper Volta, Mr. Hacklestone. The name of the country is Burkina Faso."

"Please, Ingrid, call me John. Anyway, doesn't matter what it's called, it's not getting any more help for its family life program from the United States of America. Not when I make these documents public."

"Did you travel around a little, Mr. Hacklestone? Get to see the country some?"

"Not much to see, is there? Just those mud huts and dirt. I know enough about Africa from TV and I know just what you're going to say but I'm a step ahead of you, Ingrid. Look, I'm not the pope. I have nothing against Christian family planning. What's to stop these people from using the good old fail-safe methods of family planning? Nothing, that's what. They're just plain lazy and they think murder is easier than slipping on a rubber or popping a pill. Or, think of this, just saying *No*. Worked for our grandmas!"

He was grinning like a male baboon trying to subdue a naughty member of the harem as he ordered two bottles of wine to go with dinner, asking her if she didn't want to celebrate with him as they ate. He was quiet while he ate and when his tray was empty he asked her if she was going to eat her pudding and roll before moving them onto his tray and tucking into them with great gusto. "Waste not, want not!" he cried, so loudly that she ducked her head to avoid the bemused smiles of fellow passengers.

She had begun to despair when the film began and Hacklestone finally put on his headphones. She read her book, keeping an eye on him, trying to exercise the patience that Kwashie had been trying to teach her. When that didn't work, she tried casting a spell, using telepathic control that she thought was behind so much of the healing power of traditional medicine. But it was probably the wine that made Hacklestone finally doze off as they were crossing over the Mediterranean.

It was much easier than she expected — she had been afraid his briefcase would be locked. She took everything she could reach and without looking at it slipped it all into the zip pocket on her computer case. Then she leaned back and returned to the murder mystery. The pathologist had accepted Morse's offer of a drink this time and was — at long last — sitting on the couch with the detective, listening to Wagner.

Hacklestone didn't wake up until they touched down in Paris and he seemed subdued by his sleep. She felt magnanimous and escorted him to his departure satellite at Charles de Gaulle; he seemed unable to fathom the layout of the airport. She wished him a pleasant flight to Atlanta. He thanked her several times for all her help. She smiled and waved as he stumbled off into the boarding lounge.

She wasn't sure what to do with the pilfered material until she saw an airport cleaner — a worn-out looking African woman whose security tag said her name was Henriette — coming towards her with a cleaning trolley. Henriette was sweeping up cigarette butts and collecting lipstick-stained styrofoam cups. Ingrid asked if she could put some rubbish into the garbage bag on the back of the trolley and Henriette nodded sullenly.

She pulled the stack of documents out of her computer case and shoved them as deep as she could into the bin, soiling her hands on ashes and butts and styrofoam cups and soggy newspapers. She was surprised to see a tiny dictaphone tumble out of one of Hacklestone's fat file folders and disappear into the mess of rubbish inside. She hesitated, wanting to retrieve it from the rubbish bin, see what kind of material Hacklestone had really collected in Burkina Faso, a country the West viewed with suspicion because of the revolutionary young president whom she and Kwashie so admired. See who John Hacklestone really was. "Wait a second . . ." she said, but Henriette was already wheeling the trolley away and there were only a few minutes before her flight boarded.

She turned and got on the moving sidewalk, trying to brace herself for what lay ahead in New York while the picture of Hacklestone's dictaphone nagged at her. She told herself it didn't really matter what was on the miniature tape; it had already landed where it belonged. Lost and buried in the tons of trash produced every day by strangers on their way to and from far-flung corners of the world for whatever reasons they had for their travels to places they knew nothing about.

Glossary

Abule: fictitious ethnic group in fictitious West African country

animatrice: French term for a community development worker whose job it is to animate community self-help activities

boys' quarters: common term in West Africa for rooms or housing provided to domestic staff on a family compound

chop bar: informal roadside eatery in parts of anglophone West Africa where cooking and serving are done outside

coni: fictitious currency (1000 conies = USD 1.00)

dawa-dawa: local name for locust bean tree, deriving from Arabic word 'dawa', meaning medicine

enskinned: official ceremony in which a chief is installed and will henceforth sit on skins

fufu: West African dish made by boiling and pounding yam, sometimes also with cassava or plantain

Goroni: fictitious ethnic group in fictitious West African country

guinea worm: a nematode that infects humans when its eggs are consumed in infected water; it then grows into a long worm inside the person's body and exits through the skin

Hausa: language spoken by the Hausa people in West Africa and used as a lingua franca and a common marketing language in several countries

high-life music: popular music from West Africa

harmattan: prevailing cool wind that sweeps south from the Sahara Desert each year, usually from December through February, bringing a sandy haze that may cover most of West Africa

houseboy: common term for adult male domestic worker

housegirl: common term for adult female domestic worker

jollof: West African recipe for preparing rice using various spices and vegetable bits

juju: supernatural or magical power associated with charm, amulet or fetish among some West African peoples

Kakadi: ficititious village inhabited by fictitious Abule people

kinkirgo: child of the Devil

kola nut: a nut produced by a tree, chewed to relieve pain or hunger or in a ceremonial occasion; standard gift for chiefs

Langadi: ficititious village inhabited by fictitious Goroni people

linguist: the man appointed by a traditional ruler to receive visitors and translate their words for the chief

mammie wagon: usually dilapidated vehicle used for public transport

market mammie: vernacular term for market woman

marabout: Muslim holy man or mystic

mineral: common term in anglophone West Africa for soft drink

mobylette: French word for moped

pito: traditional beer made from sorghum

rival: vernacular term for co-wife in a polygamous family

Sahel: semi-arid belt of savanna stretching from Sudan, west to Senegal in Africa

sheanut and sheanut butter: oil or butter that is used in cooking, healing or as a cosmetic creme, which is extracted from the seed of the sheanut tree, indigenous to West Africa

Taali: fictitious village inhabited by fictitious Abule people

Talon: fictitious regional capital, inhabited mostly by Goroni people

tuo: traditional West African staple dish made by boiling maize or millet flour into a porridge

zomkom: traditional Sahelian non-alcoholic drink of millet and ginger